Tim Ashley was born in Sussex, England in 1961 and educated at Oxford and Cambridge. In 1995 he left a career in investment banking and went on to start, merge and float an internet company. In 2001 he gave up full-time employment to fulfil his long-held ambition to write. *The Island of Mending Hearts* is his first novel, though he has previously published a mixture of journalism and short fiction, most recently 'Best Eaten Cold' in Peter Burton's anthology of gay murder stories, *Death Comes Easy*, also available from GMP.

Tim lives in London and Sussex with his partner of 17 years. He has recently completed a second novel, *Henry*, and is now working on a third.

The Island Of Mending Hearts

TIM ASHLEY

First published 2004 by GMP (Gay Men's Press),
an imprint of Millivres Prowler Limited,
part of the Millivres Prowler Group,
Unit M, Spectrum House,
32–34 Gordon House Road, London NW5 1LP

www.gaymenspress.co.uk

A CIP catalogue record for this book is available from the British Library

ISBN 1-902852-47-8

Printed and bound in Finland by WS Bookwell

Distributed in the UK and Europe by Airlift Book Company,
8 The Arena, Mollison Avenue,
Enfield, Middlesex EN3 7NJ
Telephone: 020 8804 0400
Distributed in North America by Consortium,
1045 Westgate Drive, St Paul, MN 55114-1065
Telephone: 1 800 283 3572
Distributed in Australia by Bulldog Books,
PO Box 300, Beaconsfield, NSW 2014

To the memory of John Ashley,
a wonderful man and a much better father
than the one portrayed in this book.

Acknowledgements

For putting me up and putting up with me,
I would like to thank Richard, Rick and David.

Contents

Prologue

I am staring into the near-blackness. The warm smell of the sea floats in from the deck nearby, twining itself around the steel band's rhythm. I strain forward in the darkness, knowing that this is a dream but making it real. I follow the flickering, upside-down flame reflected in the stranger's eye as I raise the cigarette to my lips. There is a moment of perfect silence, full and rich and rare.

Suddenly a shrill noise issues from somewhere over my shoulder. It is Selina, and she is holding the cordless phone that she keeps by her bed. She is shouting my name, 'Michael, Michael, Michael,' and she reaches towards me and shakes my shoulder. I'm disorientated, hyperventilating. It's the middle of the night and she has left her room to come to mine. She is trying to wake me, but I do not want to be roused.

'Michael, it's the police. It's James. He's collapsed. They're taking him to St Richard's. Michael.' The last not a wail, not a whisper, not even my name. Just a sound.

The calm of sleep is sluiced away and the focal length shifts brutally shorter, distorting everything, separating me from everything. I reach for the phone but the line is dead.

The next part doesn't seem to happen in the right sequence. I see the face of a surprised pedestrian scrabbling for the safety of the kerb as we speed past. I'm not aware of dressing. I'm in the car but not driving. We don't speak. Suddenly we are in the hospital, where the lens of nightmare shifts to fish-eye. Everything in bleached white and blue metal, the corridors lengthening as we move through them, everything speeding up but not progressing. I flash my staff ID card at a figure in the shadows, then run into the operating theatre, where I see the final charge administered, the last convulsion rise then settle. I stand looking at the flat line on the monitor and hear the steady beep and see the doctor waiting silently, holding the discharged paddles in his hands while a nurse scribbles down the time of death. I know that everything is over.

I turn to Selina, who shouts, 'Michael, do something, save him. SAVE HIM. For Christ's sake, Michael, don't just stand there. You're the fucking specialist. *Do something.*'

The last thing I notice is Selina's lipstick. I turn to face her and see that she is wearing fresh, deeply red lipstick and I wonder when, in all this horror, she found the time to put it on.

The lens pulls back to its widest now, and she is further from me than the stars, as far as the blackest, furthest, coldest void.

I'd been having a similar nightmare for years, this endless me, standing impotently by while a patient dies on a table in front of me. At this point I would usually wake and spend a few frightened moments gasping for the reassurance of wakefulness. But recently everything had changed. Because just a few weeks ago and for the first time, my nightmare had come true. And the man on the table had been Jim.

Book I
A Kind of Innocence

1
Cruise

Suicide is like masturbation: they both hide their obscenity behind euphemism, using the back doors of language to introduce their sordid intent. So I wasn't going to kill myself; I just wanted to 'end it all'.

It wasn't self-indulgent or any of the other things that suicides get accused of by people like my father. I didn't want attention, it wasn't a cry for help and I certainly didn't expect anyone to feel sorry for me because, in true family tradition, I didn't feel sorry for myself. In fact, I didn't feel anything; that was the whole point. My life had pretty much stopped and the real obscenity was that my body just carried on without it, like a decapitated chicken circling a farmyard.

I didn't even plan anything; the opportunity arose quite naturally in the course of events and I pursued it without question. It was the obvious thing to do.

The cruise itinerary was to be something like this: Fort Lauderdale, Key West, Cozumel, Grand Cayman, Fort Lauderdale. A round trip, circular and pointless; the perfect send-off. In truth, I'd forgotten all about it until the tickets arrived, by which time I had been on my own and anaesthetically drunk for more than three weeks. I was getting bored with the hangovers, and I needed a change.

I decided that I would jump unobserved from one of the ten decks at night while the other guests were in any of the seven restaurants, the theatre, cinema, casino or spa. I imagined myself surfacing in the wake of the ship and watching its lights slipping swiftly away to join the stars on the horizon, then slipping away myself. It was a cold and comforting thought, the anticipation of nothingness.

I would leave a note for the crew saying that I'd gone intentionally over the side and that there would be no point in turning around to look for me. And then I'd leave another note, for my sister Lolly, the only living person I cared for.

These tasks were the last things left for me to do, as if my life had been a shopping trip armed with other people's lists and, when I'd finally turned to my own page, there had been nothing on it. *Que será*, I thought. The dogs bark, the caravan moves on.

I packed a single piece of cabin baggage with a few things and as I caught the train to Heathrow, as I waited at the club-class check-in, as I flew at thirty-five thousand feet listening to the steady fizz and crackle of my neighbours' headsets, I mulled all this over. While the others watched their movies, I sat quietly drinking miniatures and staring at my seatback LCD. It displayed a small graphic of the plane tracing a curved trajectory across the globe towards the warm Caribbean as if it would, at the end of the journey, slice into the darkening blue and save me the trouble of catching the ship.

At Miami Airport, a woman tour guide with a power-drill voice met several people from my flight. I told her Selina had been detained by an emergency at work and I would be travelling alone. She crossed out a name from the manifest, hiding her speculation with a perfectly compiled smile. Then she pushed through the crush, creating a bow wave that allowed us to pass easily to a waiting air-conditioned transit.

There were plenty of empty seats and I chose one well away from the other people. We emerged from the airport into a maze of intersecting freeways and waterways, their glare dulled by tinted glass, their reflected heat neutered by the hiss of a nozzle above my head. I closed my eyes and sank into an insulated limbo for a while, until I felt a sudden sharp turn and a slowing of speed. Blinking out from the controlled twilight of the cabin I saw the enormous pockmarked side of the ship consuming the whole horizon in every direction and, for the first time since Jim's death, I felt a twitch of interest and excitement.

Not at the ship itself, but because I had finally arrived at the last stage of my journey.

The only recollection I have of the process of embarking is the horrid sensation of being led down the long white corridor to my cabin. This set off an echo of the hospital, a reverberation from the night it all happened, creating in an instant that same fish-eyed horror of an endless convergence of walls and floors towards a terrible point. I paused and gripped the rail and, while the steward made his quip about us not yet being at sea, I caught my breath and my nerve. Then at teatime, as we set sail, I watched the docks slide past my porthole into the distance while my fellow passengers were up on deck, waving goodbye to the empty quayside.

As we ploughed past the coastline towards the start of the Florida Keys, I stayed in my cabin watching the flat strip of distant land unfold monotonously. At dusk I ordered a light dinner in my cabin, then didn't eat it. I was starting to shut down.

A while later I opened my minibar and helped myself to a large Scotch, then another. However numb I already was, I wanted to become more so; I drank a miniature of brandy too, and then made my way to what seemed likely to be the least scenic and therefore least populated deck – the Plaza Deck.

Arriving through a heavily sprung glass door, I was met by the warm salt smell of the sea. It brought back a powerful image of the sun deck in my dream; the sun lounger beside me, Selina with her blanked-off eyes, the lure of the darkened bar nearby.

I moved towards the rail and gripped it, squeezing its hard reality. Black water pounded far below, a foaming mass carving before and behind it, dark horses riding the night.

I looked left and right. Fifty feet away a hugely fat woman stood alone, staring out to sea. Automatically, I started to guess at her weight, to calculate the strain on her heart, to estimate her age and to perform the same basic actuarial calculations I would with any overweight patient who walked into my consulting room. Calculating their time of death with a smile and an invitation to sit.

The woman turned and saw me looking at her, then smiled, waved and stepped out of view through a door.

Now that I was alone on deck, I focussed on the faraway shoreline. It was alight with a billion watts of coastal development, a soundless distant holiday a whole state long, repeating itself like a cartoon backdrop.

As I watched it glide past, the realisation grew that I did not want to die there; I would be better off waiting for the real deep, between the end of the Keys and Mexico, out there in the Gulf where there was nothing on the horizon. I didn't want to go overboard in sight of land, within easy reach of the rescue services; nor did I want to die in shallow waters. I wanted depth, darkness, a far more private oblivion. I would wait another day, until after we had left Key West. I was serving no one but myself, and there was no particular hurry.

I returned to my cabin and started to write a note to my sister Lolly, but after two more brandies and a small bottle of red wine I set it aside and picked up another piece of paper.

Dad,

You won't remember this but when I was a kid, Mum once asked you to give me a swimming lesson. I was looking forward to it but when we got to the pool you were furious with me because I wouldn't let go of the float. Then you just pulled it away and watched me thrash around. Well, I'm going for a bit of a swim soon and you'll no doubt think that it is a characteristically weak thing of me to do, an easy way out. That would be your typical reaction, but it isn't true, because finally and for the first time in years this is something that I have chosen to do even though I know you'll disapprove.

I used to want you to be proud of me and I'm sorry for both of us that that's not going to happen. I suppose it's the correct form in a note like this to end by saying 'I love you'. You brought me up to follow form, didn't you, Dad? Well, this time you'll have to excuse me.

Michael

After I had finished I sat blankly for a while before reaching for the much longer note I had started writing to Lolly earlier. I read the first few paragraphs back to myself in a muttering undertone, suddenly aware of how drunk I was. It sounded horribly wrong, too matter-of-fact. I wanted to leave her something better than that so I ripped it in half and dropped it in the bin. Then, afraid that the steward might see it and alert someone to the clearly stated intention of its opening sentence, I picked the bits out and flushed them down the lavatory. I reread the note to my father and found it sounded maudlin and incontinent, or so he would doubtless think. I wasn't going to let him have such an easy let-out, so I ripped it up and flushed it away as well.

I woke with a headache the next day. We were just easing into port at Key West and, though it was breakfast time and I was hungry in a mechanical way, I couldn't face eating on board; the gaggle of people and the Technicolor buffet repelled me. So I decided to go ashore.

It was a brilliantly sunny day and I winced in the sharp morning light as I slipped down the gangway; I had not packed sunglasses.

The first street I came to seemed to run the whole length of the town. It endlessly repeated the same string of stores and restaurants, halfway between New England clapboard and Caribbean Plantation. At that time on a Sunday morning it was mostly quiet apart from a street-cleaning crew, and all the restaurants and cafés were closed. This district was clearly for the tourists and would follow their daily rhythms; if I wanted coffee and something to eat, I'd have to look further afield.

But as I continued to walk, an odd sensation settled over me. The repetition of such similar-looking buildings, block after block, created a surge of unreality, a powerful impression of *déjà vu*. The perfectly straight line of the street had become a circle, trapping me within it.

About half a mile from the ship I found myself waiting unconsciously at a red traffic light, even though I was on foot. I felt strange, weak, afflicted by the sunlight. I wanted to put this down to my hangover but I'd had enough hangovers in the previous weeks to know that this was something else. Phantom letters to Lolly and Dad had begun to form and re-form in my head whilst I'd been walking and when I realised that I had stopped without reason at the red light, I experienced something like a convulsion. This upsurge of panic felt both viscerally physical and oddly disconnected. I struggled with it briefly, forcing it down, and then the light changed and I moved on, turning left.

I walked for some distance until I came to a building that looked like a petrol station but instead of petrol pumps and cars the forecourt was filled with rows and rows of passengerless mopeds. There was a large sign on the roof, two red crosses, stark and medical at either end of the words 'Moped Hospital'. I looked at it for a few moments and started to sweat coldly, my vision closing in on it and my peripheral vision darkening. I ripped my gaze from the sign and, muttering something like 'this is crazy' to myself, I crossed the road and turned right.

I quickly became lost in a maze of narrow streets and lanes. Still feeling dazed, I wandered aimlessly until I saw a sign that said 'Blue Lagoon Café – All U Can Drink Coffee & Good Home Cooking'. There was a convenience store opposite and without pause I crossed over, went in and bought a packet of Marlboro, the only brand I could think of, my first and last cigarette.

As I left I was unnerved by a fleeting glimpse of someone turning the corner of an aisle towards the rear of the shop. He was carrying a wire basket filled with groceries and, though I only saw him for a split second, it went off like a flashgun: a frozen image of Jim in sweatpants and a pale blue T-shirt.

Back across the street and seeking sanctuary now, I peered through the window and saw with relief that the café was empty. The sign on the door said 'OPEN' so I pushed it and a bell tinkled as I entered. There was no one there at first so I shouted 'Hello' and was immediately aware of the alien sound of my voice, bizarrely overdubbed by a stranger.

After a few seconds a tired-looking, pretty blonde woman appeared through a green plastic strip curtain at the rear. It swayed like strands of wet kelp behind her.

She said, 'Hey,' in a friendly if somewhat distracted way. It was a gentle voice.

'Do you serve breakfast?' I asked.

'Well, yes. No. I mean, I don't actually serve it. I'm the chef and Alex is the waitperson except he just went out to get provisions. But he'll be back in a moment.' She looked around her as if waiting for a prompt, then said, 'What would you like to eat?'

'What do you have?'

'Well, we have coffee, ham, eggs, hash browns, beans, grits, toasted English muffins with butter, croissants, most other types of cholesterol, artery-hardening materials and death on a plate. That's what most folks want. Or I can do you a wonderful plate of fruit.'

Seemingly surprised at the length of her own sentence, she gave an embarrassed half-smile, as if seeking encouragement. I didn't feel like smiling but neither did I want to appear rude, so I forced a grin. It felt unreal, like a carnival mask.

'I'll have a plate of fruit, please, and an ashtray.'

'Healthy combi*nation*!' she laughed. 'Not in here, you won't, but if you're extra nice you can smoke out back, there's some tables there. Follow me.'

She disappeared through the plastic curtain and I followed her down a short corridor into a dappled green yard full of dense tropical foliage. Patches of blue sky showed through the leaves of a huge banyan tree, which stood in the corner, covering most of the space with its canopy. Four large and two smaller tables were carefully placed to create a series of private spaces, all empty. A scrawny chicken pecked away at the sawdust-covered earth.

'Meet Lunch,' the blonde said.

I felt, and must certainly have looked, bemused.

'The chicken,' she continued. 'She's a little lost missy we took in from the Chicken Store on Duval. They run, like, a chicken orphanage, I guess you'd call it. She's very imprinted on humans. She's called Lunch, which was Alex's idea of a joke, only she doesn't think it's funny.'

'What does "imprinted on humans" mean?' I asked, smiling again, but this time less uncertainly.

'You know, I never asked that when we adopted her. It's just what they said at the store. I guess it means she thinks we're her family, like she's a human too. She's certainly a picky little eater, aren't you, honey? Only the best for you.'

She made a gentle clucking noise and bent down briefly, pulling what looked like a piece of croissant from a pocket in her apron and holding it towards the chicken, which clucked in reply and scampered towards her. I thought again how pretty she was.

'Anyway, I have work to do,' she said, rising. 'I'll send Alex out to you with coffee and an ashtray when he returns. After you've abused your heart and lungs, he'll bring you a plate of fruit. We have great fresh mango this morning.'

She disappeared through the curtain and I looked around me. There was no noise apart from the stirring of leaves and a soft burr in the throat of the scratching chicken. The air was perfumed with frangipani and the scent of baking bread and I felt a sudden release of tension, as if a taut string had been cut somewhere within me. I sat down at the furthest of the tables with my back to the door, opened my pack of cigarettes, took one out and placed it on the table.

Looking around, I took in the sheer bulk of vegetation. To my side a recently planted vine of some sort was gently gripping its first tendrils around a trellis, three or four tiny buds evident, impossibly delicate and tenuous.

After a few minutes I heard the rustling squeak of the plastic curtain. I turned around and was jolted to see a young man, around the same height as Jim, though maybe three or four years older and with darker hair, carrying a tray. It was the man I had seen in the store just minutes earlier, wearing sweatpants and a pale blue T-shirt.

'Hey,' he said, gently. 'My name's Alex. Coffee and ashtray as requested, fruit *en route*.'

'Hi,' I said, unnerved again. 'Thank you.'

Then, as I watched him for the few seconds it took him to cross the yard, he seemed once more to be replaced by an image of Jim, so that by the time he reached me I was starting to crack. The same casual energy in the way he walked, the same carefree expression. Now he was beside me, bending to set down the tray, close and real enough to touch.

The feeling that had been welling up all morning was trying to burst out now, but I made one last effort to dam it. I looked the other way as he poured the coffee, hoping to keep control until he'd gone. But then he said, 'Cream?' and I had to reply.

'A little, please. Thank you.'

'*De nada*,' he replied.

This was one of Jim's favourite phrases, delivered unawares but so full of him. I floundered after it, trying to hold my head together. But the coup de grâce came when, with his next move, Alex accidentally reproduced a scene from my long-familiar dream.

'Care for a light?' he said, and before I could reply he crouched down, took out a book of matches and tore one off. As I lifted the cigarette to my lips, as he lifted the flaring match to my cigarette, as I looked into his eyes, I saw a beautiful, tiny, upside-down flame reflected there.

2
Drowning

The dam burst, and the flood I had been holding back washed over me until I was choking, drowning on dry land.

I sat blinking, my eyes stung by tears, unable to speak, sobbing and rocking with this sudden and unexpected release of grief. Alex continued to crouch silently by my side, an uncertain look in his eye. After a few moments he placed a hand on my shoulder and said, 'It's OK, it's OK. Whatever it is, you're OK here.'

I carried on crying for a while until eventually he said, 'Is there someone I could call, sir?'

I didn't try to reply; speech would have been impossible, so I shook my head instead.

'OK. You'll be just fine.' His voice took on the rocking lilt of a lullaby. 'Don't go away, I'll be right back.'

He stood and walked away through the curtain, returning a few moments later with some paper napkins and a glass of water. Over his shoulder I could see the blonde woman standing tentatively, half in and half out of the curtained doorway, the strands of the kelp-green plastic mingling mermaid-like with her hair.

I don't know how long the three of us remained in these positions. They didn't speak and I couldn't. But after some time, my voice returned at least enough for me to say, 'I'm sorry, I'm so sorry,' and then, after a few more moments, 'I should go.'

'Not until you've had your plate of fruit,' came the woman's voice from the doorway. 'And I'm glad to see you changed your mind about the cigarette.'

She smiled, again in a tentative sort of way, and disappeared behind the curtain.

'I don't mean to intrude,' said Alex, 'but you look pretty miserable to me. Where are you staying? Do you live here or are you on vacation? I mean, is there anyone with you, like, someone we could call to come meet you?'

'I arrived this morning on a cruise ship. It's in the harbour. I'm travelling alone. I...'

My voice trailed off as I realised I had no idea what to say or do next. But I felt I owed some explanation, some way of showing that I was not just a random, deranged stranger who had walked in from the street; that my tears were rational.

'I'm sorry for the drama, it was just something you said, it's an expression my...'

I couldn't bring myself to say the word.

'Something someone very dear to me used to use,' I said instead. 'And you reminded me of him.'

'*Used* to use?' Alex asked, with an infinitely gentle stress on the first word.

I nodded, trying to fight back my tears.

'Jim was almost the same age as you. He was always picking up these expressions. Too much American TV, I suppose.'

I said this to try to defuse the embarrassment of the situation a little, even tried a laugh, which came out as a blub.

He took my hand between both of his and squeezed it for a few seconds, then stood and busied himself with the things on the table. As he did so, the blonde came back through the curtain.

Placing a plate of sliced fruit in front of me, garnished with a purple flower, she said, 'I'm sure you worked out by now that this is Alex. I'm Sue. What's your name?'

'Michael.'

'Hey, Michael. Now eat.'

They left me alone in the yard for a while, picking at my plate while the little chicken pecked around at my feet. In the distance the rest of the town started to come to life. I could hear music, a little traffic, and faraway laughter. A breeze stirred the green yard. It seemed to breathe and I breathed with it.

It must have been fifteen minutes later that Alex came back and by then some sense of calm had returned.

'You're English, right?' he asked.

I nodded.

'How long is your ship in town for?'

'It leaves this afternoon.'

'Where to?'

'Somewhere in Mexico I've never heard of.'

'You don't sound like a happy holidaymaker to me.'

'I'm not.' I smiled. 'This was never really going to be a holiday. I shouldn't have come. It was already booked and there just seemed nowhere else to go. Autopilot, you know.'

'When do you have to be home? I mean, like back at work or whatever?'

'Whenever,' I shrugged. 'Maybe not ever. I'm a heart specialist. The hospital's given me… indefinite leave, because of all this.'

He nodded, clearly confused but deciding not to probe any further.

'Well look, here's a thought,' he said. 'Do you know your way back to the ship? It's quite a way from here.'

I shook my head. 'Not really, but of course I'll find it if you can point me in the right direction.'

'Look, Michael, it's not so busy here right now, won't be until around eleven. I could ride over to the ship with you, if you could use the company. There's a spare bike.'

'That'd be very kind but I don't want to inconvenience you. Either of you. I mean, there must be a lot of preparation to do before lunch, and I've imposed myself enough already. I… that outburst earlier, it was ridiculous, I'm sorry.'

He looked at me gravely for a moment but with a slight smile around the corners of his mouth before replying, 'I don't know how people in England *do* grief, but that looked pretty normal to me. Nothing ridiculous about it at all. Better out than in, you know.'

'Thanks, but really, I'm all right now; I can find my own way back.'

He held his hand up. 'Enough, already! Sue will be fine for a half-hour on her own. Besides, I need to spin by home and get a spanner; the dishwasher broke down. It's kind of on the way. Almost.' He grinned. Actually, when he smiled he looked nothing like Jim at all, which made it easier to say 'OK.'

We left a few minutes later, Sue refusing my offer of money and reaching to squeeze my shoulder briefly, saying, 'Goodbye, it was nice meeting you. See you again, I hope. And I hope you feel, you know, better.'

There was a gate at the back of the yard and once we were outside Alex unlocked two bicycles. He gave me the larger one, obviously his own, on the grounds that I was the taller. Pedalling like a clown on the smaller machine, he led us off further away from the main street, turning from time to time to see that I was still with him. We cycled in silence for a minute or two, and I looked around me as we rode.

The houses were the same mix of styles as the commercial area I'd walked through earlier, but smaller and more intimate. Some of them were carefully tended and painted in cool pastel shades. Others were peeling and rusting, slumped over their crawl spaces. They were crammed tightly together on what appeared to be tiny lots, narrow fronted but with roofs going deeply back in shining metal waves. Through and on and over everything grew the most decadent vegetation. Improbably large boughs and fronds of flowers curled and arched their way, softening the uprights of the architecture. Every few moments, we'd cycle through a patch of their perfume.

On the sides of the road, Key West went through its Sunday morning routine. An old black man with a white beard rocked on his porch. A Cuban woman strapped twins into a pushchair whilst her shirtless husband tipped a bucket of soapy water over his car. Another car further down the street stood below a tree that had shed a thousand yellow flowers, turning it into a carnival float. We passed a flaking, castellated church, a mounting frenzy of gospel choir escaping through its half-open windows. A jogger dodged the huge puddles left by a recent storm and the sun rose high and strong.

A couple of minutes later, Alex stopped suddenly, pivoting his right leg over the saddle of his bike until he was standing on the left pedal while he coasted to a halt.

'Here we are,' he said, unlocking a rusty padlock from a gate in a high fence. 'Come in.'

I followed him through into a large yard, bigger than the one at the café. It was totally overgrown, impenetrably so in many places, with an uncontrolled abundance of palms and vines. We had come in by a side entrance and to our left was a large, rather run-down house.

'Pretty grim, hey?' said Alex.

'It's certainly...' I struggled for a word '... poetic.'

'Well, that's charitable.' He laughed. 'Stay here for a moment.'

He disappeared into the house through an unlocked door and left me standing there. I looked around me at the chaos. Rusting garden furniture stood a few feet away, half eaten by rampaging greenery. A few smaller palm-like plants stood in cracked terracotta pots. One of them had forced a root out through the wall of its container, the escaping white tendril snaking down and away into the earth nearby. Clearly nothing here was willing to be constrained.

A rear deck hung crazily off three-quarters of the back part of the house before losing hold and sagging unconnected to the ground where an old barbecue struggled to avoid its advances. The roof appeared to be a series of rusting metal tiles, their lustre dulled by corrosion so as to give the appearance of the scales of a fish gasping for life on the quayside. At the back of the house on the right-hand side, the roof failed to meet the guttering, which stood off at a useless angle, just out of reach. But there was some evidence of temporary repair: the rear of the roof was patched in places and new, unvarnished strips of wood were nailed neatly over the worst areas of disrepair on the back wall. A small space had been cleared in the yard to make way for a wooden table and four mismatching chairs.

In the trees behind me I heard a rustling noise, then a loud squawk. It was clearly some kind of bird, but the foliage was too dense for me to see it. In the foreground two enormous multi-coloured butterflies flew in a spiral around each other, drifting upwards in the heat. The rising path of their fluttering appeared random, but the distance between them remained constant.

Alex reappeared, a small hessian tool-sack over his arm.

'Speechless, eh?' he said.

'Do you rent this place?' I asked. 'I mean, it's quite beautiful in a way but it barely looks habitable.'

'Believe me, you're right. I don't know what's holding it together. First sign of a hurricane, I'm outta here. It's kind of a long story but I had a mad great-aunt, a real sweetheart. Aunt Peggy was a pretty famous local artist. She died a while back but she left this place in trust for me until I was twenty-one, provided some other requirements were met. That was three years ago. I always knew it was coming to me, and I'd dreamed about it for ages so when I finished college I decided to put off grad school and come live here for a while. My parents are *not* pleased. For all sorts of other reasons too. Kind of ambitious for a first-time fixer-upper, hey?'

'You're a braver man than I,' I replied. 'My grandfather's hobby was carpentry; he'd have loved this place. I used to spend my summers with him on the north Norfolk coast as a kid, and one year he and I renovated a large Victorian beach hut. Actually I would imagine it was a very similar construction to this, but about a tenth the size. He was always teaching me how to fix things – he said it was much more satisfying to mend a broken thing than to make a new one.'

'That's pretty poetic too,' said Alex. 'I could sure do with your grandfather around here. The sad truth is, I'm completely without the right skills, though I do try. I have two jobs just to get fed so I never really have enough time to make inroads on the house. You know, this place is worth an absolute fortune, though I'm totally broke just from trying to keep it patched. But I won't *ever* sell it, I've really promised myself that. So I just have to find some way of stopping it falling further apart.'

'As they say,' I replied, 'where there's a will...'

'I guess so.' He trailed off, looking absently into the undergrowth for a few moments, then snapped back into life. 'Come on, Michael, let's get you to that ship. Are you feeling OK?'

'I'm fine, thanks. I don't know why, I just had a bad morning.'

'That sounds natural under the circumstances.'

'Yes, I suppose it does.'

Alex paused as if he were trying to work out how to phrase his next sentence, but then a look crossed his face that seemed to say he'd changed his mind.

'I hate to hustle but I can't leave Sue for too long. And I could daydream here all day given half the chance.'

We were closer to the dock than I'd realised, just a few minutes' ride. It was a shock to round the corner of a narrow street and see the huddle of roofs give way to the stark, huge whiteness of the ship. I felt a hint of my earlier discomfort begin to re-emerge.

We dismounted a few yards from the bottom of the gangway and Alex switched bikes, taking hold of the handlebars of the smaller one in order to steer it alongside himself as he rode back to the café. I think that for a moment neither of us knew what to say, so we just looked around at the busy dockside scene. People were arriving and setting up stalls and stands, preparing for a day of frying conch fritters or selling handmade necklaces and tie-dye T-shirts. The moment lengthened.

Then Alex turned to me and said, 'Maybe I shouldn't ask but, your... umm. Jim. Did he...' A brief pause, eyes averted and then moving back to meet mine.

I completed the sentence for him. 'Did he die recently, you mean?'

Alex nodded and I said, 'Less than a month ago.'

'That must be very hard. I'm sorry. You must have been feeling terrible.'

I looked up at the expanse of hull besides me, my eyes coming to rest on the Plaza Deck. 'Yes, I suppose I have.'

There was another pause, maybe half a minute, then Alex said, 'I really have to go. Michael, I...' The same look I'd seen a few minutes before in his garden reappeared, as if he wanted to say something but couldn't phrase it.

'It's been nice meeting you,' he said. 'And if you return in happier times, drop by the café. You'd be very welcome.'

He moved to extend his hand in a formal way, balancing the spare bike against his knee, but it slipped and clattered down to the ground. I bent to pick it up and as I set it on its stand he spoke again, his words tumbling out.

'Michael, are you *sure* you want to get back on the ship? You could always stay here for a while. I mean, forgive me if it looks like I'm intruding but you said yourself that you were on autopilot, that you didn't really *want* to be on the cruise.'

I looked down the quayside towards the gangway, thinking. A family was disembarking, two adults in matching shorts and Hawaiian shirts in acid tones, their two children wearing miniature versions of the same outfits. The father was dragging the younger of the children, a girl, by her hand. She was screaming in protest, her face puce with rage while her brother trotted sullenly alongside. He appeared calm, but my mind drifted over to him, an empathic spectre hovering by his side, and I knew that he was the angrier of the two.

'Michael?' said Alex, trying to regain my attention.

I reeled my thoughts back in and tried to focus on what Alex had said, but my eyes were drawn back to the silently resentful boy as the family walked towards us.

I replied mechanically. 'Why would I stay? I don't know anyone here.'

Alex balanced on his bicycle, placing his hands on my shoulders and looking me straight in the eyes. 'You don't know anyone on the ship either. Why would you want to be on it?'

The group was almost level with us now, the little girl still straining and shouting, 'Let me go. I don't want to. I don't WANT TO!'

Her father snapped. He reached behind him and scooped her up with one arm, slapping the back of her legs viciously as he swung her in front of him and shouting, 'That's enough now, Mary-Anne. That's *enough*!'

She fell into a moment's stunned silence, staring him in the face with a look of astonished hatred, then she started to scream again. He shook her this time, so hard that her head wobbled like a doll. Then he slapped her again.

'Michael, are you OK?'

I was about to answer when the boy, a few years older than his sister, flew into a rage. He began to pummel the back of his father's legs with his fists, shouting 'Don't hit her, stop it, *stop* it!'

The man turned to him and barked, 'Shut *up* now, Junior, and mind your own business or you'll get the same treatment.'

I was suddenly aware that Alex was restraining me. I was tensed, coiled, utterly involved in the nearby conflict. Alex's hands were firm on my shoulders now, as if he feared that I was about to spring free and join the fray. Then he spoke, clearly and deliberately, loudly enough for the man to hear him: 'It's terrible, isn't it? I would never hit a child, my own or anyone else's.'

The man moved towards us, his eyes straining to escape from his face. 'What would you know, faggot?'

Alex turned his head and regarded him intensely for a second before replying. 'I know what any decent person of any sexual orientation should know. Which is exactly what I said. If you're angry, find some other way of taking it out.'

The man's face was the same colour as his daughter's now, his black pupils shrunken into concentrated dots of fury. He moved closer, so close that I could smell the tobacco on his breath, and said, 'Do you want to make something of it?'

The woman stepped forward, placing one hand on her son's head and the other on her husband's shoulder and saying in a calming tone, 'Dave, not now, honey, OK? We'll miss the start of the game.'

He and Alex stared each other down for a few more moments, both children open mouthed and silent now, until finally his wife pulled him gently backwards and took the little girl from him. Then she turned, took her son's hand, and started to walk away.

The man's stare intensified for a moment, then he said, 'Fuckin' faggots. What would you know about children? What would you know about being a father?'

Alex didn't reply this time. He was looking over the man's shoulder to where his wife had stopped and turned towards us. She mouthed, silently, 'Thank you.' Then she regained her voice. 'Come on now, Dave. We don't have much time.'

The man deflated slowly, his chest and shoulders falling like a cockerel after it has crowed, and a few moments later they were gone. Alex turned his head back to me as if nothing had happened. He was completely calm and relaxed.

'Here's a suggestion. If you can get packed and off that ship in five minutes tops, or Sue will kill me, I can drop you off at my friend Penny's guesthouse. It's a great place and Penny's a very nice lady. It's on the way, sort of. Alternatively, you can just tell me to mind my own business and I'll go away. But then you'll be back on board with the dad from hell.'

I looked up at the ship again, aware that a clock was ticking. Then I looked back at Alex's face. He fixed his eyes directly on mine as he spoke again.

'Then maybe we could get together later, if you feel like some company. Maybe with Sue, some other nice people?'

A series of possible futures hung in the space between us. After a few moments, I plucked one out of the air.

'Five minutes?' I said.

'I'll be waiting.'

In just under five minutes I was back, my small bag slung over my shoulder. And as I left the ship, I handed my cabin key to a surprised cleaner, saying, 'Please tell the purser that I'm staying in Key West.'

3
Paradise

We cycled off down the main street, now thronged with tourists and thumping with music from a thousand loudspeakers. Alex pedalled frantically and I struggled to keep up, a duckling being led into new waters. After a few blocks he swung right, shouting over his shoulder, 'Welcome to Cuba,' and even as he said it we zoomed past a corner shop with a group of Hispanic children playing outside and salsa music dancing through the air. I was trying to stay with him as he cut in and out of the narrow streets, so things were no more than an impression of colours, of fleeting sounds and smells. I swerved to avoid a chicken and nearly crashed into the back of Alex's bike as he halted abruptly outside a pretty, medium-sized house. It was swathed in flowers, like everything seemed to be, but here the riot of colour was out of control.

'PENNY!' he shouted, just as I saw a painted sign with 'Penny's Paradise Guesthouse' in large letters above a picture of two women standing naked, except for fig leaves, holding hands in a jungly garden. Alex followed my glance and laughed. 'It's OK, this is just a regular guesthouse. I mean, Penny's a lesbian but this is no Dyke House of Horrors. Relax. No trucks parked in front, see?'

He winked and, as I scrabbled for a reply, I heard a woman's voice coming from inside the open front door.

'Is that my favourite waitperson screaming my name out in the street, like I'm some common-or-garden hooker?'

As she spoke, she emerged through the door and paused, leaning coquettishly against a wooden pillar on the porch, flickering her eyelids in self-mockery. She was huge. Not fat at all, but at least six foot two or three with a hefty bosom. And she was an explosion of colour. Clothes, hair, makeup, all were subtly larger than life. She had a tropical flower of some sort behind her ear and thick, anchor-chain necklaces.

'Penny, this is my friend Michael. He needs a room for a night or two. Can you look after him?'

She looked at me with mild interest for a moment, then said, 'Any friend of Alex's is a friend of mine, and as it happens a dreary pair of leisure-suited miseries from Minneapolis just checked out three days early. Key West "Not What They Expected", by which I take it that they either did or didn't get laid, depending on what they expected. I just finished cleaning their room myself because that cow Juanita's off sick, again. It was repulsive. Empty fast-food packages and something else too unspeakable to mention. But it's OK now. I sprayed.' She mimed a high-and-low spraying action. 'So that's three nights maximum, then I'm booked solid for a month. What's Mr Friend's name again?'

'Michael,' Alex and I said together.

'Let the man speak, Alex,' Penny said sternly. Then, turning to me, 'Hey, Michael. I'm Penny. Penny Heron.'

The accent was clearly Southern Belle, but I had a sense that this was another piece of self-mockery and that a different voice lay beneath it.

'Pleased to meet you, Penny. I'm Michael Stuart. Thanks for finding space for me at such short notice.'

Alex made his excuses and, shouting 'Catch you later,' pedalled off at speed, leaving us alone. I felt slightly deserted, a sudden sense that things were moving too fast for me, that I was out of control. The combination of Penny's sheer scale and up-front manner overwhelmed me.

'You look tired to me,' she said. 'Peaky. Almost English. You need some sun, so it's a good job your room's got a sun deck in back. One hundred forty-five dollars a night plus taxes plus service, which you won't get much of, what with Juanita playing Marie Celeste. Is that all you got?'

This last was accompanied by a glance at my bag.

'I'm afraid so,' I replied.

'Don't even look big enough for sandwiches to me. Still, each to his own. Follow me.'

Whistling 'Travelling Light', she took off through the doorway. I ran up the steps to catch her, just in time to see her disappearing through another doorway at the end of the long corridor that continued off the reception hall. This further door was brightly lit by daylight from behind and as I approached it I could see through into the space beyond.

There was a large decked area with a few dining tables close to the doorway and, as I stepped through, the view opened out to include a long, narrow swimming pool, brilliant blue in the sunlight with a ring of darker blue tiles at water level. Beyond that was a series of doors into handsome cottage-like units. At intervals the decking was neatly cut away to make room for palms and flowering shrubs and in one place two stone herons stood, their heads nestled together. From concealed loudspeakers came tantalising wisps of an aria I did not recognise.

We skirted the pool and headed towards the right-hand hut, the door of which Penny threw open as she stepped inside. I followed into a medium-sized room, simply but well furnished in dark wood and ethnic fabrics, prints of Rousseau paintings depicting fantastical jungle scenes on the wall. A carved wooden bowl full of fruit stood next to a pitcher of iced water on top of a chest of drawers and a fan rotated slowly on the ceiling. Opposite the entrance a French door stood open to reveal a glimpse of further decking beyond, more plants, a green picket fence with trees behind, and an Adirondack chair with a white towel draped over it.

I had the strangest sense that the room had been prepared for my arrival.

'Humble but honest, and clean,' said Penny. 'Well, at least it's clean now.' She mimed the spraying action again. 'I'll leave you, OK, honey? Take a nap. Ring if you need anything: food, whatever. Oh, and you may want this.' She reached into her hair and produced a hand-rolled cigarette. 'If you know what it is, you can have it. If you don't know, you won't want it. Think of it as a little welcome gift from the Management. My personal homage to the great Mrs Madrigal.'

I was entirely mystified, vaguely feeling that I'd just failed some kind of test. But I took the gift from her outstretched hand and said, 'Thank you, this is a lovely room, I'd like to take it. I think I will sleep for a while. Maybe out in the sun.'

'Good idea,' she replied. 'Now I have to go clean up after a strange woman from Provincetown who's been here for two months and doesn't know how to pick up a towel from the floor. Like I said, ring if you need. OK?'

'Thank you.'

She walked out, shutting the door behind her, but just before she did so she turned on the threshold and gave me a huge wink. I had no idea why.

I had slept so deeply the night before that I wasn't physically tired. Mentally, however, I was exhausted. There were too many things to think about and too many feelings circling around me, like planes around a fog-bound airport. But for now I needed a break and time to adjust to this sudden change of plan – or rather, to suddenly not having a plan – so I sat down in the Adirondack. Settling the towel as a pillow I lay back in the shifting sun and shade of my private deck and, straining to catch the tiny fragments of music in the breeze and to push out the fragments of thoughts that tried to enter my head, I nodded off.

4
An Invitation

A while later I was woken by a telephone ringing in my room. I opened my eyes to find myself in shade, the sun having moved round beyond the edge of the next-door hut. The phone rang again. I felt a sudden shot of fear. Who could it be? Half awake and quite confused, I could only think of Jim, Selina, the hospital – and of being sucked yet again into the dark tangle of my nightmare. By the time I had worked out where I was, the phone had stopped ringing.

I poured myself a drink from the jug; the ice cubes were shrunken to hailstones now but the water remained cool. I returned to the deck and the Adirondack, sitting and holding myself as I allowed memories of Jim to wash around me: the certainty and force of the way he moved; his easy smile and open manner; the sheer power of his presence and thus of his absence.

I drifted through the past like this for a while, walking through the walls of memory, unable to touch anything in the rooms through which I passed.

It dawned on me, after a few minutes of wandering like this, that it was no longer possible to put off thinking about certain practicalities. I had to acknowledge that for now at least, I wouldn't be throwing myself off any ships. But I also felt slightly foolish. I had jumped ship in a different way, onto an island full of people I didn't know, on the basis of a few kind words from a friendly stranger.

Having had time to pause for thought, it was clear to me that Alex's instinct to help could have been no more than a reflex: he was young and spontaneous and had acted on impulse. In short, I didn't have any place here. He had just been too well meaning to turn away from my immediate distress and would certainly be embarrassed and inconvenienced by my continued presence. So, as I came down from the mild elation of the cycle ride from the ship and the brief interlude of friendly company, a renewed depression started to set in.

This was somewhat different from the feelings of the past month. It wasn't blank, or numb. It wasn't a desire not to exist. It was the delayed start of something painful and inevitable. Of course, I did not see this clearly at the time; I simply felt sapped, sad, and alone.

Related to this, I also felt an older, more familiar pain. It was to do with my father, triggered by my drunken scribbling of the previous night and by the scene at the quayside that morning. It had been the subtle counter-current of my life for so long that I had given up trying to swim against it.

I sat like this for a while and then a thought struck me. I got up, went into the room and rummaged in my bag. Of course, I did not have my address book with me – I'd hardly been planning on needing it – but I thought I knew the Toronto number by heart. I glanced at my watch. It was four o'clock in the afternoon and I reckoned it would be the same time there.

I took the handset from its cradle. It was a wireless model so I went back out to the deck with it, took a deep breath, and dialled my sister's number.

'Hi, Lolly and Pete aren't here right now, please leave a message.'

The familiar, amiable voice of my brother-in-law.

Beep.

I gathered myself.

'Hi Lolly, hi Pete, hope you're both well and the baby's not arrived early and taken you by surprise. Just calling to say that... I... had to get away for a while. I don't know why really but I'm in Key West. In a hotel. Anyway, I really can't face anyone so, whatever you do, please don't tell a soul you heard from me. I want some time. I don't want anyone else to have the slightest clue where I am. But anyway, I'm OK, really, and looking forward to unclehood. If you've got any news, call me. The number's...'

I scrabbled my way back to the phone's base where the relevant numbers were written neatly on a sticker, read the sequence out, then said, 'Goodbye.'

As I replaced the handset, there was a gentle knock on the door. Startled, I paced over and opened it. It was Penny.

'Alex tried to call you earlier but you didn't answer, so he figured you were out. He left a message. He and Sue do this thing, Sunday nights at the café, because they're closed on Mondays, rest for the wicked.' She smiled. 'Anyway, they do this thing, when the last customers have gone. It's like a potluck thing where friends just come round and chill out, finish off any food, maybe take something along with them too. You know, like pizza or whatever. And some wine. Nice crowd.'

'Oh, I don't know, it's very kind but I mean, I hardly even know them, and...'

'... you don't want to be a burden.'

'That's not how I was going to put it.'

'Come on, Michael, I don't know you from Adam but you're miserable as shit and anyone can see it. It doesn't make you a bad person. Maybe they actually liked you and maybe they don't know yet, and neither do I. And yes, maybe they're just being kind. But they asked you and I'm going because I always do. And as the landlady around here, I make the rules. So you're coming unless you can show me a sick note. OK?'

'OK,' I said, unable to think of any other response. Penny had taken control.

'Good,' she continued. 'Now, I don't want to appear rude but if you're staying for more than a day, and if you're to be my walker tonight, and if I'm correct in assuming that that weedy bag of yours contains no more than underwear, a toothbrush and a lethal dose of sleeping pills, you'll be needing some clothes.'

She smiled again and looked me up and down, eyes shining with mischief. 'Looks like Gap's your style. Forty-something goes preppy. But we don't have a Gap in Key West. Hmmm. SearsTown's too bleak for you right now and it's a hike from here. So that leaves Fast Buck Freddie's and Banana Republic. You want to look like a Fashion Conscious Local or an Ad Man On Vacation? No, don't answer, I love dressing people up. All clothing is drag. It helps us all explore who we could be. I think for now we'll go Ad Man, subject to later revision. Leave by the front door, take a left, two blocks. Left at the lights onto Duval, our sensitively adapted main street, then around four blocks on your right.'

'But...' I started to reply.

'No buts. I will look stunning this evening and so will you. What do you do? I mean, for a living?'

'I'm a cardiologist.'

'Well, you're in the right town. Half the people here are recovering from broken hearts. I'll meet you by the front door at 11 pm. And if you haven't smoked it by then, bring that joint I gave you earlier.'

5
Banana Republic

Duval was heaving with people that Sunday afternoon. While lithe-limbed local kids chased chickens in the back streets, on Duval the chubby offspring of well-fed tourists ate them deep-fried. Where the narrow streets of the old town were perfumed with a shifting landscape of tropical scents, Duval offered the stink of stale cooking fat, tobacco and beer.

It seemed that most of the tourists in town were confined to this one street and, unlike the subtly engaging areas through which I had cycled earlier, it lacked the ability to cast a sudden spell. Leery-faced men in bulging-bellied T-shirts argued with blowsy women in too-short shorts. In the shadowy recesses behind brightly painted bar-fronts, hulking banks of TV screens pumped out a frenetic diet of sporting highlights to listless, chair-bound audiences.

This wouldn't have been an attractive sight for any observer but for someone fighting a vague and unpredictable sense of unreality it was disorientating in the extreme. I kept my eyes down until I came to Banana Republic, where I almost panicked. There was a sale on, and the place was crawling with people.

I wasn't in the right frame of mind to deal with this zoo of activity and stood uncertainly in the doorway. I must have looked lost because, as I was about to turn away, a young girl with short black hair, purple eye shadow and a nose-stud came dancing up to me. Above my head Elvis Costello sang 'I Don't Want to Go to Chelsea'. The girl bobbed to its reggae beat.

'Can I like, you know, help?'

'Well, I...'

'I know, it's grossly busy, you wanna run away, come back later, tomorrow, whatever. Except I know exactly what you need because you have these really pretty green eyes. So follow me.'

She didn't quite take my hand as she danced towards the back of the shop, but it felt like that. As I trailed behind her, I noticed she had a purple braid sprouting from just above the nape of her neck, dotted with powder-blue beads.

There was a non-sale section off to one side, near the changing rooms, and from a rail she took a buttonless short-sleeved shirt with an open-necked collar. It was in a shimmering green shot silk.

'Face the door for a moment,' she ordered, weaving past another shopper in time to the music until she stood with her back to the entrance. She held the shirt up at head height and rapidly switched her eyes backwards and forwards between it and my face. Then, standing still for a moment, she nodded solemnly, as if she had received a sign. A moment later she was off again, spinning towards a rail of trousers.

'32 long, right?'

I nodded, not even trying to speak. I was way behind the action, had handed the whole process over to her by default.

Next, she plucked a pair of dark olive trousers from the rail and held them up to my waist for the briefest moment, then said, 'Perfect fit. I mean, you could try them on but,' she nodded in the direction of the changing rooms, 'it's like, gross in there. Too many, you know, like really large ladies trying to bargain-hunt themselves into things that do *not* fit. Anyway, I'm really great at this and my friend bought some of these last week and he's like exactly your height and they didn't need altering at all. Now, anything else? Like, socks and box?'

'I'm sorry, I didn't quite catch that?'

'I KNEW it!' she shouted delightedly. 'Tall, handsome, killer green eyes, accent like Hugh Grant. You must be Michael.'

I nodded. 'This is a set-up, isn't it?' I asked.

'I'm like, *so* busted. This is great!' she laughed. 'Yeah, Penny called me earlier, told me you might be coming by. Gave me a verbal photofit, that kinda stuff. I've been watching that door for a while.'

'Why do I get the feeling that someone else has planned every move I make in this town? How does a man get some privacy around here?'

I smiled as I said this, but in truth I did feel uncomfortable with the fact that Penny's unseen hand had followed me across the island.

'Chill,' she said. 'Everyone knows everyone else around here.' She pronounced the word 'else' as if it had a 't' in the middle. 'You'll get used to it. Actually, it's cool. All things will be good. I'm Phil, by the way.'

'Phil?'

'Yeah, Phil. Now, let's go choose the rest of your stuff.'

I left the shop fifteen minutes later with a jacket, a pair of khaki shorts and a polo shirt, socks, boxer shorts, a cashmere sweater and the shirt and trousers that Phil had chosen for me. It struck me as I walked further west down Duval towards the port that I wouldn't be able to fit all of these new things in my bag when I left. I paused briefly outside a shop with a display of suitcases in the window, then walked on. My hands were full; I could always come back tomorrow.

It only took five minutes to get to the dockside, and I heard the huge noise of the ship's horn before I rounded the corner. Thousands of people were milling around, a carnival feeling in the air. My ship was sliding out of dock towards the sunset, its huge whiteness softened and coloured by the incredible red, purple and orange-tinged evening light. Impossibly perfect clouds stacked up behind it on the horizon, piles of cotton backlit into startling hues. From deck upon deck up the side of the ship, people stood and waved at the dockside and thousands of strangers waved back.

Off to one side I heard laughter and applause so I turned and climbed some steps parallel to the oceanfront, walking along to where a series of street entertainers had set up their pitches. The first one I came to starred a performing pig which, encouraged by its owners – a youngish-looking couple – stepped over small hurdles and jumped from platform to platform wearing pearls and a hat, then snuffled at the audience's feet for snacks. Towards the back of the impromptu stage sat a young boy, nine or ten years old, playing in a bored way with some props from the show while his parents and the pig worked the crowd. And I thought to myself that the strangest life could seem normal, once you were accustomed to it.

After a few more minutes I became aware that there was a general movement away from the sideshows towards the water's edge. The sun was a huge, fat disc now, its top obscured by cloud and its bottom edge just starting to slide into the sea. As it dipped into the horizon, a mirror image of it reached out from the water and for a few moments the two suns touched, forming a slender serif at their conjunction. Along the whole length of the bay, people turned their heads towards the spectacle, synchronised like sunflowers at dusk. We all watched for a minute or so as it sank towards its end and then at the last moment, when just a slice remained, it paused dramatically until the crowd grew almost silent. Then it speeded up until it finally dipped from view, a last ray remaining, trapped in the amber afterglow.

Tentatively at first, the crowd started to clap. A growing wave of applause swept across the water towards the sunset and as whistles and cheers arose from a thousand mouths there was a long, distant toot from the departing ship's horn.

I'd been holding my breath without realising it and now as I breathed out an elderly woman at my side turned to me smiling and sighed, 'It don't get any better'n that.'

6
Outerwear

When I returned to Penny's some time later, there was no one about. Lights shone from behind the curtains of some of the windows in the main house, but the huts by the pool were dark. The pool itself was brightly lit from within, shimmering like a huge blue cocktail sprouting a surreal garnish in the form of the plants around its edge. Another unknown thread of something operatic hung in the air for a moment, the last note dissolving slowly into the warm evening. I wanted to swim but had no appropriate clothing, so I settled for a long shower.

When I had finished, I shaved and put on the soft towelling robe that hung waiting. I opened the bathroom door and let the hot, wet air escape into the fan-stirred atmosphere of my room, where my new clothes lay neatly on the bedside chair. They looked like a person who had been put into storage, folded up to save space. I walked gingerly around the foot of the bed, trying not to wake this stranger, and opened the doors onto my deck.

The night was cooler now and the scent of jasmine hovered in the air. Far away I could hear the faintest rumble of life, the throb of a distant engine. Absurdly, given that it was dusk, a cockerel crowed, long and throaty, a chest-expanded mating call. I strained to hear if any music was drifting in from the main deck area, but there was nothing.

I had to decide what to do now. It was 10.30 and soon I'd be expected to appear. Part of me was fearful of being alone and needed to see some friendly faces, however new. And although another part of me felt apprehensive and aware of that morning's unpleasant sense of disorientation, I came down loosely in favour of company. So, clad in my new shirt and trousers, I emerged from my room twenty-five minutes later.

Penny was waiting for me on the front porch. I heard her before I saw her; she was singing 'Some Enchanted Evening' quietly to herself, crooning gently like a mother hen and rocking in a chair that hung suspended on slender chains from the ceiling. As I came out of the front door, she heard my footsteps and turned to look me up and down with satisfaction on her face.

'Well,' she said, 'quite a transformation. You do scrub up well. You want to watch it, you know; you'll be breaking hearts looking like that. How do I look? Good enough to be seen with?'

She stood up and performed a graceful revolution. She was wearing a long swirling skirt in a colourful sarong fabric, slit almost up to her hip on one side. On her top half was a dark blue bodice-like blouse that pushed her breasts up and out impressively. A gold-threaded shawl was draped over her shoulders. The effect was South Sea Maiden goes Gypsy, accentuated by the wild pile of her hair into which some of her colourful beads had escaped.

'You look very attractive,' I said, determined to charm her. 'Mysterious and dusky.'

'Good. The problem with being my height is, the only people who make clothes my size are the drag queens over on Duval and that's a look I have to avoid at all costs. Can you imagine it? I'd look like Doctor Butch'n'Femme's monster.'

'Pardon me?'

'You haven't heard of butch and femme? It's a dyke thing. Lots of lesbians form his 'n' hers pairs, you know, where one of them is all flannel shirts and work boots and the other is exaggeratedly lipsticky.'

'Oh, I see. You'll have to forgive me. You're the first lesbian I've ever...'

'... had?' she said, laughing raucously.

'No! You know what I mean.' I was blushing now. 'You're the first lesbian I've ever *met*!'

'That you *know* of,' she said. 'We're all around, you know, secretly plotting to take over the world. A few squirts of sperm and we won't need you lot ever again. So you'd better watch out.'

'Thanks for the tip,' I said, warming to her. 'How do you plan to get the sperm?'

'Oh, there are plenty of gay men willing to oblige. In this town, we could get all the sperm we need in an afternoon, believe me. Now come. If we're late the food will all be gone and I didn't eat yet.'

She reached out her arm for me to take, and we walked in time down the steps to the street. Piloting me to our left, she said, 'God, it's such a relief to get escorted by a man my own height for a change. Alex is a couple of inches short where it counts for me. But then, I am not other women.'

'Talking of which,' I replied, 'the lady you paid homage to earlier when you gave me the, umm, joint. Who is she?'

'Oh, Anna Madrigal you mean? My poor man, you did look confused! Well, I'm not telling you. Not yet. If I like you as much as I think I'm going to, I'll show you where you can find out. And if I don't, you'll never know. So you'd better put some effort in, OK?'

'OK,' I replied. 'You know, lots of women these days are over six feet tall. More protein in the diet and so on.'

'These days,' she said with a sigh. 'You're right, these days. But years ago, when I started dating, I was a freak. I mean, girls from...' She paused. 'Girls where I grew up were just not this tall. Hell, the guys weren't this tall.'

I took a deep breath of scented air as we walked past a sweet-smelling bush. It was good to be having a real conversation again, a conversation held with another person rather than conducted fitfully in my head.

'Started dating?' I asked. 'Boys or girls?'

'Boys, of course. Actually, not "of course" at all. How could you know that? Look, I may seem very "out" to you, meeting me now, at this age. But getting comfortable with it took me years. And in truth I'm not sure that anyone raised in suburban America in the 50s ever really gets one hundred percent comfortable with being anything but a regular suburban American. But I'm ninety-eight percent there, and it's easier in Key West than in most other places.'

'Why is it easier here?' I asked. 'I mean, people here seem very friendly, sort of tolerant and laid back, so what's the story?'

'Next time you come to Key West, come by road. That's what I did the first time. Then you'll understand. You see, this place is the end of the line, nearly two hundred miles from Main Street America. You reach it via a series of scrappy little islands joined by enormously long bridges. It's literally out on a limb beyond a limb and it's nearer to Cuba than America, so it's always danced to a different tune. It's tolerant, arty, independent...'

She explained that it was originally populated by smugglers, pirates and wreckers. Then later, after the collapse of its native industries, Key West became very poor, which made it a magnet for drifters – it was possible to survive on almost nothing and everybody did. 'And unlike Hawaii or the Virgin Islands,' she continued, 'you could get here by just hitching a ride, so it never became exclusive. Over time it built up a population of people who didn't fit in anyplace else, and I guess they just had to be pretty tolerant and broad minded to get along with each other.'

'But what about all the military installations?' I asked. 'I saw some while I was out walking today. It doesn't usually make for a very liberal town, such a big military presence.'

'Are you kidding? Listen, stick a few thousand young sailors in a barracks for months on end this far from civilisation, fill them with beer every night and pretty soon they won't care what they screw! My pet theory is that the reason this town has such a strong drag tradition is that the resident gay community realised they were infinitely more likely to get a cute young lieutenant to hump them if they made even the slightest effort to look female! Anyway, the military's mostly gone now.'

This talk of the military was creating uncomfortable shadows of my father somewhere at the back of my head, so I changed the subject.

'What brought you here in the first place?' I asked.

'Pretty much the same thing as you,' she said gently.

I paused momentarily before replying.

'And how do you know that?' I asked.

'Alex is no fool and he knows I can be, well, a little questioning. So he called and asked me to go easy on you, before he brought you round this morning.'

'Before he brought me round? But I was with him when I decided not to catch the ship. I don't think he had a phone with him. I'd have seen him make a call.'

She stopped walking and turned to face me, taking both my hands in hers.

'Like I said, Alex is no fool, he called from his house while you were in the back yard, just to check that I had a room available. He had a hunch that he might be able to persuade you to stay. He could see where your head was going. Listen, don't freak out about it. He's just an extremely nice and very intuitive guy. And... well, whatever.'

'And what?'

'Oh, nothing. Just... whatever.'

'I'm not freaking out,' I continued. 'It was nice of him. I'm just... not accustomed to people making such an effort. It's very nice if a little disconcerting, but it's pretty much new to me. Where I come from, people aren't usually so thoughtful.'

'Well, you and I effectively come from the same place then, and maybe that's why we've both ended up here.'

She took my arm again and steered me across the street before continuing.

'So, I came here for pretty much the same reason as you. Or rather, that's why I stayed. I am, or rather was, an opera singer by training. Nothing special, no top-billing diva, but reasonably successful at least. I was on tour in Europe when I had a phone call from my brother Carey.

He was living here in Key West, had done for years, with his boyfriend Karl. You'll meet Karl tonight, I think. Anyway, Carey called to say that he was sick.'

I looked at her sideways. Her face was perfectly composed.

'He had been HIV for years; lots of HIV-positive people come here. The climate makes it easier for them to stay well and the social climate is very sympathetic too. Anyway, things just stopped working for Carey. He got pneumonia and by the time I got here from Europe he was dead. I spoke to him on the phone while I was waiting on a connecting flight in London, the day before he died, and he actually said goodbye. He knew he wasn't going to last the night and from his voice, so did I.'

I tightened my grip on her arm momentarily and she returned the pressure as she continued.

'I had been here once before but only for a few days one August. I don't really remember my first trip; just the heat and needing to sit in a car for the air-con. Anyway, I arrived three days before Carey's funeral in the most terrible state. I'd been weeping and wailing the whole way across the Atlantic, like the diva I'm not, people staring at me like it was bad manners to cry in public, then I got here and people behaved so differently towards me. Admittedly they were Carey's friends but they really looked after me, particularly Sue. Karl had gone AWOL, couldn't cope, though he did show up for the funeral. By which time I had five or six new friends, people who'd been close to Carey, possibly saw me as an extension of him, whatever. The thing was, they just seemed altogether nicer than the people I'd become used to elsewhere. So after the funeral I stayed. At first it was just for a couple of weeks, but pretty soon I was back and I bought my own little slice of paradise and settled down. Happy ending, so far.'

'What was he like? Carey. How old was he?'

'He had his thirty-eighth birthday a week before he died. He would have been around the same age as you now. And he was beautiful. Well, you'll probably see a photo of him at some point, but this is not just his sister speaking. He was the same height as me, ridiculously strong jaw, eyes so blue they looked like they'd seen heaven. Black, black hair.'

She trailed off and I turned my head towards her to see that her look of composure remained.

'I'm sorry,' I said. 'I mean, I'm so sorry for you, for him. That I reminded you.'

'That's OK,' she replied. 'Honestly. There comes a time when you feel like the loss is warmer than it's sad, and that telling someone what happened is a way of keeping some part of the person you loved alive. Really.'

For a few moments we walked in silence. Then she said, 'I don't want you to feel that you've walked into a community of emotional cripples or whatever, but you'll find that what I said earlier is true. There's an above average number of mending hearts in this town, and they generally help each other out. I mean, provided they don't turn out to be psycho or something...' Suddenly she laughed. 'God, there was this guy, two years ago, turned up at someone's pool party with this awful story. His wife had been murdered in Chicago: raped and killed during a burglary in their home. He'd arrived home from a trip two days later and found her. We were all falling over each other to bake things for him for days... until Phil saw him on TV in this "Most Wanted" slot, and he disappeared. Turned out he'd done it himself. Yuk. I'm always convinced he's gonna turn up some dark night. That's why I need such a big, brave escort.'

The Deep South accent and coquettish manner from that morning had returned and she fluttered her eyelids, mugging the face of a helpless bimbo. Every inch a performer.

We had reached the intersection I'd stopped at in my stupefied state that morning. The lights were green and we walked straight across. In the air above us and about fifty feet up, an impossibly large American flag rose into the breeze then subsided, caught in a massive spotlight.

We walked in a companionable silence for a while until we were no more than thirty yards from the café, then Penny turned to me and said, 'So, is there anything you'd like to ask me before we go in?'

Bemused, I asked, 'Such as?'

'Oh, I don't know. Nothing you want to know about any of the people you've met?'

I thought I detected a cryptic tone.

'Not that I can think of,' I replied. 'Am I missing something?'

She turned and took a step back, ran her eyes over me briefly and said, 'Not as far as I can see. Come on.'

She took me by the hand before I could pursue the topic any further, and led me towards the door. But just before we got to it, she stopped and slapped her forehead with her hand.

'My God, Michael, I'm so sorry. I forgot to give you this.'

She fumbled in her purse and pulled out a folded piece of paper. It had my room number pencilled on the outside.

'Someone called for you earlier. Sam – he's the night-clerk – took the message. Here.'

She handed me the piece of paper. I opened it slowly. The date and time were written neatly at the top of the form. On the 'To' line it had my name and, on the 'From' line, that of my brother-in-law.

And the message read:

James Angus McGrath, named in Jim's memory, born today at 19.03. Weight $5\frac{1}{4}$ lbs.

Michael Donald McGrath, named after his fabulous uncle, born today at 19.12. Weight $5\frac{1}{2}$ lbs. Non-identical twins. Mother and babies doing well. All love. Call us tomorrow.

7
Party

After a lifetime of keeping my emotions buttoned down, this news threw up a combination of feelings that was far beyond my gamut. So for the second time that day, Alex encountered me in a highly charged state. He was grabbing a couple of bottles of wine from the fridge when Penny and I came in. There were a few other people in the café but Alex's head rose as we entered and he came straight over before Penny had the chance to introduce me to anyone else.

He repeated a gesture of Penny's, facing me full on and taking both my hands in his, which caused me to register a slight feeling of embarrassment.

'Wow, what a change since this morning,' he said. 'You look like a million dollars. It's amazing what a few hours with Penny can do for a man!'

His eyes danced over me, catching and returning the points of candlelight in the room. He had changed into shorts now: baggy white shorts that came down to his knees, baseball sneakers, and a dark blue T-shirt with 'Konichiwa' written in large letters across the chest. His face was one big, white, American smile.

'Thanks. Actually, I just had some quite wonderful news, I...' I handed him the piece of paper. 'It's from my brother-in-law. Penny just gave it to me. Here.'

He took the note from me and as he unfolded it he raised his eyes to meet mine again in question.

'Should I...?'

'Sure, please, read it.'

He scanned for a few seconds and then, taking me by surprise, he threw his arms around me in a tight bear hug and swung me from side to side saying, 'Michael, that is such great news!'

'Alex!' It was Penny. 'Put the poor man down. He's in a delicate state.'

It was true. I was laughing and almost crying at the same time; happy, sad, elated and confused. Also very self-conscious at being so visibly emotional in front of a room full of people. So what came next went over my head. Or rather, it made no conscious impression at the time, though I remember it clearly now.

Alex said, 'Well, let's hope the twins are as handsome as their uncle Michael. Now come with me.'

He took me by the arm and led me over to the fridge, looking over his shoulder as he did so and shouting, 'Penny, you gorgeous dyke, get Sue in here right now. It's French champagne time. We have two babies' heads to wet!'

Despite the increasingly familiar feeling that my life was being taken out of my own hands, I did not resist. Alex's buoyant enthusiasm was a licence for me to feel the same way, and I accepted it gladly.

Within moments Penny reappeared with Sue. Phil followed them through the curtain and blew a wolf-whistle at the sight of me wearing the ensemble she had chosen for me earlier.

'Hello Phil,' I said. 'My own personal style consultant.'

I heard myself speaking, and felt the shock of sounding like myself again, like someone with a sense of humour.

'Just don't blame me for those shoes, OK, buster?' she said, looking down at my scruffy brogues with affected disdain. 'Groovy pants, though. God, they are such a good fit. Spin around so I can see your butt.'

As I turned to show her my rear, Phil whooped. Then, just as the champagne cork popped, someone patted my backside. I didn't see who. It was a neutral kind of a pat – it might have been any or all of congratulatory, reassuring, jovial, exploratory.

Sue appeared at my side and slipped her arm quietly through mine, saying, 'Penny told me the news. That's very sweet. It's a lovely idea to name your nephews like that. You must feel very mixed emotions.' She spoke with the same tentative tone I remembered from that morning, as if someone else might interrupt or contradict her with a more incisive comment. Then she reached up to me on her tiptoes and brushed my cheek momentarily with her lips. I smelt perfume, cooking, the faintest whiff of something more earthy.

Champagne was being passed around. As soon we all had a glass, Alex raised his and said, 'To babies James and Michael, inheritors of our wonderful, wild, fucked-up, beautiful world. May they love and be loved with abandon.'

'James and Michael!'

'James and Michael!'

'James and Michael!'

'James and Michael!'

8
Another Surprise

A second bottle of champagne quickly appeared and soon I was slightly drunk. While Alex and Sue greeted a group of newly arrived guests, Penny steered me through into the yard.

'I want to introduce you to Karl, Carey's boyfriend. He's a little more sedate than some of these high-octane youths. He's also somewhat of an antidote to the Moonie love-fest you've gracefully endured from the rest of us without gagging. In fact, he was weaned on pickles. Actually that's not fair. He's a good man, he just can be a little arch sometimes. But you know what they say: behind every cynic there's a disappointed romantic. He hasn't found another partner since Carey died. So he's a little lonely, underneath the hard shell.'

As she spoke, she manoeuvred us past a group of tall, elegant women who were talking animatedly. 'Evening, boys,' she said to them. She was greeted with a few theatrically frigid air kisses.

One of them, an extravagantly dressed creature, replied, 'I see your nose is still as finely tuned to the oestrogen-testosterone divide as ever, my dear. And who, may I ask, is this delicious young man?'

The voice was husky and left me in no doubt as to its owner's true gender.

'Mine. Keep your painted claws off him,' said Penny, imitating the drag queen's camp tone and making a clawing motion at the air.

'*Daaarling*!' This was addressed to me. 'Welcome to Green Card *Hell*. I'd rather get a job in Bosnia than marry her to get residency. How much is she charging?'

Throwing further sarcastic air kisses over her shoulder as she went,

Penny swept us past them, muttering in the loudest possible stage whisper, 'And I'd rather be in hell than in *that* frock.'

We found Karl standing on his own in the far corner of the yard, smoking. He was somewhere in his late sixties and around six foot but he looked taller, due to his poised, architectural thinness. Dressed in a cream linen suit with a white shirt, holding a bottle of sherry and wearing a Panama, he was the Englishman from Central Casting. Until he spoke.

'Penny, my luff. Vot is zis tasty morsel you are bringing me now? I do hope zis vun is more affordable zan se last. He left me feeling qvite drained, in *every* way.'

'Michael, this is Karl. Karl, Michael. Give Michael a drink, Karl, and you can cut out the German Count act. He won't buy it. He's from England so he knows a real aristocrat, and a real German, when he sees one.'

Karl shrugged in mock defeat and lapsed into a standard East Coast WASP accent, which still sounded subtly fake. He took my hand and raised it to his lips as if to kiss it, but instead he sniffed it, then shook it like a businessman might, and said, '*Willkommen, bienvenue*, welcome.'

He took my glass and filled it to the brim with sherry, shooing Penny away as he did so. Surprisingly, she went.

'Talking of cabaret, I see you met those delightful young ladies.' He nodded in the direction of the drag queens. 'It really is *so* dreary the way they insist on crossing claws with Penny. For some reason that I've never understood, dykes and drag just don't mix.' Karl said this as if it were a well-known rule, enunciating the words like a familiar ditty.

'Hilaire Belloc should have written a cautionary tale about it,' he continued. 'I would love to do the illustrations. Now, how did you end up here, my dear? Ripped from the bosom of Mother England into this seething hormonal ferment of crazed colonials. Surely, it was not by choice? And yet they're all so *nice*. Have you been sick yet?'

I took a considered swig of my sherry before deciding how to play the situation. I plumped for neutral, with a tone tending towards Karl's own. With Penny gone I felt a little abandoned and uncomfortable; but a childhood filled with Forces parties had given me an automatic line in polite chat.

'I arrived on a cruise liner this morning.' I paused. What next? A bad Oscar Wilde impression came out. 'Crippled by seasickness, I decided to remain ashore. A gentleman by the name of Alex introduced me to Penny's Paradise and here I am.'

'From one cruise to another then,' he replied. 'And has Penny given you what I believe is known in some circles as "the low-down"?'

'I'm sorry, I don't quite follow you.'

'Has she performed her weekly act of Gestalt? Has she told you of the connection between Penny and Karl, star-crossed in-laws? I'm sure she has. She rarely introduces people without applying pre-emptive emotional first aid. Don't worry, my dear; I'm as tough as old nails by now. No need to be sensitive on my account.'

I swigged again at my sherry. 'You mean Carey. The connection between you and Penny? Carey, her brother?'

'Ah! Dear Penny has expelled all, again. She is *quite* spent. Until next time. She is a serial offender, but I adore her nonetheless.' He stared at the ground for the briefest of moments, then said, 'I do approve of her little paradise. She certainly shares Carey's good taste. And of course you're very lucky to get a room there at such short notice – it's more solidly booked than the Hyatt Ritz Carlton Regency. Dykes, male homosexuals and increasingly these days, swingers. A few lost heterosexuals too, I shouldn't doubt.' He looked at me in open speculation. I chose to ignore it.

'Swingers?'

'Hideous people who take refuge from doing it with their own hideous partners by doing it in groups with other, equally hideous, people. Mostly Germans, or from Wisconsin.'

'Is that who stays at Penny's place? Really? I haven't seen any of the other guests yet.'

'Oh, they don't get out much. They travel right to the end of Interstate 1, charge their camcorder batteries, invite some friends they met in an internet chatroom, and get on down.' He wrinkled his face in a withering look.

I had a sense that this was a game of tennis: he had served and, on the assumption that he would eventually prove the superior player, was indifferent between fault and rally. I reached for his sherry bottle but he moved it sharply away, then in a guarded manner beckoned my glass towards him and poured me a reasonably generous amount. 'So,' he said, 'over to you.'

'Tell me about the swingers. Why here? I mean, I've never been to Key West before but all I hear is Gay, Dyke, Swinger and so on. Why here in particular?'

Of course, I'd already asked Penny a similar question; but this town was clearly one that its inhabitants liked to talk about, so this seemed to be the best way to divert further questions about myself.

'My dear innocent boy,' Karl answered. 'Here's a potted socio-sexual history of Key West, and I speak with the detachment of an émigré. Take one town: hot climate, humid, sweaty, miles from anywhere. Half sensual Cuban, half repressed American. Fill it with a mixture of everybody else's social outcasts and add thousands of young sailors on heat. Bake for a short while, then reach for the tissues. Splat. America's first officially off-its-face, does-what-it-wants town. Clear enough?'

'But from your tone of voice I'd guess the swingers are more recent and less welcome. Why is that?'

'Here's the thing; go down to Atlantic Shores, it's a sort of adult beach resort without a beach. It's where people go to sunbathe in the nude and check out the talent. It's a good old-fashioned meat market. Now, that place has been gay for years. Years! I should know, God help me. Then slowly a few dykes creep in. Even though most gay men secretly feel on some level that lesbianism is unnatural, nobody actually complains. We can't argue against it, you see. It's hard to square the circle between our own heartrending pleas for equal rights and our natural lack of affinity for the double horror of *two* women doing it. The arguments would be too subtle for mass consumption, like trying to argue in favour of single-sex schools.

'Anyway. So there you are at the Shores, snoozing in the sun. You wake, look up and there's a vagina staring you in the face. But you have to act as if it's perfectly acceptable, because she's lesbian, you're all gay people together, and together you fight the good fight for acceptance. However.'

He paused dramatically.

'This is the thin end of the wedge! Soon enough, with the aid of some less-than-reputable niche tour operators, word gets around that Key West is "anything goes-ville".

'Next time you wake from your afternoon nap at the Shores, the vagina is sporting a mohican, pierced by what looks like Philippe Starck door furniture, and its proprietor is holding hands with a man. And you find yourself asking, "Where now?"

'We used to fear segregation. Now we crave it. Gay men are like Jews – and I should know. Put us in a ghetto and we hate it. Don't put us in one, we'll create it.'

Penny reappeared. 'I've come to rescue you, Michael. Karl will hold forth all evening, getting you progressively more drunk, then pounce. I've seen it all before.'

'Thank you, but I'm managing quite well on my own. And Karl is keeping me both entertained and educated. I'm perfectly happy.'

This wasn't strictly true, but I was doing better than I would have thought. Karl's acerbic manner was carefully ironic rather than bitter in delivery.

'What a sensible young man,' he replied. 'And so good looking, too. I don't suppose by any chance that you're *available*, are you?'

'Karl!' exclaimed Penny.

'Shut up, you silly woman, let the boy answer. He's perfectly capable of looking after himself.'

'I'm flattered,' I said. In fact I was flustered. 'But I'm afraid I have to disappoint you. I'm actually married.'

I just caught the look of surprise on Penny's face before Karl continued.

'Oh Michael, so disingenuous – or maybe naïve? I'm not interested in your marital status; I'm trying to find out if you have sex with men. The fact that you are married gives me *precious* little to go on. If I had a dollar for every married man I've slept with, I'd be even richer than I am.'

I considered my reply briefly.

'I'm sorry to appear naïve, but as far as I'm aware, married men tend to be heterosexual. It goes with the territory. Though I should add that I am currently going through a divorce. Does that improve my potential?' A slightly tense edge was creeping into my voice now and I knew that Karl could sense it. For whatever reason, he decided not to pursue the scent.

'You have the potential to be whatever you want to be, as long as you have the power to imagine it. That's where most people fail. Dear, oh dear, young Alex *will* be disappointed.'

Penny interjected. 'Karl, you're over-sharing, that's very unfair. Michael, I will steer you away from this poisonous old man now, and you mustn't listen to a word he says. Whatever Alex's sexual preferences may or may not be, at least he has manners. Unlike Karl.'

'Oh Penny, don't be so pompous. I'm quite sure Michael can look after himself. And now, this sherry is almost finished. I must go in search of another bottle. It has been a pleasure meeting you, Michael. I do hope our paths will cross again. Perhaps you'd care to dine with me?'

And with that, he was gone.

Penny stood uncomfortably by for a moment. I looked around the yard. There were twenty, maybe twenty-five people present now, forming and re-forming fluid groups. Conversation and laughter drifted in and out, weaving with the sound of an acoustic guitar, which I at first took to be issuing from a loudspeaker but which was in fact coming from over by the curtained door where Sue sat on a stool, strumming away.

Penny broke our silence. 'I should never have left you with him for so long. He really doesn't know where to stop.'

'Alex and you have both been very kind to me today,' I said. 'And it's already made something of a difference, it really has. I certainly don't care who either of you sleeps with, as long as you enjoy it.'

'Karl, for a whole lot of reasons that predate Carey by a long shot, has a bitter streak a mile wide, but he can also be very funny and very interesting and often even rather nice. He's just a *teensy* bit irritated that you're not a prospect. Now, let's go listen to Sue play and I'll introduce you to some of the others.'

'Would you mind if we didn't, just for a moment? I'm not sure I feel like meeting too many strangers right now.' I scoured my head for something to say to cover my embarrassment at admitting this. 'I'd like to ask you about Sue and Phil anyway, if you don't mind.'

A short, plump man walked past with a bottle of wine and Penny stopped him and recharged our glasses.

'Well, let's do it chronologically,' she replied. 'I've known Sue since before Carey died; she was a friend of his. You see, Carey and Karl owned this café. Karl still does, though frankly he's so stinking rich that it's just a minor toy for him. Anyway, about ten years ago, when Carey was running this place, Sue walked in off the street and asked for a job. She'd been travelling around the country with a group of itinerant hippies, her whole childhood long. Her parents were members of this group, all Woodstocked out and nowhere left to go. So they drifted here and there and ended up in Key West for a while. And Sue decided to stay.

'Like a lot of hippies' kids, she's very conventional herself. She craves normality. I sometimes think that she'd be best suited to life as a suburban housewife. And yet, she has this strange, insubstantial quality, as if she were a candle flame.' Penny paused for a moment before continuing, as if she were addressing herself. 'She can sometimes gutter quietly almost to nothing then suddenly flare up again. She needs love, like all of us, I suppose.'

'And Phil?'

'Ah, Phil. Phil also defies easy summary. She's actually from Key West. Did Alex tell you about his aunt, who left him the house? The artist?'

'In passing.'

'Well, Aunt Peggy had a Mexican lover called Enrique who she refused to marry for some obscure reason. Which made her double anathema to her rather conservative family, of course. Anyway, she apparently couldn't have children herself, so she encouraged him to, everywhere. By some accounts he had as many as thirty or forty, scattered from here to Miami and back. And she used to remember all their birthdays, send them Christmas presents, the whole thing. Even put some of them though school and ended up spending most of her inheritance on them, which is why Alex won't get any money with the house. Anyway, Phil is one of the lover's grandchildren, so she's a sort of unofficial cousin of Alex's. She lives at home with her bed-bound mother who sounds rather like the woman in *What's Eating Gilbert Grape?* – did you see it?'

'I'm afraid not,' I said, aware of a slight slur to my voice.

'It's about an enormously fat woman with what you might call a "differently functional" family, bringing them up on her own without ever being able to leave the sofa. Anyway, Phil's dad died when she was young. He used to do game-fishing trips for tourists, the boat got caught in a storm and he was never seen again. They never found his body. Which left her mother with eight kids. Cuban Catholics. Phil comes somewhere in the middle. She's tremendously conscientious, more so than the older kids. So she gets to be the breadwinner for Ma and the younger ones. But – and this is the key – not only is she smart and hardworking, she can sing like you would not believe. Now, like I told you earlier, I used to be an opera singer. But my first love was the blues. And Phil has quite simply the best blues voice I have ever heard, anywhere, without qualification.'

'Does she ever perform anywhere around here, in clubs or bars or anything?' I asked, taking another swig of my wine.

'You bet she does. Every single night. She's just waiting for some big shot from the music industry to come through on vacation and spot her. And she's saving up to cut a demo. She is unspoilt, sweet and totally determined. Get her autograph while you can.'

'Will she sing tonight?' I asked.

The plump man was back, this time with a tray of pizza slices. I realised that I hadn't eaten. It was midnight and I was getting quietly drunk on an empty stomach. I reached out to take a piece but the moment had passed, the tray had moved on.

'For sure. She loves to be accompanied by Sue, says she's the only guitar player in town with any real soul, but Sue only plays for friends, here, on Sundays.'

Alex had been working his way through the yard towards us and had just come within earshot, so I turned to him with my next question. 'OK. So I see the connection between Alex and Phil, and I know how Sue and Penny met. Who joined the dots? How did all four of you get to know each other?'

Penny and Alex exchanged brief but uncomfortable glances. It was immediately clear that I had asked the wrong question.

'Via Sue, I suppose,' Alex said, after a moment's pause. 'Sue and I are married.'

9
Over the Rainbow

Loosened up by a combination of champagne and sherry, I took the unexpected news that Alex and Sue were husband and wife in my stride. In fact, being drunk suited the circumstances well – after a day as odd as this, nothing seemed unlikely any more. Even the most contradictory pieces of information seemed to flow together with ease. And drink had been my way of coping recently.

'I had no idea! How long have you been married for?' I slurred.

'Just over a year, but...'

'Alex!' It was Penny. 'Not now, dear, I suggest you explain your complex marital history when Michael has a few hours to spare. Anyway, Phil's about to sing.'

Alex and I looked over to where Sue was sitting and saw that Phil had joined her. They were flicking through a sheaf of papers together. Sue gazed at one particular page intently and quietly strummed a few chords to herself.

'Did you bring your joint?' asked Penny.

'Oh, I'm sorry, I forgot.'

'Never mind. I have an emergency supply.'

Just as she had that morning, she fumbled in her hair and pulled out a crumpled joint. 'Poor baby,' she cooed to it as she straightened it out. 'There.' She reached across to a table in front of Alex and picked up a disposable lighter which somebody had left lying there, lit the joint with an intensely focussed look on her face and, after one or two exploratory puffs, took a long draw and held it in. I had an image of her on stage, taking a deep breath before letting loose a devastating high-note. But when the sound came it was no more than a satisfied sigh. Penny handed the joint to me.

'I'm afraid you're going to think I'm terribly square,' I said, 'but I'll pass for now. I didn't even attempt my first cigarette until this morning, and that was hardly a success.'

'Michael, don't you ever take up smoking cigarettes at your age. That's not pleasure-seeking, it's pure defiance, of something or some*one*. But marijuana is quite different. You're probably aware of its widely proclaimed medical benefits. And I am an excellent teacher, so you've no need to fear.' She took my hand firmly and put the joint between my fingers. 'Since it's your first time, you can only have one puff to start with. Then after a few minutes we'll see how much of an impact it's had and adjust the dosage accordingly. Draw it into your mouth, but don't inhale yet.'

She was like the Sister in the sanatorium at my boarding school; it wouldn't have entered my head to argue with her.

'Now, slowly, very slowly so you don't cough, inhale through your mouth and nose. When your lungs are full, exhale immediately but slowly. That's it.'

The smoke burned my throat, but not excessively. I easily controlled the cough that tried to come, and within a few seconds the procedure was complete.

'Gooood. Now, it may take a minute or two before you feel anything – assuming that you do. The classic first-timer mistake is to take another few drags immediately because you feel no impact. That's the quickest way to knock yourself out. Luckily this is very mellow grass indeed. Quite mild, unusually non paranoid-making. The very finest, in fact. But please go easy, nonetheless. A little bit will loosen you up but too much is not a happy mix with... well, just go easy on it.'

I didn't respond. I was watching Phil, who stood up from her crouching position next to Sue and picked up a small microphone from on top of a box that looked like a portable karaoke machine. Sue strummed a few chords, randomly at first, but then I realised that Phil was humming along to them. Over the course of a few meandering bars, the humming developed into a soft croon. It dipped and weaved in between Sue's chords as if the two were playing tag gently. Then slowly it resolved itself into an immensely familiar tune. It was the haunting, wordless female vocal line from *Dark Side of the Moon*, sometimes sinking to a whisper and sometimes growing to a wail. It was spine-tingling. The yard had grown quiet, all heads turned towards the two girls.

'Class act, eh?'

It was Alex whispering from beside me, the joint glowing red in the corner of his mouth. I suddenly realised I could not speak at all; or rather, that I didn't want to speak. I was entirely insulated, as if packed in invisible bubble-wrap, aware of nothing but the red glow of the joint and the sound opening itself in front of me. In slow motion, Alex linked his arm through mine and squeezed it. Penny did the same from the other side.

'How are you feeling? Any effect yet?' asked Penny.

I didn't speak, just nodded and smiled. Alex held the joint up towards my mouth, but I gently shook my head, still smiling. There was a faint buzzing sensation at the back of my brain, and the briefest moment of fear – a shadow of a sense that I might have a bad trip of some kind. But the warm insulating glow was too strong to take second place to anxiety, and all I wanted to do was to stand arm in arm with these two people and listen to this incredible music.

The rest of the evening dipped in and out of focus, though I have clear memories of certain things. I can remember my glass being filled with red wine at least once, because it's what I usually drink at parties and it was the first I'd been offered that night. I remember laughing at something, though I don't know what. But most of all I remember the music. Phil skipped fluently between soul, blues, jazz, a whole range and fusion of genres. Some of it she had written herself, but many of the songs were familiar. It was the performance, and voice, of a life-worn woman in her forties, coming from the mouth of a girl barely out of her teens. This gave it a poignant but double-edged quality that matched my mood; it was strange to hear how intimate she was with songs that I had first enjoyed before she was born.

At some point Penny excused herself. She had guests arriving early the next morning and needed to be up at a reasonable hour. I offered to walk her home, but she wanted me to stay until Phil had finished, so she left me with Alex.

As soon as Penny had gone, I helped myself to a more liberal supply of grass. By this stage I felt confident that I could regulate my own intake, but of course that confidence was itself bolstered by the mixture of alcohol and marijuana. Soon things slowed down almost to the point of stopping. My last clear memory was of Phil's final song. It was a fantastically sad rendition of 'Somewhere Over the Rainbow'.

I don't know if it was the drug, the song, or the combination of the two, but this song transported me to an entirely new place. It started conventionally enough: a few simple guitar chords, the briefest of pauses, then a voice like sadness itself flowed through the yard. Each familiar line was nuanced with a depth of feeling that turned it into a love song and a song of mourning, until I understood for the first time what a thoroughly adult song it is. Lullabies, dreams and fairy tales, wishing on stars, troubles melting like lemon drops. These things, all capable of the most saccharine rendition, became altogether more serious and more directly significant to me.

Halfway through the song, Alex appeared beside me and gently removed the joint I was holding, saying, 'It might be a good idea to go easy on that, Michael.'

I just nodded.

As she hit the last verse, Phil's voice opened up into a new range. She chased each crescendo higher, traced each descent more bittersweetly, taking a group of silent people up and over their own rainbows, then on a last, aching and fading note, gently lowering them back to earth again. For the second time that day I found myself crying, not because of any particular thing but simply because this twenty-year-old girl appeared, in my stoned state, to have sung directly into my soul. And from the subdued but intense nature of the applause, I don't think I was alone.

I felt the gentle pressure of a hand on my shoulder and half turned to look at Alex. A quiet candlelight flickered all around him and I thought: everything looks beautiful.

'Gets me every time,' he said. 'She should be banned from singing that song to anyone over the age of twelve; it's a public health hazard. Listen, it's late and I think we should get you home to bed. Penny'd kill me if I let you walk back alone as stoned as you currently look.' He smiled an unreadable smile. 'Pablo over there,' he nodded his head to indicate the chubby man who had been serving drinks earlier, 'is going to clear and close up, so I'll walk you back. It's kind of on the way. Almost.'

I have the vaguest recollection of trying to say something in reply, I don't know what, but no words came out so I simply allowed myself to be steered mutely through some 'good nights'.

10
A Familiar Dream

It might have been the relaxing effect of the marijuana, but my favourite dream came to me that night for the first time since Jim's death.

I am lying on a sun lounger on a wooden deck, somewhere that feels familiar. Below and beyond is the sea. I can smell the tang of salt, feel the sun and the breeze. Selina is lying on a lounger beside me, with sunglasses on. I cannot tell if she is awake or asleep because I cannot see her eyes. Her lips are red.

I whisper, 'Would you like a drink?' as quietly as I can, so as not to wake her if she is asleep. I want to get away unnoticed.

She doesn't answer, so I get up quietly and walk towards the bar. I'm shuffling in sandals and swim-shorts, carrying a towel draped around my neck. I'm aware of the movement of air on the skin, on my bare chest and midriff. I can feel the sun on my back.

The bar is twenty yards away. Its roof is made of some woven, natural material, desert island style. I wade towards it through the humid air. As I pass under the eaves, the sound of steel-band music swells from ceiling-mounted speakers. And it gets dark. Not shady, but suddenly dark, as if I've entered a basement nightclub with only the flicker of candles and a few concealed downlighters.

I sit on a stool and catch the bartender's eye. Ordering a beer, I look around. There's almost no one in there, but in the darkness I can just make out another man standing next to a barstool a few yards away. I nod and almost imperceptibly he nods back.

Everything is very soft, very slow and calm.

Then I do something that puzzles the part of me that knows this is a dream: I pull a packet of cigarettes from my shorts pocket. In real life I've never smoked. With my wife, when would I have dared?

I'm surprised to find myself tapping the packet on the bar like a pro, like a rugged stereotype from the movies. Flicking the flattened underside with my middle finger, I angle the pack to my mouth then my mouth to the pack in order to let my lips intercept the highest of the little pyramid of cigarettes that slides part way out. Sitting upright, I reach towards the candle on the bar, intending to use it to light the cigarette.

As I draw the candle forwards, I become aware of the other man moving out of the shadows towards me. He pulls out a book of matches then, stopping beside me, tears one off and lights it. Everything is slowing down now, and the focal length is zooming lazily in, compressing things closer together.

I swivel a quarter-turn towards him as the match flares. I am perfectly still on my stool, facing him with the cigarette in my mouth. He holds the match up towards my face. The flame stabilises and I take a draw, but what I'm really doing as I light the cigarette is looking at a beautiful, tiny, upside-down image of the yellow fire dancing in the other man's eyes. His face spreads into a slow smile. I am aware of the match burning close to his fingers. I am aware of him extinguishing the match with a gentle puff of breath without shifting his gaze. I am aware that, even though the match is gone, the flame is still there in his eye – and everything is perfectly still.

Usually this part of the dream lasts until I wake or drift away. Sometimes it seems like forever, and sometimes I seem to doze off within my own dream and not wake until I actually wake. But this time I was woken by the telephone next to my bed. It took some moments to work out where I was.

I was lying naked, face down, in my room at Penny's with sunlight streaming through the diaphanous curtains. I had a powerful erection and a terrible headache. I rolled slowly over and reached for the phone and as I did so I noticed that a pile of clothes was folded roughly on a chair near the bed. On top of it was a pair of boxer shorts. They were not mine.

11
Underwear

I froze. The telephone rang again. I was in no state to think clearly but there was a rush of thoughts to deal with and I had to decide what to do about the phone. A sudden, fearful possibility gnawed at me and I looked quickly over to the other side of the bed, seeing with relief that it was empty.

Who could be calling? It had to be either my brother-in-law, whom I didn't feel well enough to speak to, or someone from last night's party. It might be Penny, but then again it might be Alex. And I really did not want to speak to him at that moment, at least not until I had solved the riddle posed by the strange pair of boxer shorts. So I decided not to answer. But the phone rang and rang until eventually I decided that it must be important, or surely whoever it was would just give up.

'Hello, this is Michael.' My voice came out as a rough croak and I realised that my throat felt sore. An image of myself with a joint in my mouth flashed in front of me like a police photograph.

'Good morning, Michael.' It was Alex. 'God, you sound terrible!' he continued. 'You sound as bad as I feel. Worse. It took you forever to answer the phone. Did I wake you?'

I was sweating. 'Morning, Alex. Yup, I feel pretty bad.'

'I am not surprised. Talk about the dope monster. And you had quite a lot to drink, too. By the time I finally got you into bed, you hardly knew what was happening.'

I was silent, crazily trying to sort through the implications of this. My head was a sore, thumping haze and I couldn't focus clearly on the thoughts that were trying to emerge from it.

'Michael, you still there?'

'Uh-huh.'

'You OK?'

'I feel rather queasy. Bad headache too.'

'I'm not *that* bad,' he replied. 'In fact, I probably remember last night a whole lot better than you do.'

Again, I did not answer. This was getting to be too confusing. I couldn't fathom how many *entendres* deep we might be going.

'Alex,' I eventually said.

'Yeah?'

'Thanks for putting me to bed last night. I suppose it must have been you that undressed me and everything.'

'No, there was a whole group of us.'

I was really starting to feel sick now, physiology and psychology working together to churn my stomach. I replied weakly, 'You're kidding, right?'

'No, I'm deadly serious. You were wild.' He paused and for a moment I could hear nothing but his breathing. Then he continued. 'Of course I'm kidding, dumbo, it was just the two of us.'

I didn't know whether I should be relieved at this.

'Just the two of us?' I asked.

'Yeah, I undressed you alone. With very little help from you, I might add. I was most impressed.'

'Impressed?'

'Well, you're in great shape.'

'Alex, stop it, this is really unfair.'

Gales of laughter emerged from the handset. 'You really don't remember a thing, do you? Well, I can set your poor mind at rest. I undressed you, took you to the bathroom where I kept a respectful distance while you peed, then put you to bed, alone. I left immediately and came straight home.'

I couldn't stand the confusion.

'Alex, if that's what happened, why is there a pair of unfamiliar underwear here?'

Silence. Then, '*Underwear*? *Whose* underwear?'

As he repeated the phrase I focussed on the offending underwear. And slowly, as I did so, the truth filtered through to me. These were the boxer shorts that Phil had chosen for me at Banana Republic – unfamiliar because they were new and I was disorientated. My underwear.

'Alex...'

'Yeah?'

'I think I owe you an apology.'

'Yeah?'

'These boxer shorts.'

'Yeah?'

'They're mine.'

'Just now you thought they were... *mine* or something,' he said. 'Suddenly, they're yours. How can you be certain?'

'What brand do you wear?'

'Mostly Calvin Klein briefs or Ralph Lauren boxers.'

'Not Banana Republic.'

'I don't think so.'

'Hold on for a moment.' I got out of bed and grabbed the shorts, then climbed back in and read the label.

'Alex?

'Yeah?'

'I just read the label. Actually, they're Banana Republic; I bought them yesterday, but I'm so befuddled this morning, I didn't recognise them.'

'So you automatically assumed they were mine, right?'

'Well, you're the only other man who's been in this room since I arrived. You woke me up with the phone, and I saw these unfamiliar boxer shorts by the bed and I didn't know what to think.'

'But you decided in your confusion that *I*, a married man, undressed you while you were close to unconscious, and had my wicked way with you, then left my underwear behind as a souvenir?'

'No. Well, I didn't know. I mean, first Karl tells me you're gay, then it turns out you're married. I can't remember a damned thing and...'

My stomach gave a more threatening lurch. I was starting to feel radically worse.

'This is terrible,' I continued. 'I'm so hung over, I can't say what I mean. I feel sick, I don't know what I'm doing here. I have to go now. Goodbye.'

'Don't hang up! Don't hang up! End of underwear subject, I haven't even told you why I was calling yet. You still there?'

'Just.'

'OK, listen; I know I don't deserve it after teasing you. I couldn't resist. But I want to ask you a favour.'

'Ask away, but be quick. I really need to get to the loo.'

'Well, you know you said that your grandpa was a carpenter, you renovated that beach hut together.'

'Yup.'

'It's my day off today, and I was planning to spend it at home. I have to make some fairly serious assessment of what needs doing – it'd be criminal just to let the house fall apart. Anyways, I'd really value your opinion. I mean, after all, the whole place is just a glorified beach hut.'

I was silent, frantically trying to think of an appropriate excuse. I felt awful; all kinds of thoughts were crowding in on me and the sense of unreality from the previous day had returned like a slap in the face. But after the concern he had shown me, what could I say?

'Come on, Michael, please. If you just lie there all day, you'll only feel worse. Please?'

'But I have the most appalling sick headache. I'm not sure that I can even get out of bed. And I have to phone my brother-in-law.'

'OK, here's the deal. I will be with you in ten minutes – you'll never find the house on your own. We cycle back here past Eckerd's...'

'Eckerd's?'

'The drug store. We pick up some things I need. It's pretty much on the way. Then I treat you to Key West's answer to the hangover. No, listen, I know everybody has a hangover cure, but this one is absolutely guaranteed to have you human again inside of fifteen minutes. I need you up on my roof this afternoon. OK? Then call your brother-in-law from here later, when you feel better.'

'Well, Alex, you know I'd really like to help, but I have to think about booking tickets out of here and...'

'Michael, you've got two more nights' reservation at Penny's, so I'm not letting you leave yet, OK?'

'Well...'

'So that's arranged. Ten minutes, so if you're going to puke, make it quick. And Michael?'

'Yes?'

'I knew they weren't my boxer shorts all along. I clearly remember putting mine back on afterwards.'

'You absolute...' I gasped, but the line was dead.

12
I Spy

Alex announced his arrival by knocking on my door ten minutes later. I answered it wearing a towelling robe, a layer of shaving foam on my face. I had just showered and, somehow, I had managed to keep my roiling stomach together. Alex was wearing a pair of grey cut-off sweatpants and a T-shirt, with a small rucksack in his left hand.

'Have you made the first incision yet, Doctor?' he asked, looking at the razor in my hand. I shook my head. 'OK, back in the bathroom. Wash and go, that's today's motto. With *your* hangover I think it's best to leave shaving until tomorrow when your hands have stopped shaking. It's not as if anyone around here's going to mind a bit of stubble.'

I stood there, mouthing my way towards protest. But Alex was a wall of energy this morning and there was no point resisting. 'Come on, let's boogie,' he said, rubbing his hands together vigorously.

While I slipped into my new shorts and polo shirt, Alex stood out on the deck, whistling to himself. He came back as I was lacing my brogues.

'Somehow I feel those are less than tropical,' said Alex, looking at the shoes. 'We'll get you something a little more appropriate at Eckerd's.'

'OK,' I nodded.

'The dope monster finally speaks,' he replied. 'Think you can cycle in that state?'

I nodded uncertainly, not really convinced that I could stand up for long, let alone pedal half the length of Key West. My bile was rising again, but I fought it back.

'Alex, I really do feel awful. Maybe I should just go back to bed.'

He grimaced. 'Get your sorry ass together, right now, and follow me.'

I stood carefully and looked around for my room key and wallet. Realising that they must be in the pocket of the trousers I had been wearing last night, I moved towards the chair. The offending boxer shorts were on top and I had to move them to get to my trouser pocket. As I did so, I caught Alex's eye. He smiled without saying a word.

As we locked the room and started off around the pool, Penny emerged from the main building, followed by a grim-looking, moderately overweight couple dressed in matching outfits. They were struggling with their bags.

'Michael, Alex, how lovely to see you. Say hello to Mr and Mrs Olsen. They're visiting our beautiful island for a week, and they're staying in the room next to yours, Michael. They've driven all the way here, it's taken them *ages*, hasn't it? The poor dears are exhausted, aren't you?'

They both made dissatisfied grunting noises.

'That's too bad,' said Alex. 'Where you folks from?'

'Madison, Wisconsin,' they said as one, before Penny bustled them on with a smile.

I just about managed the cycle ride to Eckerd's. While Alex was inside I finally vomited, quickly and (I think) without being seen, into a bin in the parking lot. Alex emerged a few minutes later, reached into his rucksack and pulled out a pair of sunglasses.

'Here, I think you'll be needing these,' he said, handing them to me. 'There were no decent sandals your size but it's OK, I remembered I have a spare pair someone gave me last Christmas, they're a little big on me but I think they might fit you. We'll try. So anyway, I got the ingredients for your cure. Let's go do it.'

It took us another five minutes to get to the house. The streets were quieter than the day before and, it being a Monday, the family activity of Sunday had given way to a more businesslike atmosphere. Men in flatbed trucks loaded with timber, metal piping or plants drove slowly down the narrow streets. A postman cycled past us in the opposite direction, shouting 'one-way street' in a friendly way. Alex just waved. I noticed the absence of tourists, though we were only a few blocks away from Duval. The air was fresher and less humid today, with a gentle breeze, but it was still very warm. I felt dizzy and disorientated.

Just as we had the day before, we swung into a narrow lane and drew up parallel to the fence that ran down the side of the house. I vaguely wondered why we weren't using the front entrance, but still felt too feeble to follow the thought through. Alex opened the gate and went into the yard. As I followed, I saw Lunch, the little hen from the café, pecking around on the fringes of the undergrowth. Alex followed my line of sight and smiled.

'I can't leave her alone all day in a closed café, now, can I? Besides, she loves to ride in the basket on my bike. It's the closest she gets to flying. Don't go away,' he said, disappearing towards the house. 'I'll be right back.'

The sun stood almost overhead and there was little shade in the yard other than that offered to the deck by the house itself. I grabbed a chair and walked up the steps carefully. They creaked, but not alarmingly, being somewhat more solid than they looked. Hearing Alex whistling somewhere in the interior, I walked along to the end of the deck and peered through a screened window into a rather basic kitchen. An old gas range, a tap and basin, some cupboards and shelves, a large and very old Frigidaire. Alex was nowhere to be seen but I could still hear his whistling. Then he walked into the room from a door to one side. He didn't see me at first and for a few seconds I watched him bustling around, fetching a variety of things and assembling them on a tray. He was slightly shorter than I had first thought, around five-ten or eleven, and broad shouldered bordering on stocky. His hair was a dark chestnut brown. Brown eyes, too, with very clear whites. It was his face, however, now seen in repose, which held the attention. The only way to describe it would be 'perfectly imperfect'. He was close to the classical ideal of male beauty but with some minor flaws: the lips a little too full and the nose, though very straight, perhaps slightly too small. His eyebrows were prosaic too, being strongly defined and almost meeting in the middle. The most arresting feature was an openness of expression that was present whether he was smiling, frowning, laughing, puzzled or, as now, wearing no particular expression at all.

However sophisticated he might seem in certain ways, it was the face of an innocent, the sort of face that draws people to it. The initial resemblance to Jim had been, I now realised, a trick of my mind, amplified by the strange echo of my dream and by my own heightened emotional state at the time.

I coughed to signal my presence and said, 'Hi,' and he peered, smiling, through the screen.

'Oh my God! The bearded dope-crazed stalker approaches.' He made a crucifix out of his index fingers. 'Now hold on for just another few moments and don't look. I'm about to assemble the secret formula. Get thee hence!'

He gestured me away, so I turned back towards the yard and sat for a while. Plenty of thoughts were trying to get through my hangover, but I managed to push them away. The old familiar feeling that there was some duty I should be performing, some unfinished task that someone else was waiting for me to complete, was stilled by my hangover to a Zen-like calm. I would need to call Lolly and Pete at some point that day, but otherwise no one, anywhere in the whole world, had any expectations of me at that moment. In fact, no one even knew where I was, except Alex.

He came through the sprung screen door backwards, carrying the tray. The door snapped shut behind him, nearly knocking the tray from his grasp, but he caught his balance and turned to face me with a broad smile. He had taken his shirt off to reveal a well-proportioned but not overly muscled chest. His skin was lightly and evenly tanned and there was a fine trace of hair running up from the line of his shorts, which were slung low over his hips, to his navel. Otherwise he appeared hairless.

'Going to seed, eh?' he said, aware of my eyes on him. He looked totally unembarrassed at being stared at, though I felt a sudden jolt of guilt.

'Not at all,' I replied, blushing. I hadn't intended to look so obviously. He appeared oblivious.

'You know, you're actually in much better shape than me and you're what? Fifteen or twenty years older. You must work out loads.'

'I swim a lot, it's very solitary, you can just empty your mind. I generally do at least a mile a day, often more. Which reminds me, I must buy some swimming trunks; I'll go to flab if I don't get some exercise soon.'

'You're so full of shit. Remember, I undressed you last night. You could eat junk food every day for a month and still be in perfect shape. It's sickening.'

'Alex...' I said, in a voice intended to warn him that I was serious about his not teasing me any more. A small sensation of panic was bubbling in a corner of my head.

'OK, OK, it's a fair cop. Zip.' He made a zipping motion across his mouth and put the tray down on the ground in front of me. He then hopped off the deck into the yard and grabbed the table, lugged it up the steps and set it down in the shade in front of me before returning to fetch the other chair. As he lifted the tray to the table, my eyes shifted to it. There was a jug of water and a glass, a bowl of sugar, a carton of tomato juice, a frosted, half-full bottle of vodka, a tall green tube with the circumference of a stack of coins and a blister-pack of soluble ibuprofen tablets.

'I really don't think this is going to...'

'Shh. I have to concentrate. Now, firstly, Berocca.'

'What?'

He handed me the green tube. The rubric on the side said, 'For

Hectic Lifestyles', and listed a number of vitamins and minerals.

'I think "Hectic Lifestyles" is wonderful, don't you?' he said. 'I mean, it implies Successful Career Women rushing from the daycare centre to the office to the gym and back again, grabbing a sandwich on the way and Not Always Having Time To Eat a Balanced Diet. Or alternatively, it means, For Dehydrated, Hungover People Who Forgot to Eat Anything and Probably Took Some Drugs. Whatever, with some minor adjustments, it works.'

He flipped the top off the tube as he spoke, extracting a fat orange disc and placing it in the glass. He then added two ibuprofen tablets and filled the glass with water. It effervesced like something from a Frankenstein movie, a fluorescent orange colour with a faint mist hanging over it. After a few moments the contents had fully dissolved.

'Now, this is Stage One. Drink.' He handed me the glass with a look that dared me to challenge him.

'I feel so completely terrible, I'll try anything. But if this comes straight up again, you'll have only yourself to blame.'

I drank it down slowly but steadily. It tasted fine and, after a few moments of monitoring its progress, I was relatively certain that we wouldn't be seeing it again.

'Stage Two has to wait for a few minutes while that takes effect,' said Alex. 'So don't touch anything. I'll be back.'

I was confused to see him head away from the house and through the gate in the garden fence. I heard him unlock his bike and listened as his whistling disappeared rapidly into the distance. Curiouser and curiouser.

The temptation to look around the inside of the house was intense and had I been feeling better I might well have done so. But I didn't have the energy, so instead I sat quietly in the shade watching the little chicken peck around the yard. From time to time the whirr of bicycle wheels drifted past on the other side of the fence. Sometimes, from further away, I could just hear the low throb of a slow-moving, big-engined car, the boom of its bass speakers vibrating through the porch.

I also heard, coming from somewhere far back in the foliage, the same rustle-and-squawk I'd noticed the previous day. A few minutes after Alex had left, an aeroplane hummed low overhead. It looked fairly small, as if it would seat no more than twenty or thirty people, and it had propellers. It occurred to me that the island was probably too small for a full-sized airport, which might explain the relatively contained impact of the tourist trade.

And so I sat pondering irrelevancies and managing to ignore my shadows.

I was nodding off into a light doze, my head and arms resting on the table, when Alex returned. The sound of the gate opening woke me and I looked up and saw him come whistling through the overgrown entrance, framed by a powder-blue sky, wearing nothing but his shorts, sandals and a smile.

He was carrying a brown grocery bag with 'Fausto's' printed on the side in large letters. He held it defensively to one side as if I were trying to peak illicitly into it, and said, 'Feeling any better yet?'

'Maybe a little – I still feel sick but my head's not as bad. I was just nodding off.'

'Stay awake for another few minutes until you've had Stages Two and Three, then we'll nap for an hour or so. I'll soon turn you into an upright citizen again.'

With this he disappeared inside again and then I heard the sounds of frying through the kitchen window. I was just wondering what impact this might have on my stomach when he reappeared with two glasses filled with ice and topped with lemon segments, a dark fluid swilling around in their bases. He quarter-filled each one with vodka, and then topped them to the brim with tomato juice. Stirring a little sugar into them with a spoon, he held them up, clinked them together and said 'cheers' before handing one to me.

'Are you really sure about this?' I asked. 'Medically speaking, it'll just put the hangover off until later.'

'Who cares about later? Anyway, what do doctors know? Taken in combination with Stage Three, this is a winner. Talking of which...' Glancing towards the kitchen window, he took his glass and went back into the house saying, 'Sip it down like a good boy, now,' as he went.

I took a sip as instructed. Though it was powerfully spicy, the cool velvety tomato juice combined with the subtle kick of the vodka to send a calming, warming path through me. My stomach relaxed almost instantly and a few moments later a pleasant sensation seeped into my head.

When Alex returned with two enormous bacon and egg toasted sandwiches, I was feeling notably improved.

'May I introduce you to Stage Three? Are you in touch with your hunger yet?' he asked.

'Just about. I'm certainly in touch with this vodka. Where's Sue?'

I don't know why this question popped out at that particular moment, but it had been at the back of my mind. Maybe the alcohol helped ease it forward.

Alex's brow furrowed briefly, his eyebrows meeting. He wore the same expression I had noticed the previous night when he exchanged glances with Penny.

'She's freelancing today. There's this guy she sometimes works for; he's got, like, a private island and he has parties there sometimes. Sue does the cooking. She's in a lot of demand.'

'What time will she be home? I mean, will I see her later?'

In truth I was being polite. I was relaxing into Alex's company but the thought of dealing with other people still created a sense of unease.

'Well. She... she doesn't actually live here.'

'But you said last night that she's your wife. I mean, you look like you're on pretty good terms, not, you know, like me and Selina.'

I wished I hadn't said it. The strategy of keeping real-world thoughts at bay had been working reasonably well and I felt something like superstition at having broken it.

'Who's Selina?' he asked, a puzzled expression crossing his brow.

'My wife,' I answered, aware that he was hearing this information for the first time. He was about to say something when I interrupted by saying, 'Anyway, don't change the subject.'

'Oh man,' he replied. 'Please! Give me a break?'

I held him with a brief gaze before continuing. 'All right, I don't have any right to ask any of this; I unconditionally back off. Nice weather we're having.'

He returned my gaze for a few seconds, then said, 'Shit. OK, it's too late anyway. I've already let too much out. First, and I know this will sound weird, you have to promise me you're not a spy of some sort.'

'A spy? You must be joking! This is the strangest thing yet, and that's saying something.'

'All right, I throw myself on your mercy because I think I trust you. Here goes. But you have to promise not to tell a soul. Only Penny, Sue and Karl and like, four or five other people, know anything about this.'

'You promise never to tell everyone that you had to put me to bed because I got stoned and I'll promise you anything.'

This was better. A jokey approach felt safe and familiar.

'Christ, I can't believe I'm doing this. OK, here goes. My aunt, right, I told you about my aunt?'

'You told me she left you the house, and Penny told me bits and pieces last night when she was telling me about Phil.'

'OK, so my aunt, she was actually my great-aunt, she couldn't have children...'

'... so she encouraged her Mexican lover to behave like a stud horse.'

'Right. Now, she had this absolute *thing* about children. And because of the way our family panned out, I'm the last of the Crawfords. She was a Crawford, and she never married. Anyway, when she last made her will I was eighteen and I'd already come out to my parents.'

'Come out?' I faltered as I said the words out loud. 'Oh... *Come Out.* I see.'

In fact I didn't see at all. If he was gay, why was he married to Sue?

'So in any event,' he continued, 'my parents were totally cool about it. They're like that. They happily told everyone. Including Aunt Peggy. Now, she was cool about homosexuality, she had to be – she'd lived in Key West for like, thirty years. But she still put this typically loopy clause in her will: I could only inherit provided I'd finished at least undergrad and provided that I had a wife.'

My confusion lifted. He'd married to satisfy the terms of the will.

'Aunt Peggy wanted me to have kids and continue the line,' he went on. 'I mean, she wasn't trying to turn me straight at all. She was just saying that, if I got married and had at least one child within three years, I could keep the house, otherwise it goes to a distant cousin who's not a Crawford but who does have children. The rest is detail, except for one thing, but that's not really my business to reveal. Anyway, I knew Sue, I'd met her here quite some time ago and she'd been a friend for a while. She suggested the arrangement.'

'So, what's this about spies?' I asked.

He shifted uncomfortably without replying. The alcohol had made me brave, as it sometimes does, so I continued for him, making it up as I went along.

'Someone's already tried to contest the will,' I said. 'The distant cousin. They suspect that you contracted a marriage of convenience and you're worried that they might hire a private detective to prove it, invalidating your ownership of this place,' I gestured around me, 'thereby claiming it for themselves. And you thought that a strange Englishman blundering into your life might be the perfect cover for an investigator. Right?'

Alex stared straight at me, a rapt expression on his face, as if he had been hypnotised by a snake. I had obviously stumbled on something more than I'd expected, so I went on. 'You decided to check out this possibility by helping him get stoned out of his head so you could take a look at his hotel room on the excuse of putting him to bed – and whilst he was unconscious, you briefly rifled through his things, but found nothing.'

Alex was silent, amazed and frightened looking.

'Well?'

Nothing.

'Well, Alex? How about it?'

'Good guess so far, apart from the fact that you needed absolutely no encouragement to get off your face. It wasn't until the party last night when you were asking about Sue that Penny became mildly suspicious. I promise you, I never suspected anything. Penny thinks I'm too trusting. Anyway, Penny was going to check your room on the pretext of cleaning it, just to make sure – so, I didn't plan the putting-you-to-bed part. But I did have a quick look around before I left. Sorry. Shit! You must have spent a lifetime reading Sherlock Holmes or something. You're really good.'

'And you're really busted.'

'What?'

I stood up slowly, reaching into my pocket as I did so. 'I said, you're really busted. I caught all that on my tape here,' I nodded towards my pocket. 'Which is all I need to prove my client's case.'

Alex was motionless. The colour had drained completely from him. His eyes were fixed on my hand as I withdrew it millimetre by millimetre from my pocket, to reveal, slowly, nothing. I smiled knowingly and revealed my palms like a magician who had just made something disappear.

His colour returned in a rush as he exploded.

'You total, total bastard. I can't believe you did that. Why have I been nice to you?'

'Somehow I don't think you'll be teasing me again in a hurry, Alex. You wouldn't dare. I'm much better at it than you are. So, no more funny comments about last night. Agreed?'

'No. This is war. Now eat your sandwich, you sadistic fuck. Anyway, Nancy Drew, you didn't quite guess everything. And as punishment for your atrocities, you may never know the rest. Now eat your breakfast and I hope you choke on it.'

A few moments passed with Alex pretending to ignore me while he ate his sandwich. Then the phone rang and he picked up his plate and went inside with it, pausing at the door to throw me a finely tuned grimace so that I knew that, now he'd got over the shock, he was more amused than rattled and was already planning his revenge.

By the time he re-emerged, I had finished eating and was trying to interest Lunch in some leftovers. She seemed remarkably snooty.

'That was Karl. He's invited a group of us to dinner tonight at his house, it's a sort of a regular Monday thing. We should go. It's worth it; he has the most amazing house.'

'Who'd be there?' I asked, planning to refuse politely if I could.

'Oh, the Groundhog Day cast. Me, Sue, Penny, Phil, Phil's boyfriend Maxo, some mystery guest. You wanna go?'

'I am feeling a little better, I must admit. But I don't know how long it'll last. I think I'll be a pooper and say no, get an early night.'

'Wait here,' Alex said, and he disappeared into the house. I heard a clatter and a muffled curse before he appeared triumphantly, dragging two small foam mattresses with badly worn covers. He propped them against the wall and went back into the house, emerging seconds later with two towels. Placing the mattresses a few inches apart, one in the sun and one in the shade, and covering each with a towel, he said, 'This is your early night. You can take a nap in the shade now but I'm afraid there's to be no party-pooping. I accepted for both of us and, what's more, I pretended to come outside and discuss it with you first, so to all intents and purposes you've already said you'll go. I think it would be very rude to change your mind now, don't you?'

I signalled my temporary submission by a slump of the shoulders as I stood up and moved towards the mattresses. This wasn't what I wanted at all but there seemed little I could politely say. My mind was half-consciously flicking backwards and forwards between mild anxiety at the prospect of the dinner and a mild fear of being on my own; a miserable and unresolvable sensation. I wanted to turn off for a while to try to stabilise.

It was hot and I took my shirt off and rolled it into a pillow, positioning it under my neck as I lay down on my side, facing away from Alex.

Then he said, 'Michael?'

'Hmm?'

'Do you want to know how I really knew that the underwear didn't belong to me when we were on the phone earlier?'

'How?' I said sleepily, not turning to where he stood.

'I never wear any,' he said.

I saw his shadow stoop down while he removed his shorts. Then he stood for a few moments before lying down behind me.

13
An Intimate Touch

I shut my eyes again in feigned sleep, as if Alex's striptease had had no impact, though in truth my heart was pounding.

As I lay there in the warm shade, several strands of thought weaved in and out of each other. Sometimes they took distinct and individual shape and sometimes they were so tightly woven that it became hard to tell them apart. Pictures of Alex mixed uncomfortably in my mind with older memories.

While dozing through these thoughts, I was suddenly reeled back into more immediate wakefulness by the sensation of being touched very gently on the back of my upper thigh, along the line of my shorts. My first reaction was to brush the spot, as if it were a fly. But it was gently insistent. My second thought was to ignore it and continue to feign sleep, but I was alarmed to find that I wasn't able to control my physical reaction comfortably for long. I needed to adjust myself.

I was close to panic as I opened my left eye a fraction but I couldn't see anything of Alex, since I had lain down with my back to him. The delicate touch continued its explorations.

I was aware of a rapid change of the light in the yard, matched by a rise in my own heart rate. Out of my line of sight, the edge of some clouds must have been skimming the rim of the sun causing a pulsing effect, as if we were on a film set and the lighting man was adjusting the main bank up and down, trying to find the right level for realistic sunlight. I was still not fully awake, and all this felt unreal. The touch on my leg was far from illusory, however, so I slowly uncurled my arm from where it lay foetally tucked into my side, my fist balled under my chin, and reached out behind me towards my lower buttocks where the caress was now focussed. My fingers met and briefly interpreted the texture they found, diagnosing, after a few confused moments, feathers. I turned slowly over to see Lunch pecking away nonchalantly at the ground between our two mattresses, the filigree of her tail brushing my leg as she did so. Alex lay, eyes closed, beside me in the sun. He too had rolled over and was now lying peacefully on his side, facing me, the expression of a sleeping angel on his face.

14
A Shaft of Light

I drifted off to sleep then, waking a couple of hours later feeling dehydrated but otherwise better. The mattress beside me was empty and the sun had moved around so that only a small part of the yard was still directly lit. Though the fiercest heat of the day was gone, the humidity had built again and black clouds were loitering on the horizon opposite the sun. The slight breeze from earlier had dropped and an uncertain calm had crept in.

I could hear the sound of a shower running somewhere inside the house, so I opened the screen and the inner door and shouted through, 'Alex?'

There was no reply. I shouted again more loudly.

'Upstairs,' he replied.

The sound of water stopped. I shouted, 'I'll wait 'til you come down.'

'OK, listen, I know you need to use the phone. There's one in the front hall or if you wanna wait a couple of minutes I'll bring one out.'

I waited for a few moments, then I opened the inner door fully and went in. Once my eyes had adjusted to the comparative darkness, I saw that I was standing at one end of a long corridor. Just then, the phone rang, but the sound seemed to come from more than one place, its source impossible to locate. It stopped after the third ring. To my right was a door, partly open, through which I could see into the kitchen. To my left another door stood ajar, with darkness beyond. At the far end of the corridor I could see daylight filtering through the fanlight above what I assumed must be the front door. I followed the light and after about ten yards the corridor opened out into a spacious, triple-height entrance hall. The space was dimly lit at ground-floor level, its windows obscured by blinds imprinted with the dim pattern cast by louvred shutters beyond. But, two floors up, a ray of sunshine pierced a stained-glass window in the roof and sent a spotlight charging through the darkness, illuminating parts of the first- and second-floor internal balconies with a cool blue beam.

I heard feet somewhere above me and a door closing, then Alex's voice cut the gloom. 'Hold on for a second, Penny. Michael? You there?'

As he spoke he emerged from the shadows into the beam of light on the first-floor balcony and stood for a moment. He was clearly unable to see me in the dusk below, with the blue-tinged light full in his eyes. A white towel was wrapped loosely around his waist and he was gripping a cordless phone between his shoulder and ear in order to free his hands, with which he was trying to open a packet of razorblades. His still-wet skin refracted the light.

'Michael?' He listened for a response. And then, with a slightly sung intonation, 'Where are you, Michael?'

I don't know why I didn't speak. Somehow he seemed to hold all the available space to himself.

'Penny?' he said into the handset. 'Sorry, I thought he might have come in.'

Pause.

'No, it's OK. I'll tell him.'

Pause.

'Sure, sure.'

Pause.

'Penny, go easy on me, OK? He's a grown man. Look, I know he's vulnerable right now and I am very sensitive to that. He's got this, abandoned look, like an orphaned bunny or something.'

Pause.

I tried to make myself smaller and more silent, to absorb more light.

'It's perfectly simple. He drifted off the street and into my life less than 48 hours ago, bereft and lonely. I looked into his eyes and saw something there that I think we both need to explore. End of Chapter One.' His voice implied that Penny was missing something that should be self-evident.

'He's funny, kind, clever, handsome and so *straight* acting. It's terribly attractive – you know how I hate faggy men.'

Pause.

'I'm fully aware of that. He told me about her this morning. She's called Selina, and it doesn't sound as if they're on good terms. Probably something to do with whatever was going on with Jim – you know, the guy who died recently.'

Pause.

'Because I can *tell*.'

Pause.

'I just can.'

Pause.

'No, he must still be outside. Anyway, fine, I am very much taking care of him and I will do so for as long as it takes and as long as he will let me. If there's room for change over time, we'll see. And if there isn't, I'll have to settle for being friends, which would be better than nothing.'

Pause.

'I think he's only just starting to deal with his partner's death, like a sort of delayed reaction thing? I don't quite get where the wife thing fits in yet but I'm sure I'll figure it out soon.'

I almost gasped in the darkness. He thought Jim had been my *partner*?

'Anyway,' he continued in the half-light above me, 'yesterday was almost like watching someone come out of a coma. He's quite up and down. I think he might be having like, anxiety attacks or something. Which sounds like a pretty normal thing under the circumstances. But he's coming to Karl's. I twisted his arm.'

Pause.

'Thanks, honey. OK, trust me. See you later.'

Before I could panic and scuttle, he turned and went back into the shadows. Then I heard the sound of water running again and Alex's semi-tuneful whistling of 'Someone to Watch Over Me'.

I walked carefully back to the other end of the passageway, as if treading on something that might break. On reaching the screen, I eased it open and slipped outside, taking a deep breath of the sticky, still air. The atmosphere was oppressive and I felt trapped, as if everything around me was racing beyond my control. I was going to have to explain things to Alex before the situation got any more out of hand.

But through the ocean of miserable feelings that threatened to sweep me away ran a counter-current of simple relief – at least someone was concerned about how I felt.

And as for the unthinkable? The things Alex felt he and I both needed to 'explore'?

An internal voice, implanted long before, said, 'No.'

Rhythmically, over and over, with stern and absolute disapproval, 'No.'

It did not give a reason; it would not leave itself open to argument; it could not accept the aspect of desire.

15
Where Do You Go To?

I was lying on my mattress, absently watching the bruised storm clouds scud closer, when Alex came out onto the porch. He was fully clothed, slightly more formally than I had yet seen, and he was carrying a small canvas holdall.

Noticing the sky, he said, 'Wow, looks like we're in for a cracker. They never last long though, 'cept in hurricane season. How you doing? Has the cure worked?'

I found it hard to meet his eye. 'I'm close to OK, thanks, feeling much better.'

'Any weird feelings you're having may be the grass. It can give you a slightly altered state for a while. That stuff we had last night was very good, very chilled, but all grass can be a little paranoid-making if you have too much. It's the something-or-other-anoids in it. Just ignore it, it'll go soon.'

'The cannabinoids, you mean. Very good, you should be a professional physician.'

'God, you sound like my dad. Please.'

Very briefly, his mouth tightened into a '*that was the wrong thing to say, wasn't it?*' expression but he moved quickly past it.

'Listen,' he said, 'I have to go to work now, I'll be done by around 7.30, just in time to pick you up from Penny's. Think you can find your way back there?'

I nodded.

'You'll need to change and shave – even I shave for dinner at Karl's. He appreciates a little formality.'

'I'm sure I can find my way back,' I replied. 'But I thought you were off work today.'

'Oh. Yeah.' Alex looked a little shifty. 'It's my other job; it's only, like, a few hours a week.'

'What is it? I mean, what do you do?'

He looked evasive.

'It's kinda dull. I, um, I guess I... well, I sort of show people the sights of Key West.'

He looked so uncomfortable that I did not push him any further and, at that moment, I wanted to engage with him less rather than more. But I was intrigued. Why was he so embarrassed about it?

'Oh, by the way, Penny called to say your brother-in-law phoned the guesthouse. Says your sister's doing fine, so are the twins, and he's off to the hospital now for a while, so call him later when you have a chance. There's something he wants to ask you. No rush, he'll be out for a few hours.'

'OK, thanks,' I replied. 'Listen, do you mind leaving me here and giving me the key? I want to take a look around the place like I said I would. I can spend an hour or so doing that, then go back to Penny's and shower, then call my brother-in-law. You can pick me up when you're ready.'

'For sure. Just be careful on the outside upper porch. It's basically stable but the railing is unsafe, so keep well back. The floors are OK though, as far as I can see. Otherwise feel free. Take a good poke around.'

'You know, I'm not sure how much use I can be... I'm not a professional and I don't know anything about local construction techniques, that sort of thing.'

'Michael, whatever you know will be more than I do, so please don't worry. Just, well, any thoughts you have would be appreciated. All I can tell you is that I had this guy look it over a few months ago and he said there was a whole load of stuff needed doing but he'd have to write a whole report, which I couldn't afford. Here...'

He handed me the key saying, 'This opens the gate we came in through, that's all you need to lock. See you later.'

'Bye, see you later.'

He left me in the gathering silence. The yard was still now, no breeze whatsoever. The occasional squawking noise from the undergrowth had ceased. It was clearly going to rain soon, so I picked up the two mattresses and pulled them through the screen into the hall. With the sky so dark, it was very gloomy inside and I searched for a light switch. I couldn't find one in the passageway but there was one next to the front door and when I switched it on a series of dim wall-lights flickered into life. The hallway was probably fifty feet wide by eighteen deep and thirty-five feet tall into a vaulted ceiling. I felt a little spooked by the Gothic gloom but, aware that this was probably the after-effect of the marijuana, I tried to ignore my jumpiness.

The walls and floors were simply made, of tongue-and-groove pine in a deep honey colour. The carved and turned staircase was made of a darker wood, possibly mahogany, and rose from the left-hand side of the hall to the balcony of the floor above. Some very large, dark, modern paintings hung on the downstairs walls but otherwise there was little furniture: a chair, a day bed and a nondescript desk. In places the walls were scarred a lighter colour by vertical stripes, showing the outline of previous divisions. The hall had once been considerably smaller, with rooms to either side.

I went to the window next to the front door and raised the blind, only to see the shutter beyond, still holding back the light. Looking more closely at the door, I saw there were bolts at the top and bottom, but they were not drawn shut. This implied the door was in regular use. The lock had a large, metal, ridged knob on it that turned easily to the left, and the door opened.

I stepped out onto the front porch and was arrested by the view in front of me. Across the narrow street, instead of the row of similar-looking houses I had expected, stood a sagging, rusted chain-link fence. Beyond it was a cemetery. It was laid out in a grid pattern, the single and multi-stacked tombs forming houses and apartment buildings divided by a series of paths and interspersed with trees and green spaces – a miniature city of the dead, there were so many.

The white marble facades were lit by a powerful clean ray from the sun, backed by towering black and purple storm clouds that now filled most of the sky. The scene appeared extra-dimensional, as if the light itself had substance. A scattered host of white angels shone in this unreal light, their heads bowed over the tombs they guarded as if caught in a painting by Blake.

I stepped out further onto the porch and saw that a table and chairs were arranged in a group there, more comfortable looking than the ones in the yard. The seat cushions bore the imprint of their most recent occupants and a newspaper lay roughly folded on the table, held down by a heavy glass ashtray. This domestic still life was clearly in frequent use. In using the side entrance so as to avoid my seeing the cemetery and being further reminded of my grief, Alex had been 'taking care' of me.

I descended the broad steps that fell to street level, unlatched the front gate and crossed the street, then turned and faced the house. It was considerably larger than those on either side, rising two and a half storeys above its crawl space, the area below the ground floor that protects a house from ground moisture. Its neighbours kept themselves more modestly to between one and two storeys and most appeared to sit on narrower lots.

The front porch sloped slightly and was subdivided by four square columns that reached up through the balcony to support a flat roof. Beyond this rose another roof, pitched away at a forty-five-degree angle and holding the blue stained-glass skylight. The front door was flanked by two shuttered windows on either side, with sills at waist height. Below these sills, the centre-lines of the windows continued down to floor level to form, in combination with the windows, an effect somewhat like a French door with a blind lower half. The porches on both levels had faded blue ceilings and were fronted by slender but sturdy carved and turned banister-posts in the same style as the internal staircase. The appearance overall was part Caribbean, part New England, part Victorian Gothic with maybe a hint of Dutch. But this once-beautiful architectural crossbreed had, in its decay, taken on the appearance of a sad mongrel.

All over the house, pale grey paint was flaking away to reveal the weathered silver-grey timber beneath. Below the porch a latticework of wood obscured the crawl space. Bizarrely, strapped to the front of the railing on the upper balcony hung an old bicycle, laced through with a string of fairy lights that blinked incongruously in the daylight.

The neighbouring house on the left-hand side stood no more than eight feet away, but on the right a distance of some fifteen feet separated Alex's house from the boundary fence. In the space between the house and the fence ran an alleyway with a rotting wooden gate halfway down, bound shut with creepers like Sleeping Beauty's castle.

I guessed that the lane down which Alex had led me to the house must end somewhere on this side, with the yard of his house extending further back than that of its neighbour. I looked up at the line of the flat roof, which was straight and true between the supporting columns. The paint might be flaking but the basic structure of the house appeared to be sound. I found myself wondering automatically what my grandfather's opinion would have been.

The thought of him transported me to the salt-bleached Norfolk coast of my childhood, as if the house had shrunk to the size of a beach hut and I to that of a ten-year-old boy.

Thunder growled lazily in the distance and a few fat raindrops fell. I mounted the steps to the porch and searched for the catches to the shutters but couldn't find any, so I went back into the house. From the hallway, the stairs to the internal balcony rose to my left.

It was very dark now, with little light filtering through from outside and the wall-lights casting an inadequate glow. As I started to ascend the stairs, the first flicker of lightning slashed the dark air followed within a few seconds by a closer rumble of thunder. I gripped the banister and continued upwards.

There was a switch at the top of the stairs and as the lights came on they revealed a series of faded, framed posters. One was from the Theatre Royal, Haymarket. It was for a production of *Sweet Bird of Youth*, starring Lauren Bacall. Another was for *A Streetcar Named Desire* and a third was for a reading of *The Roman Spring of Mrs Stone*, a novel I remembered from long before. The posters were brown and foxed, signs of mildew creeping in from the edges. Lightning flickered again, thunder sounding soon after.

A corridor led from the balcony towards the back of the house and I followed it until I came to a room on my right, its door standing ajar. I could hear violent rain beating down on the roof, drumming an insistent rhythm. I reached inside the door and my fingers located a switch in the darkness. I flicked it on and, pushing the door with my elbow, stepped inside.

The room was lit by a single unshaded bulb dangling from the wooden ceiling. A double bed was pushed up against the far wall, its covers pulled roughly over. On top of the blanket lay a pair of jeans and a white shirt, casually thrown there, almost joining at the waist so as to form the outline of a person. Opposite the bed and at right angles to a side-facing window stood a shabby antique dressing table, the edges of its mirror stuck with several photographs. A glance showed them to be a mix of family, friends, sports teams, holidays, pets. I took in an image of Alex and Sue, Penny, Karl and others I didn't recognise, smartly dressed, possibly a wedding photograph.

Against another wall stood a large wardrobe with a chest of drawers beside it. Next to the bed was the half-open door to the bathroom where a white towel lay crumpled on the wooden floor.

Lightning flashed across the sky again and this time, through the window, I could see it forking towards the ground. The thunder was immediate. I was suddenly aware of the immense humidity of the room and the musky locker-room smell; sweat intermingled with traces of talcum powder and lime, slightly stale linen.

A tangle of laundry lay in a wicker basket at the foot of the bed.

Socks, a vest, another white shirt – this one amputated and sleeveless. More lightning splintered as I looked back at the figure on the bed.

Caught in sideways spasm the shirt appeared to be embracing itself, its arms at crazy angles. The charge in the air was tangible as this writhing shape was brought briefly to life by another crackling flash before lying still again. Then as the lightning ripped through the room once more, the body on the bed resumed its convulsion and a series of terrible recent images flashed overpoweringly before me.

I moved quickly from the room and down the stairs, desperate for air and light.

As I came into the hall, the phone rang. I stopped, casting my eyes around to see where it was, but as I did so the answering machine clicked in.

'Hi, this is Alex. If you have my cellphone number, try that, if not, please leave a message.'

After the tone a male voice said, 'Alex, you little rat, you're late again and I'm unfortunately not one of the privileged many to have your cellphone number. I have sixty members of the Gay Accountants Society of Philadelphia – that's GASP to you – waiting for your matinée performance. I've had it with you being late. If you're not here in ten minutes you're fired. There're plenty of other equally qualified guys around here would gag for the job. *Comprende?*'

16
Buttocks & BarFlyz

The storm was moving away when I came back out into the yard, though it was still raining heavily. By the time I had locked the side gate behind me, I was completely soaked. I cursed as I tried to unchain my bike, water streaming down from my hair and into my eyes. As I emerged from the lane and onto the street, I could still hear sheets of rain pounding on the tin roof behind me as insistently as the pounding of my heart.

Caught unawares and umbrella-less, people were either cowering in doorways and porches or continuing to walk, drenched, as if nothing were happening. I passed one young couple who were running along holding hands, their wet hair plastered gruesomely over their faces like the moulded plastic hair of a doll.

My pulse was still racing and I pedalled at a frantic pace, swerving to avoid gigantic puddles or ploughing through them where there was no way round, sending water pluming to either side. In places, large palm-fronds, dislodged by the storm, lay across the road. I went past a parked car with all its lights flashing and an alarm shrieking attention to its shattered windscreen – a fallen coconut from a tall palm was lodged against the wipers. After a few blocks I slackened my pace as I approached a red four-way warning light at a junction, where I had to stop while a large flatbed V8 throbbed slowly through the street-wide puddle like an idling powerboat. When it had gone I resumed pedalling but more slowly now, a child who had run far enough to put the bogeyman behind him.

I couldn't avoid Duval since it was my surest route back to Penny's.

It was as crowded as ever despite the receding tropical rain, which the partying crowds had taken in their stride. I waited at another junction while a long, yellow road train carrying scores of tourists crossed Duval, the voice of its driver repeating from loudspeakers along its snaking length. On either side of me The Bull and Fogarty's Inn pumped out live music, a cover version of the Eagles' 'Take it Easy' duelling with a frantic country and western song. The lights changed and I pedalled on, moving faster than many of the fat-engined cars being lazily piloted down the strip. It had stopped raining now, and the tarmac and roofs were starting to steam, the heat stored earlier in the day causing the rainwater to vaporise in slowly rising drifts. I stopped at the tail of a body of traffic that was backed up from some lights further down the road. As I waited, a bright yellow sign on a bar-front billboard to my right caught my attention. It said:

BarFlyz Welcomes G.A.S.P.
Let Our Cute Guys Dance 4U
Monday Matinee Special
No Cover
All You Can Peep!

The traffic was moving on now, but I stayed, rooted. Through the doorway of the bar I could see what lay within. At the far end, about sixty feet away, a bank of glaring monitors was showing a rap video: a black woman lay handcuffed to the leg of a table, writhing in time to the music, while a lip-synching black man in a white fur coat, open to the chest to show a bundle of chains and medallions, cut the dress off her with a pair of scissors. In the background a choreographed group of dancers twisted and pumped their leather-clad hips, then kaleidoscoped into a hydra and swayed as if underwater.

The bar formed an island in the middle of the room, thrown into silhouette by the light from the video screens. Men sat around it on stools, watching four near-naked male dancers perform on the counter top.

They ground their torsos in slow circles, screwing the air in front of them, feet planted a few inches apart, unmoving. Sometimes their arms went swaying up above their heads and sometimes their hands would slide down their bodies, caressing their chests, nipples and stomachs as they went, until they reached their groins where they would slide their fingers into their skimpy underwear and rub their genitals in mock ecstasy. One of them appeared to be wearing a short towel instead of underwear and, as I watched, a customer leaned forward and rubbed his hands up the young man's legs and under the towel. The dancer allowed him to explore for a moment, then bent forward and whispered something in his ear. The customer took a wad of bills from his pocket, counted some out and tucked them into the dancer's boot. The dancer crouched to kiss him on the cheek before standing, pouting his buttocks and gyrating slowly away.

I couldn't believe that Alex would do this sort of thing, but what did I know of him or his life in any detail? Besides, the wording on the billboard was surely reason enough to wonder, especially given the phone message I had overheard and Alex's earlier shifty countenance. Nonetheless, I was relieved that none of the four looked like him. One was dark-skinned, one had too-short hair, one was too tall and the other too muscular.

Just as I was starting to cycle away, the music faded and a male voice boomed out over a PA system.

'And now, gentlemen and gentlemen, a little later than planned, the very moment you have long been waiting for. Our very own island paradise favourite – and remember he likes a warm hand on his entrance – please give it up for the one and only, super hot...'

The voice faded behind me as I picked up speed and entered the raucous sound sphere of another bar. If it was Alex, I did not want to know. Why should I?

17
A Light?

No one was around when I reached the guesthouse but a pair of swimming shorts had been left in my room with a note from Penny saying she thought I might like to borrow them. I went out onto the deck and hung my damp clothes over the fence to dry before slipping into the shorts. They were a green and purple plaid, and fitted well.

I was about to go out to the pool when I heard a noise from the private deck of the room next door, on the Wisconsin side. It was a low, persistent grunting and just as I was drawing conclusions as to what it might be I heard a man's voice saying, 'Yeah, the Jolly Roger's been bulldozed, it's like a Marri-ot or some such now, Ah thank.'

A woman's voice replied, 'Ohh, that's a real piddy, we was sure lookin' forward to goin' there again, warn't we, Greg?'

Another man replied, 'When you gon' stop yurr yackin' and see if that li'l thang's recharged yet, woman? We ain't got all day.'

A second woman answered, 'Well, honey, from what I remember, all day's about as quick as it gets when yew gets up and at it!'

There was laughter and then the second man said, 'Very a-musing, honey. Well, in the meantime, pass me that chicken. Cheers everybody, welcome to Sodom and Gomorrah.'

For the second time in twenty minutes I did not want to stay around for the dénouement. What was it with this town? Was everybody here obsessed with sex all the time? Or was I reading more into things than I should? Somehow I didn't think so. I shut the French doors, turned on the air-conditioning unit and went out to the pool. A hundred laps would help clear my head.

I thrashed up and down for a while, thinking of nothing as I usually do when I swim. It was immensely calming to push all thoughts and feelings away and just feel the force and energy of my muscles and the clean, cool water.

I built a steady rhythm, breathing under my left arm on every fourth stroke. After forty lengths of crawl I changed to butterfly for ten lengths, then reverted to crawl to catch my breath. My fitness level had clearly dropped. I stopped for a moment to set the timer on my watch, then took my pulse for fifteen seconds and multiplied by four. At peak fitness it would have been around 145 by now but instead it was nearer 155, so I slowed down to a steady breaststroke. It was exhilarating to be this breathless, my heart pumping from exercise rather than anxiety.

At this more relaxed pace I started to think things over. I was relieved to be on my own for a while. I liked Penny, Sue and the others but I was uncomfortable with their over-attentive manner. And I was even more uncomfortable with what I'd overheard in the conversation between Alex and Penny earlier, so I was not looking forward to the evening which, I feared, might bring more of the same. I was just wondering how I might politely find an excuse not to go when I became aware, above the sound of the water, of someone calling my name. I stopped, panting, and looked up. It was Sue, holding a portable phone and standing at the edge of the pool.

I said, 'Hi,' and swam over.

'Hi, Michael. It's your brother-in-law. Here.' She darted across to where I'd draped my towel over the back of a chair and as I levered myself out of the water, handed me first the towel and then, when I'd rubbed my hair and face, the phone. I mouthed 'Thank you' to her as I lifted the handset to my ear.

'Hi, Pete, how's my favourite brother-in-law?'

'Michael! Great, great. We're all doing fine. Twins're sleeping right now. Actually I'm at the hospital with Lolly. She didn't want to wait to speak to you 'til they let her home. Here.'

There was a brief rustling sound before my sister's voice came on the line.

'Hi, Michael. How are you?'

'First things first,' I replied. 'How are you?'

'Oh, a little tired. I can tell you that giving birth to twins is very much not my idea of fun. But I'm happy. I don't want to be a gushy mum but they really are rather beautiful.'

'Lol, I am proud of you. And very chuffed at how you've chosen to name them.'

'Well, you didn't expect me to name one of them after *Dad*, did you? I mean, Bastard might sound inappropriate at the christening.'

I laughed. This was an old joke we'd evolved as teenagers to help us deal with the old man's ways.

'So tell me more about my gorgeous nephews.'

'Oh please, I've talked about nothing else since they were born. I'll send a photograph. I mean, they're all scrunched and smelly like generic babies, only more adorably so, of course. Listen, Michael, before I forget, Selina called, wondering if we knew where you were. Pete spoke to her. She wants to send you a letter, says it's too personal for email. She wanted to know your address. Pete says you're in Key West.'

'Yes, I've been here for a couple of days. It's a long story but I had to...'

'Get away? I know, Michael. And I think you're right to. As far away from Dad and Selina as possible. You know, I've always thought she was a real cow, but this really takes the biscuit. I'm sorry.'

'Yup, well, I... listen, you know, Lolly, I'd rather not talk about it at the moment. I'm feeling a little odd about everything and I just feel I need a break from it all. And in terms of Selina, I don't even want her knowing what continent I'm on.'

'OK. How about if I tell her to write to you care of us? Then we can forward it to you. Pete has the address. He got it from whoever takes messages there.'

'All right, but I can't guarantee to read it. Thanks, though, Lol. Thanks for protecting me. Again.'

'Well, if anyone needs it right now, it's you. What do you mean by "odd", anyway? Are you OK?'

'I think so. You know I'm not very good at self-analysis. I'm just trying to get on with things. But I...'

I paused for a moment, taken aback by my sudden urge to cry and frustrated that this feeling kept coming back whenever I thought I had conquered it.

'What, Michael?'

'I just get a little weepy, you know. I keep on seeing things that remind me of Jim and it's... well, it's difficult. I'll be fine. I don't want you to worry.'

'Sweetie, stop being so much like Dad, for Christ's sake! It's perfectly normal to get weepy, you know. You need to mourn. It's what normal people do.'

'I suppose so. I'm just, you know, thawing out a bit at the moment from how I felt immediately afterwards. It's producing a lot of water.'

There I went again. Cracking feeble jokes to try to re-establish my equilibrium even though nothing seemed funny at all.

'Michael, I didn't say anything at the time but you were a bit like this when Mum died. I was all over the place but you were quite reserved and stiff-upper-lipped – and I'm not saying that you were being cold about it because I know you weren't. You were at least as upset as I was. I thought the same thing when we spoke last week. It's as if, well, it's as if Dad drummed it into you that it's Bad Form to show your feelings, so you don't dare. But it's your life, not his. Don't let him scare you into bottling things up.'

'I've cried enough in the last twenty-four hours to really disappoint him, believe me. Look Lol, I'm all right. I promise you. Can we change the subject? Please?'

She paused before answering.

'Well... OK... but... I think you should come up here for a while, as soon as I get home with the twins.'

'Come on, Lol. You'll have plenty to do without me hanging

around. I'll come soon, when you're settled. But in the meantime I promise that if I don't cry at least twice a day I'll get on the first plane. OK?'

This was an old trick, me reassuring Lolly, to take the focus away from myself.

'Well, all right then. As long as you promise. But I won't let you get away without reporting in every day or so.' She knew better than to push me so she changed the subject, as requested. 'So, why Key West?'

'Like I say, it's a long story.'

'Is it still a very gay town?

I feigned ignorance, guiltily aware of what my mild deception might imply.

'Does it have that reputation?' I asked.

'I don't know, it certainly used to. Dad *hated* it the first time you were there.'

This was so unexpected that I almost failed to take it in.

'Michael? Are you still there?'

After a few seconds the grenade exploded.

'WHAT? The first time I was here?'

'Surely you remember this? It was when Mum was pregnant with me. A year or two after the Bay of Pigs, so you would have been around, what? Four, five? Dad was there on some sort of top-level naval thing. Mum hated it. Well, actually, she loved the town itself but Dad was in double purgatory apparently, ranting on about queers and commies, and you know how wearing that can be. Mum showed me the pictures years ago. They're in one of the albums I've got up here.'

'Are you sure, Lolly? I mean, I have no recollection of this at all.'

But even as I said it, the previous day's sense of *déjà vu* began to crystallise. Lolly carried on.

'Well, you were very young. And the mind has a tendency to block out unpleasant memories. It's amazing either of us remembers any of our childhood at all, isn't it? Anyway, Dad was a nightmare apparently. There are a few pictures in the album but hardly any of you. Dad usually insisted on holding the camera, remember? So you and I rarely figure in the family album. The pictures of Key West are mainly of boats and planes and a few of Mum with some US naval types on a lawn. But there's one of all three of you standing next to a great big red thing at the most southerly point of America or something like that...

'I've just remembered something,' she went on. 'Once, ages ago, I was going through the photos with Mum and there's one of you in a packet somewhere, not stuck in the album. She hated it. Said it was typical of Dad to make you do something like that, to treat you like a performing monkey.'

'Make me do what?'

'Light his cigarette for him. She said you didn't actually smoke any of it. Dad just held the match up for you to light it from.'

18
If the Bike Fits

What Lolly had told me could not have been more unwelcome to someone in my volatile state: that the erotically charged dream I had been having for years was in some way related to my father. I was in unfamiliar and dangerous territory and felt ill equipped to deal with it.

I was sitting by the pool staring at the telephone when Penny came out to say that Alex had been delayed at work and would not be able to pick me up on the way to Karl's; she would take me there. I wanted to go less than ever now, though physically I felt almost back to normal.

I took a very long shower, shaving under the scalding stream and washing every millimetre of myself, then sat on the rear deck in my robe for a long while, thinking and trying not to think. My Wisconsin neighbours were quiet now. I supposed they must either be sleeping off their excess or had gone out while I was swimming. In any event I was glad of the peaceful interlude, which I used to avoid most of the questions raised by what I'd just learned from Lolly. I was already starting to plan my escape for the next day or the day after. Getting away from Key West would help me leave these confusing issues behind. Easier to move on. Maybe I'd go to Toronto after all.

Darkness slipped over me as the late afternoon faded into evening, but I didn't notice until the phone rang in my room. It was Penny.

'Hi, sweetheart. Did you fall asleep? Your date is all dressed and waiting. Well, both dates are, actually.'

'*Both* dates?'

'Penny and Sue. You can try to take your pick, but you're having us both anyway.'

'Oh, of course.' I remembered Sue having handed me the phone earlier. 'Look, I'm sorry, I was dozing. Give me two minutes to get dressed, I'll see you out front.'

When I got to the front porch, the two women were waiting on their bicycles. Penny looked startling in a dark red and black Chinese dress, a single golden dragon chasing its way from her ankle to her shoulder. Sue had changed from the shorts she'd been wearing earlier to an outfit very similar to my own: chinos and a preppy shirt.

'*Well*!' said Penny, looking backwards and forwards between Sue and me. 'You two are positively radiating conventionality this evening. No bad thing on a visit to Karl's. It'll keep him at bay like garlic to a vampire.'

I unlocked my bike but as I climbed on, they both started laughing. I shrugged my shoulders as if to ask what was so amusing. I was feeling a little defensive, my mind preoccupied by the day's events, and I found their reaction irritating.

'Michael, that bicycle's about half the size it should be,' said Sue.

I forced a smile. 'I know, pathetic, isn't it? I've been feeling so rough today that I didn't have time to hire one that fits me. Never mind, I'm sure I can keep my dignity intact until tomorrow.' I was going to add, 'When I'll probably leave,' but I decided not to raise that issue.

'You just wait right there.' This was Penny. 'I'll be back in two shakes. I have an idea.'

She dismounted and disappeared down the side of the house, so I turned to Sue and said, 'Thanks for bringing the phone out to me earlier. I was totally lost to the world, thrashing up and down that pool.'

I didn't want to steer her towards inquiring after my family so I continued, 'Have you been home since then?' Then I looked at her clothes to finish the sentence, meaning, 'have you been home to change?'

'In a sense,' she said, smiling. 'I live here.'

She gestured comfortably towards the guesthouse and smiled again, waiting for me to work it out. It took me a few seconds.

'I see. Or at least I think I do. You and Alex aren't really married in a conventional sense... you live here... does that mean you and Penny are... that you're partners?'

'Got it in one! You're learning! Yes, we are, we have been for quite a while now, since a few months after Carey died. I suppose we could have told you earlier but our domestic arrangements are too Munster-like for anyone from a more conventional universe to easily understand. We try to break people in gently. And then there's all the complications with Alex's situation. And I...'

She petered out, a strange look on her face as if she'd gone too far or been over-familiar.

'And you what?' I said it gently and felt like a kindly old schoolteacher trying to encourage a shy child. Engaging with Sue made it easier to disentangle my thoughts from myself.

She paused before continuing, her voice almost at a whisper.

'I want to be careful not to intrude, so please tell me to stop if this is, you know, inappropriate. I just feel that, after what you've been through, and so recently, we shouldn't dump too much, you know, too much of our *own* stuff on you. We can be quite invasive, without meaning to be. It even irritates me sometimes.'

'Frankly,' I replied, 'given the fact that my stuff is currently accumulating faster than I can handle it, I'd rather think about something, or someone, else for a change. Believe me, other people's stuff is light relief.' I faltered. 'I don't mean to say that other people's problems are any easier than mine. That came out the wrong way.'

'God, Michael! You sound just like me. Apologising before you've drawn breath. It's so weird, you know. I find it so easy to see it when other people do it but I can't stop doing it myself. Gets Penny really *pissed*?' Her voice rose so as to invite my understanding. 'Well, not really pissed, she's far too good at clearing up other people's mess for that but...'

She was interrupted, this time not by her own timidity but by the sound of a gate clanking shut in the alley at the side of the house. It was Penny, and she was wheeling a spectacular bicycle. It was a lady's model, no crossbar, like something out of a drug-altered Merchant Ivory film. Its tubes and forks were entirely bound with rainbow-coloured tape and it had a rubber-bulbed horn with an immense brass trumpet attached to the handlebars. A pink wicker basket was perched provocatively in front.

'This is Carey's. *Was* Carey's. My brother's. Absolutely typical of him to come to the most liberal place in America and then try to shock everybody. Anyway, if you can bear the embarrassment you can use it until you get around to hiring another one. It should be the right size for you. Maybe a little rusty, though I did oil it last year.'

She must have noticed my attempt at not looking jaw-dropped, because she went on, 'Oh come on, Michael. It's dark and nobody knows you here. Besides, the rainbow thing these days means more like, well, more a general commitment to the acceptance of difference.'

'More general than the previously specific acceptance of...?' I said, letting the question hang.

'Surely you must know what a rainbow flag means?' she replied.

I shook my head.

'My Lord! Even England isn't *that* medieval! *Rainbow* equals *all colours*, equals *colourful difference*, equals *gay*! Carey was gay, I told you that! So let's see if it fits you.'

'Oh, I see! Well, of course, thank you.'

I chained my bike back to the railing and took Carey's. The saddle was set just a little too high for me and had no easy means of adjustment, but it was otherwise right.

'Thank you, Penny. I will treat it with the respect it deserves. And thank you, Carey.'

We cycled for a few minutes, crossing into a part of town where the architecture was more modern and the streets wider, though the familiar jungle of night-scented plant life continued to sweeten the warm air.

At first it was hard to talk since the traffic on the main road meant that we couldn't consistently ride two or three abreast. But soon we were on the back streets again and I was able to draw level with Penny, who had taken the lead from the outset.

I felt I should show willing so I shouted, 'What an amazing bicycle! It looks like a girl's one, but it's got ten gears – and a dynamo, so you don't have to keep taking the lights off to stop them getting stolen!'

'That bicycle is the living embodiment of Carey. Loud and colourful on the surface, tough and practical underneath. It's wonderful to see it fly again! Almost there!'

At that moment Sue whizzed past both of us, pedalling slowly but powerfully in a low gear. Without warning she veered into a dark gap at the side of the road and disappeared. Penny slowed down so that I could move in front, then followed me into the turning.

Ahead of us at the end of a lane stood a surprising sight. It looked like the entrance to an Indian temple, a huge and intricately carved wooden screen with white stone pilasters and wrought ironwork. Two massive sculpted lions sat guard at either side of an equally massive door. The door was open, and beyond it stood another screen fronted by a large stone plinth on which stood a spotlit life-sized carving of a naked man.

'That's Carey,' said Penny. 'It's Karl's idea of keeping his spirit in the house. Rather beautiful, don't you think?'

We chained our bicycles to a railing and went in.

19
The Fine Print

As we rounded the screen a barrage of stimuli hit my senses. A mixture of perfumes hung thick in the air; part tropical night-scented flower, part temple incense. Floating strands of music competed for the attention of my senses, the same haunting duet I had heard when I first arrived at Penny's, the male and female voices twisting in and out of each other in some exquisite agony.

A huge swimming pool appeared to float partly above the ground, the sides of its upper section being made of glass. At the far end, a wall of shimmering water ran down a rippled, dark background into the pool. Light came from everywhere, but nowhere I could see. To the left was a low-built adobe structure with a number of doors and huge-fronded plants set at intervals along its facade. To the right, up a series of pale stone steps and running the entire length of the pool, was a broad covered terrace that gave through a wall of glass into one enormous, triple-height room. The room was entirely white, its central cupola supported by slender marble columns, and all around it were stone plinths carrying a variety of sculptures. The walls were hung with big, modern paintings, some of them familiar. At least one appeared to be a Warhol. The furniture was beautiful, a blend of antique and modern, and the floors were of marble strewn with expensive-looking oriental rugs.

'Karl,' shouted Penny. 'We're here.'

There was no reply and Penny was just setting off in the direction of an open door on the far side of the room when I heard a cough behind me. I turned and saw Karl, his arms spread wide, standing at the top of the steps wearing a white floor-length robe of Arab appearance. He posed frozen in the powerful downlight, his face and hands an unearthly white, a one-man *tableau vivant* portraying the beneficent host.

Penny and Sue started to clap and, as they did so, Alex came into view at the far end of the garden and, putting his finger to his lips, crept quietly up behind Karl who was lowering himself gracefully towards the floor in a deep bow. As Karl reached the lowest point of this sweeping gesture, Alex seized him from behind with one hand on each of his hips and pulled him sharply towards himself, Karl's buttocks being forced into Alex's groin.

Karl didn't flinch, just said, 'Good evening, Alex. How nice of you to come.'

Alex let him go and came bounding into the room.

'Hello, Karl. You're looking rather pasty this evening; what's that white stuff?'

'I got it from the human statue woman down at the waterfront. It's revolting, whatever it is; I must go and wash it off. I want my glowingly healthy tan to be on full display tonight. I have a *prospect* coming to dinner. Alex, be a love and mix drinks for everybody.'

'Sure. You *go* shower while *I* entertain your guests.'

Alex kissed each of us on both cheeks and then moved to the wall where he pressed a small brass square and a hidden door sprang open to reveal a bar. Without asking, he mixed a pitcher of margueritas and served them up in salted glasses.

'This is the final part of your hangover cure, Michael,' he said. 'It's very "up". You'll feel like partying all night long after a couple of these.'

I groaned in pantomime at the idea but in truth it tasted good. A combination of the cycle ride and the bizarre greeting had me feeling surprisingly alert.

'This is an amazing place. He really has quite an eye, doesn't he?' I said.

Penny replied. 'Karl is obsessed with Key West history. In the early years, the town mainly made its living from wrecking. A combination of too many reefs and too few lighthouses meant that half the cargo ended up in the homes of enterprising locals. That's why in some of the older houses on the island you'll find incredible, magpie-like collections of things from around the globe.' She swept her arm around the room. 'Like I said, Karl likes to keep the spirit alive.'

She walked across the room to an elaborate antique sideboard which had a series of mirrors arrayed around its base.

'This is a petticoat sideboard, designed so ladies could check their skirts and petticoats were properly arranged. All the mirrors are angled subtly upwards so you don't have to crane your neck. And this,' she moved to an elaborately stitched oriental tapestry, 'is an example of the "forbidden stitch". The work is so fine that the women who did it went blind. So many were afflicted that the Chinese Emperor had to ban the entire population from doing it. I guess it was an early form of public health policy.'

Penny walked me around the room, showing me an amazing array of strange and interesting items. She knew the stories behind each piece and repeated them with obvious pleasure. Then Alex took over, moving towards a framed piece of paper on an adjoining wall.

'Karl has this on perma-loan from a friend, this amazing guy who's lived in Key West practically all his life and who knew Tennessee Williams. It's an original poem, in Williams's own hand, and I don't think it's been published anywhere. Read it, it's fabulous and Karl says it could have been written specifically for him.'

I moved closer, and read it out loud.

Three

One I kept
Two I lost
Three is sheltered under frost

One I tired of
Two still wanted
Three the stony meadows haunted

One was faithful
Two was clever
Three stayed in my heart forever

'It really is quite good, don't you think?'

This was Karl, now showered and dressed in a pale linen suit. 'Of course, all poetry has its roots in witchcraft,' he continued. 'Incantations use the power of rhyme to cast their spells; the simpler they are, the more powerful they get.'

Karl turned and gestured vaguely around himself before continuing.

'I hope you like my little collection. Carey was quite a collector himself, though because he was always half-broke, he tended to indulge himself in "finds"; less well-known artists. Like this one.'

He led me through an open doorway into a study, its shelves laden with art books. Above the desk, lit by halogen picture lights, was a triptych. The left- and right-hand panels were painted with a profusion of meadow flowers, their tendrils escaping over onto the central panel, which showed two figures embracing. The man with his back to us was perfectly proportioned but had a blueish tinge to his flesh, the veins almost visible. He was embracing and being embraced by a facing figure, a skeleton whose bony digits gripped his partner's back. Ghoulish though it was at first sight, it was beautifully executed, like a Flemish Master. Karl remained silent for a time while I looked at it.

'Carey gave me this for my sixtieth birthday. Astonishing, isn't it?'

'It is, yes, it really is,' I replied. 'Did he know he was... ill when he bought it?'

'Oh yes. He had a very intricate understanding of the relationship between love and loss, how death and longing augment each other. I know that this might appear gruesome to many people but to me, it is *terribly* evocative; poignant and lovely. It represents what I had gained and what we both knew I would lose. And it foretold most accurately the eternal embrace, which I still feel we are in. I treasure this more than anything. It's as if he had painted it himself. You see, the skeleton is still alive; look at the way its fingers grip the flesh. That is Carey's remaining grip on me.' He paused for a moment before saying, 'Now come.'

I was briefly aware that this apparently casual interlude in front of the painting was as carefully stage-managed as Karl's greeting performance but I didn't have time to pursue the thought. It condensed into a mental filing-tab for later reference; he was trying to make a point of some relevance to me, but I didn't have time to work out what it might be because he took me by the hand and led me back to the others.

There was another figure in the room now, an Asian-looking man, probably in his twenties. He was laying a table and I counted that he had already set out the cutlery for eight people, though at three of the places, only spoons were set.

'Who's coming?' asked Penny.

'Well, Phyllis is singing this evening so she and Maxo will arrive in time for a late dessert. And the other guest is to be a surprise for Alex and, as I alluded to earlier, somewhat of a prospect for me. He revels in the name of Angelico Rappaport. He left Key West approximately four years ago to take up a prestigious professorship at a New England college. That position is now con*cluded*,' Karl handled the word as if with sugar-tongs, 'and so he returns. He's a little younger than I, still in his early sixties, and frightfully sexy.'

'Why's he a surprise for me?' asked Alex. 'I mean, sure, I go for the slightly older guy but sixty-something's pushing it a little.'

'The explanation is far more innocent, my sweet boy,' said Karl. 'He was a friend of your Aunt Peggy. And he's also a most distinguished architect, a specialist in, amongst other things, the domestic architecture of Key West. He knows your house very well.'

Karl's eyes were sparkling with mischief.

'But is he trustworthy, Karl? I mean, you know, with us?' Alex looked in a circular motion between himself, Penny and Sue.

'Lamb, please *do* stop being so paranoid. Your wicked Cousin Elspeth may have made a few unpleasant noises but your fantasy that she has the massed ranks of the Pinkerton Detective Agency preparing to document your every move is simply absurd, though possibly of some psychological interest. Angelico is entirely *sympa*, and the very *soul* of discretion. Now, he too will be joining us for dessert only. He's quite the toast of the town and far too busy to join us for a whole meal.'

'So, when you say that he knows my house very well,' said Alex, 'you mean he's actually done some work on it?'

'Good heavens, no! He spent his life trying to get your aunt not to hack it about in that brutal way. He was horrified at her removing all those internal walls downstairs. So, he may have a surprise or two for you.'

'Such as?'

'Well, that would hardly be a surprise now, would it? Shall we move *à table*? I think Pepe is ready for us.'

Karl hardly paused for breath as he seated us around the table, with Sue opposite Penny and Alex opposite me, himself at the head.

'Now, Alex,' he said. 'Have we got to the root of your little problem yet?

Alex blushed, immediately and powerfully.

'Too far, Karl. Wind it in and watch it, please.' This was Sue, unexpectedly assertive.

For the first time, I saw Karl look embarrassed. He also blushed and had no immediate comeback, but after a few seconds Alex saved him.

'Well, now the cat's half out of the bag, I may as well answer. Sue?' He looked at her, asking permission to continue. She looked at me and then nodded her assent. Alex looked back towards me and spoke. 'You already know from what I said earlier that in order to keep the house I needed to be married, and my wife needs to have a baby?' I nodded.

'Well, independently of that, Sue and Penny wanted to have a child.'

Karl interrupted. 'It would be my heir too. I have no other family I'd care to leave anything to, and any child of Penny's would be the closest to a niece or nephew of Carey's and therefore of mine. We would all love it. Though, of course, Penny and Sue would be the parents. There would be no confusion as to that.'

'And you, Alex, how do you feel?' I asked. He replied without pause.

'Absolutely fine. We've talked about it a lot amongst ourselves and I've talked about it with my family. I have the role of biological father clearly separated in my head from the role of extra-close uncle, which is how I'd expect to behave. I know it might sound odd to you but we don't see why we should be robbed of the opportunity to have a family just because we're gay. I, we, don't see why we should put up with having cats and dogs rather than children. Provided that we love and respect them, we should be able to be as good a family as any more conventional one.'

'Probably better than many,' I said.

Penny spoke next. 'Why do you say that, Michael? I agree with you absolutely, but why do you say it?'

I reached for my wine, feeling myself sailing closer to a personal iceberg. But I didn't have time to question why I had dropped my guard. Anyway, it was too late to back out politely. And before I knew it, I was going far further than had I intended.

'Because I had, *have*, a rather unpleasant father. My mother was sweet; my sister Lolly and I loved her very much, but she was completely overshadowed by Dad, who's a grade A bully. Luckily for Lolly and me, we both went to very good boarding schools. And our grandparents on our mother's side looked after us a lot during the school holidays whilst our parents were stationed abroad; they were more like parents should be. But Dad really shouldn't have had children. He just has no idea whatsoever. Lolly feels so strongly about this that she almost never speaks to him. She pretty much left home when she went to boarding school at the age of twelve. She lives in

Canada and hasn't been to England, or even seen Dad, for nearly fifteen years, since quite soon after Mum died. Dad wore Mum down, and Lolly has never forgiven him. His father was killed in the war while he was in his early teens and Lolly always said that's what made him so cold emotionally.'

I was almost gabbling, feeling that this was inappropriate conversation for a dinner party, so I tried to rein myself in by switching the subject back to the others.

'What I mean to say is, you can't choose your parents, but if you could, I'd much rather have had parents like you than like Dad, whose reaction to children was to treat us as an inconvenient issue of discipline and obedience.'

There was a brief silence around the table and I had the appalled sense of having finished an unsolicited soliloquy. But the others looked calm and genuinely interested, far from embarrassed.

'Well, thank you, Michael. It's very good of you to say that.' This was Penny again. 'You say your parents were stationed abroad?'

'Yup. Dad was in the navy and by the time he was forty he was already very senior. He got pretty much to the top of it before he left and then he moved into government as a defence expert. Since then he's moved even further, though his hawkish style is rather less in fashion than it once was. He's the establishment's pet Rottweiler now.'

'How old were you when your mother died?' Alex asked.

'Just a little older than you. Mid-twenties. Poor Lol was still at university. Then Mum's parents both died the year after, so it was a fairly grim time.'

Pepe arrived at the table bearing plates, which he placed in front of us saying, 'Turkey risotto with peas and sage,' and Karl poured more wine.

'So you must have gotten married at around twenty, or even earlier?' asked Sue. 'That seems very young for someone going through med school.'

My mind said *'Shut up, Michael!'* but my mouth was already out of control and I found myself continuing to tell them the most intimate details of my life. Besides, I was aware that I needed to set the record straight with Alex.

I told them about how Dad had introduced me to his new assistant Selina when I'd been eighteen. How she'd practically raped me and how, on discovering that she was pregnant, a combination of her Catholicism and Dad's temper had forced me into marrying her. Then later, when our son Jim was born with a hole in his heart, how I had steered my studies in the only direction I knew might help him, which is how I had become a heart specialist.

I told them about Jim's childhood surgery, Selina's obsession with his health and her over-protective behaviour, his rebellious response and his eventual death from heart failure whilst dancing wildly at a rave just a few weeks ago.

I told them about the nightmarish events at the hospital. And finally I told them about Selina having left me, after over twenty years of marriage, with nothing for comfort but the sound of Jim's voice on his answering service.

And I told them all of this in a perfectly even voice, as if I were reading a deposition, because though I could not bear to hear it said, I could no longer bear not to say it.

When I had finished, the others were quiet, looking at me with sympathy, and I was struck by how comforting their silence was. No embarrassed conversational reaction, just a sense of calm.

Then Sue placed her hand on top of mine before saying, 'And Selina? Where is she now?'

'I got a letter from her solicitor a few days after Jim's funeral. It said she wanted a divorce and that we'd never have lasted once Jim had finished college anyway. For years we were really only together for his sake. It was almost like a business arrangement, but I thought we were comfortable together. I thought we were a family. What was difficult was, was…'

The catch was back in my throat and I stopped talking. After a few moments Penny spoke, very quietly.

'What, Michael? What was difficult?'

I coughed and continued, struggling to stop my tears from forming. 'What was difficult was the implied *blame*. That night, at the hospital when we arrived, when Jim had just been pronounced dead... Selina seemed to think there was something I could have done – I mean, as a cardiologist. Something to save him.'

I paused and took another long sip of wine. 'Do you know, from that moment until I last saw her at his funeral, she didn't once look me in the eye.'

Penny spoke again. 'And was there anything you feel you could have done? Anything at all?'

'I could have protected him more, I suppose, though Selina did more than enough of that and I think it only pushed him to be more reckless. But when we got to the hospital? No. I don't think so. It was far too late so, logically, no. But there's always that feeling, the sense that I might have...'

'Have been able to play God? To perform a miracle?' This was Karl. He continued sadly, 'I know how impotent that feeling is.'

'No, not God, obviously.' I heard the anguish in my own voice, was aware of the drama, the fuss I was creating. But the others carried on behaving as if everything was perfectly normal. 'Oh, I don't know. Maybe... maybe. Maybe just, something a human could do.' I had picked up my napkin now, and was dabbing at my eyes.

'Then what you saw in Selina wasn't your guilt, it was her own,' said Penny.

'What do you mean by that?' I asked.

'Well, you said yourself that she over-protected Jim and that he became more reckless as a result. Perhaps she was simply blaming you because she couldn't face her own feelings of guilt. After all, why was he so determined to go dancing all night when he knew he had a heart condition? What was he trying to prove?'

'Selina never felt guilty about anything in her life, so I doubt it,' I replied.

'Well, just think about it,' said Penny. 'And maybe forgive yourself a little. It sounds as if you did absolutely everything you could have done, the whole way through. Let her handle her own guilt in her own time, but don't shoulder it yourself. You have your own life to get on with.'

I sat for a moment struggling with the implications of this thought. Then Karl said quietly, 'Shall we eat?'

'Lord, I'm so sorry, Karl, you kindly invite me to dinner and you get my drama for a first course. The food will have gone cold by now.'

'No chance of that, my dear boy, risotto is always so ferociously hot at first, don't you think? It'll be perfect now. So, eat – and please don't think this is a drama. There is nothing theatrical about the way you tell it, it's simply a very, very sad story and maybe it needed to be told.'

They started to eat and I accepted a top-up of wine from Sue. Feeling guilty at the amount of airtime I'd so unexpectedly commandeered, and wanting to avert further discussion of the topic, I returned to the original subject.

'So, anyway, about the child you'd like to have. You said there was some sort of a problem.'

Alex put his fork down and sighed, shooting another quick glance at Sue, who again nodded almost imperceptibly.

'To put it bluntly, we've tried and we're not getting anywhere. You can imagine the complications' – he smiled and looked at Sue – 'what with Sue and me both being gay, but Sue doesn't want to do anything artificial, you know, like with a turkey baster or something.'

Karl coughed. 'Please Alex, we are *eating* turkey.'

'Point taken, sorry. Anyway, Sue insists on a natural conception, for how it'll make her feel about the baby. So she and I have... you know... a few times now, but no result. So Karl offered to pay for Sue to have some tests...'

Karl interrupted. 'Well, this is my potential niece or nephew we're talking about... my family too, in a way.'

'... which turned out fine. So I went to Miami to see the specialist a few days ago and we're waiting for my results now. That's it.'

'I got tested first because I, I...' Sue started confidently but tailed off. She took a breath and continued, in a rush. 'I had a termination when I was quite young and the doctor thought that might be the reason, that it might have done some damage. But it turned out to be OK.'

'So now it looks like it's *me* that's firing blanks,' said Alex.

I felt as if Sue somehow wanted me to ask more, but I didn't want to appear intrusive. So I took a middle course, aware that they all knew I was a doctor and that I might have something useful to say.

'Selina and I wanted to have another child, but couldn't conceive. This was around the time that Jim had his original surgery. It turned out that neither of us had a problem; it just didn't want to happen so we sort of gave up. We both wanted another child, but our bodies had decided that it wouldn't be with each other. Maybe you'll just need to keep trying.'

'Well, I hope so. It's interesting that you should say that because I just think my body doesn't want to conceive. It's like it's never recovered from the first time.'

'How old were you?'

'Fifteen,' she replied, putting down her fork and fiddling with a napkin. 'It was a friend of my parents, a guy who travelled with us a lot. He didn't really, well, he didn't really ask.' She paused, then folded the napkin and laid it on her lap before continuing. 'Anyway, that was then and this is now, and now I want to have a child but it just won't happen.'

'When do you expect Alex's test results?'

'Within the next week or two.'

'Alex, what do your parents feel about this? I'm just curious, tell me to shut up if I'm being too nosy.'

'Not at all. My parents are professional liberals. They're both professors in the social sciences. They say they're totally cool about it except in one particular respect, which is that they don't approve of my having married Sue. They think it's not honest. Anyway, I can't help but feel that their approval of my fathering a child for a lesbian couple is a little more political than heartfelt, as if there's a tiny hint that they'd really like a grandchild that they could feel was more fully theirs. Of course they deny it, but I still have this feeling that I'm right. To admit it would be tantamount to their wishing I wasn't gay and that would never do. My homosexuality is a pillar of achievement in our family and it wouldn't do to question it. So instead they obsess about the details. Like grad school, qualifications, money, career, that sort of thing. It's like they think I'll turn into some trailer-park dad or something. You know, dirty baby, beer, cigarette hanging out the side of my mouth while I watch TV all day, that sort of thing.' He smiled, a little sadly, I thought.

'So what will you do?' I asked.

'Work out what to do with the house, have the baby if we can – if we can't, cousin Elspeth'll eventually get the house anyway. Then, as soon as I can, I'll go back to school. I wouldn't mind ending up as a doctor myself one day. I've completed pre-med already, it was OK, I did pretty well. But I'd hate to leave Key West.'

'Is there a university here?'

'No. I could do it at one of the Florida schools, but I'd have to spend some time away from here. It's not an easy course to do via distance learning, but you can do some that way, commute a little. Still, there's plenty of time to think about that later.'

We talked on for a while, Alex asking me more about the process of qualifying as a doctor in England while the others ate and chatted.

Then Sue interrupted us gently, saying, 'When are you planning to go home, Michael? I mean, when we have to bump you out of your room at the guesthouse, we could help you find somewhere else if you want to stay on in Key West for a while. It would be nice to see some more of you.'

I was gearing up to make my excuses and to explain how I'd soon need to visit Lolly in Toronto when Alex said, 'Now, Michael, I have a proposal to put to you. You know you said that you didn't have to go back home at any particular time?'

'Yes, well, I'm starting to think it's time I...'

'Why? I mean, if you don't mind me asking, what would you want to go back for? Do you really want to go back to work at the moment?'

'Well, no. But I should go and visit...'

'Bear me out for a moment then? Now, Penny'll need your room back after another day or so, like Sue says, no pressure, but you're welcome to come stay with me for a while. In your own room, of course.' His eyes twinkled. 'And if you feel like paying a little rent in kind, you could maybe help with some handiwork around the place. You might even enjoy it. What do you think?'

I was so concerned not to appear rude that I didn't even think clearly about what I wanted for myself.

'I couldn't inconvenience you like that,' I replied. 'I mean, you hardly know me.'

Alex cut me short. 'Look, I totally understand that you don't know which end is up at the moment and I don't want to put you on the spot. So, end of topic for now, but think about it. We could agree to trial it for a week and see how we go – if you decide to stay, which I really hope you do. You look like you could do with a good holiday to me.'

'Hear, hear!' said Penny.

'Well, thank you. I will certainly think about it. You're very kind.'

I looked at Alex across the table. He appeared flushed in the candlelight, happy but slightly embarrassed, like a child who had just plucked up the courage to give flowers to a visiting dignitary. It was surprisingly touching.

Pepe had returned to clear the plates away, and Karl replenished our glasses. He was rather priest-like as he did this, officiating at the weekly ritual of dinner with his 'family'. The dramatic temple of a room in which we were eating heightened this effect, making it quite different from the polite, English, middle-class dinner parties to which I was accustomed.

As Karl poured, he said, 'I don't mean this *à propos* of you at all, Michael, but that was how Carey and I first met. A mutual friend who was having a fling with him brought Carey here for dinner one night. I was smitten with him from the first moment; so when he said he was thinking of staying another week but his guesthouse didn't have any rooms available, I offered him one of the cabanas over there' – he waved towards the far side of the pool – 'and said he could stay for a while. The friend was furious when he accepted! Lord, we had an appalling row about it later! I was accused of cradle-snatching.'

'What was the age difference between you and Carey?' I asked.

'Twenty-five years.'

'Wasn't that difficult?'

'I was in my very late forties, still not unattractive, and I'd had two previous serious partners. I didn't really "come out" in any way, even to myself, until I was in my thirties, so my first boyfriend was predictably rather a mistake. Like the first lover in the poem' – he gestured towards the frame from which I had read earlier – 'my second partner was a better choice but after nearly ten years together it had run its course. Then, a while afterwards, Carey appeared here for dinner and the rest is history.

'But I should answer your question,' he continued. 'The age difference did worry me at first; I was worried on some level that he might be a substitute son or something like that. Then my friend, the one who lent me that poem by Tennessee Williams, said something simple but wise. I was saying how I felt a little uncomfortable about it and he just said, "Karl, happiness doesn't offer you a deal like this very often, so don't read the fine print". So I took the deal and I never regretted it. I never thought about the age issue again.'

He raised his glass to Carey as Pepe returned with plates of fish, and we all joined Karl in his toast.

Everyone started to eat, though in truth I was only picking at my plate and listening while the others discussed a friend of theirs who had just been caught by his wife in flagrante delicto with another woman. My mind was beginning to wander when Karl pulled me back in to the conversation.

'How about you, Michael? Were you ever unfaithful to Selina? Or she to you?'

If someone had asked me the same question in London, I might have found it more intrusive, but I had been playing by the local rules all evening, so I replied.

'Neither, as far as I know. Selina never seemed very interested in sex and, as I said, I didn't exactly choose to marry her.'

'So what did you do all those years? I mean, as an outlet?' he asked.

I didn't feel that 'masturbation' would have been a polite reply at anyone's dinner table, even Karl's, so I said, 'Just think of me as a dormant volcano.'

A new voice, as soft and warm as eiderdown, came from somewhere behind my shoulder: 'I certainly hope to be nearby when you erupt!'

20
An Angel

Karl stood up to great the new arrival saying, 'Angelico! My dear! Do come and sit. We'll be having dessert soon.'

Angelico accepted a glass of whisky while he was being introduced to everyone. He was a handsome man who looked younger than his age. He was Hispanic looking, quite short and a little plump but well proportioned and elegantly dressed. His mane of curling, dark brown hair and chestnut eyes gave him something of the appearance of an artist. His handshake was surprisingly strong and unusually persistent.

'Put him down, Angelico,' said Karl. 'He is not the dessert for which you were invited.' Then Karl finished the introductions with Alex.

'So, Alex,' said Angelico. 'How I've been looking forward to meeting you! You probably have little idea of what an absolute treasure you've inherited. You're a very lucky man, though that naughty aunt of yours has a lot to answer for.'

'Karl tells me that she did a whole load of stuff you didn't approve of, something about the downstairs walls?'

'Mmm. Horrific. I should have reported her to any number of preservation bodies but she was far too sweet for that. She wanted more wall space in there so she could hang her paintings. Were any of them left in the house?'

'Yes, there are some big, murky ones. One or two of them are enormous. There's one in particular which is at least ten feet long and six feet high.'

'Have you ever looked on the back of it?'

'No. Why?'

'Good. We can pop over after dinner and take a look. That may be another little surprise for you. Anyway, back to those walls. Your aunt and I reached something of a compromise. She allowed me to supervise their removal and storage. Lord knows what state they're in now, but they should be fine, they're made of Dade County pine like the rest of the house. It's almost impossible to get hold of these days; it's incredibly sought after because it has a very high resin content, so the termites hate it. I had the lumberman down at the yard bag it all up in protective sheeting and put the whole thing in my garage. Yours for the taking, and *beautiful*. Original tongue-and-groove, pretty carving around the doors. Divine. You simply must reinstall it.'

Alex looked stunned.

'I had no idea! Thank you, that's marvellous news. Karl, thank you so much for finding Angelico, for putting us together...'

Karl was returning from the bar with Angelico's whisky, and he tousled Alex's hair affectionately as he passed, leaving it standing slightly on end. Alex, now smiling inanely, tried to comb it back into place with his fingers.

'I can help,' I was surprised to hear myself say.

'You mean with his hair?' asked Angelico. 'Tell me you're not a hairdresser, my dear, you look far too butch!'

'I'm a carpenter *manqué*,' I explained. 'I'm very comfortable working with wood, though I'm a little out of practice. My grandfather taught me when I was a kid. I did a lot of it up until I went to university. So, like I say, I could help.'

'Well, Michael,' he replied, 'if you have time tomorrow I'd be delighted to show you my hidden treasures.'

'I'd like that, thank you,' I said, wondering if he'd intended this to sound like a *double entendre*.

'And then we can see about your attempting to erect those walls again. It shouldn't be too complicated.'

Alex asked, 'What do you know about the house? I mean, its history?'

'Built in, I would say, around 1850, when an earlier cottage was moved back in the lot to make way for the new, grander house. So the kitchen and the other single-storey rooms at the back are part of the original cottage. But the most exciting thing about it is its *twin*.'

'Twin?'

'Yes. Many of the older houses in Key West were built by ship's carpenters for their captains. Shipbuilding techniques are perfect for such a hurricane-prone area. You see, they generally didn't use nails, just beautifully crafted mortise and tenon joints that made the buildings more flexible so that they can literally bend with the wind. You also tend to find that there's little internal plasterwork. It just cracks as the houses move, so there are plenty of wooden walls around. Anyway, there are a small number of examples of twin houses in Key West, built by sea captains for their children as a sort of family status symbol. Sometimes they'd build a new home exactly like their existing one, on an adjoining lot. And sometimes they'd construct a new pair altogether, often one for each child. Your house is one of a pair. It's built on a double lot, which backs onto another double lot. Usually, twins were built side-by-side but in your case, which really is quite unique, they were built so that the back of your house faces the front of its twin. This was probably done in order that they might both achieve maximum southerly light, but it does have the bizarre result that your house's twin appears to have its back facing onto the street. It's the only pair like that on the whole island. In fact it's the only example anywhere, so far as I know.'

'And that would explain why I never noticed,' said Alex. 'I've never seen the front of the other house – only the back, from the road on the other side. There are too many trees in the way to see anything from the back of my house.'

'Exactly. The only difference between your house and its twin is that the twin doesn't have an older building at its rear; the lot was clearly empty when they started to build. But here's the delightful part. It's simply too appropriate! As your aunt discovered, the two houses were built by two gentlemen who were *amis particuliers*. The owner of your house was a married sea captain called Amos Fullstead, who had a house full of children but whose wife eventually died during childbirth. The twin house was built a little later by his friend, Juan Conchez, one of the first Cuban cigar makers to set up business in Key West. Conchez *never married*.'

Angelico paused for a moment to light a cigarette. 'Alex?'

Alex was spellbound, examining each new piece of information as if it were a jewel. He appeared almost to be waking from a dream as he replied.

'Yes?'

'Do you know anything about your great-grandmother? Peggy's mother?'

'A little. She's the family connection with Key West, I think her mother was born here but brought up in Virginia?'

'Quite correct. Good. Now, do you know what her *mother's* mother's maiden name was?'

'I have no idea.'

'Luckily, I do. It's a bit of murky family history that Peggy worked out years ago, and that's why she bought the house.' Angelico picked up his whisky glass and took a sip, then put it down slowly as he said, 'It was Fullstead. Amos Fullstead was your great, great, great, grandfather!'

There was an electric feeling around the table as Angelico delivered his *pièce de résistance*. He sat smiling calmly, waiting for the reaction. A look of confusion clouded Alex's face.

'Why did no one ever tell me this? I mean, didn't they know?'

'You have to remember that Amos and Juan's relationship was something of a scandal at the time and Amos's children rather swept it under the carpet. Many of them used their mother's maiden name and none of them left any clear records of this, so it took Peggy quite a while to piece it all together. And when she did, well, you know how very eccentric she was, she just made an offer to the people who were living in the house at the time, who didn't seem to be any relation. And then she kept quiet about it.

'As far as I know, I'm the only person she ever told; I was researching a book on the links between family structure and architectural development. She made me promise not to use this story, said that if her forebears had chosen to hide something strange and beautiful then it wasn't her place to undo their efforts. Somehow, I don't think she'd mind me telling you, though, and it's up to you to choose how to use the information now. But please bear her own views in mind. Have you ever thought why she chose to leave the house to you?'

'She wanted the Crawford name to continue?'

'In part, I am sure, but there's probably more. She knew you were gay?'

'Yeah, I came out a while before she died, so she knew.'

'And yet she *still* stipulated that you should marry and that your wife should have a baby. And I understand from Karl that you have married Sue to fulfil the condition?'

'That's right. Karl,' Alex looked imploringly at him. 'Are you sure this is OK?'

'Certain,' Karl replied. 'There's another piece you don't know yet which will reassure you. But don't lose the thread here. Angelico?'

'Trust me, Alex, this is all right. Now, you know what a sense of humour Peggy had in her own particular way? Think about this, think about the conditions of her will.'

Alex's brow furrowed for a moment. Then he said, 'I think I have it. It's about Amos, isn't it? He was gay, but he also married and had children. This is sort of a joke, right? Aunt Peggy wants me to bring it full circle, to be like Amos?'

'That's right, you have it! Not that she actually told me this, but I think it makes sense, don't you?'

'Yes, yes, it's incredible. Now I understand! Angelico, I cannot even begin to tell you how much this means to me. I always felt a connection to the house, like I had to fight for it. There is no way that I'm ever going to let it go now. Not ever, whatever happens.'

'What do you mean, "let it go"?'

Alex's face clouded again. 'It's not in very good condition and I can't afford to renovate. And it's not like I have any funds on the horizon either, so I'm, kind of, getting a little desperate.'

'I see. Well I'm afraid there's not a lot I can say to help, at the moment.' Angelico's eyes sparkled as if he was hiding something. 'Though I may be useful in getting some grants, provided your renovations are historically accurate. But I do think it's not as bad as you might fear. I've kept an eye on the place from the outside for a while. The last time I saw the interior was probably five or six years ago. I think there's a lot you and your *friend*,' he looked at me as he said this, 'might be able to do. I'd suggest that the problems are less drastic than they appear. And I have my own personal reasons for wanting to offer such help and advice as you might need.'

'Which are?'

Angelico took another sip of his whisky, then, beaming, he stood up and walked over to Alex's chair, placing his hands on his shoulders.

'You and I are practically cousins. Your great-aunt paid for me to go through school, right up until I qualified as an architect. I didn't know this until a few years later, but I am Enrique's son! The son of Peggy's great love!'

Alex leapt to his feet and turned to hug Angelico. They stood embracing and then Alex nodded towards Karl with a knowing expression and said, 'Angelico, do you know what this naughty old man has set you up for this evening?'

Karl smiled and rubbed his hands together excitedly, an impresario surveying a full house, as Angelico replied.

'But I thought you were the one who was set up?'

Alex was grinning madly now that he was finally in on the next surprise. 'Look how many places are laid at table! Two people are missing. That's all I'm saying.'

'Karl,' said Angelico, 'who are these places for? What are you up to, you sly old fox?'

'Did you hear a motorbike?' asked Karl.

Angelico nodded, with a 'so what' expression on his face.

'I must alert Pepe that we are ready for dessert. Please excuse me.'

Throwing us all a Mona Lisa smile, Karl rose and crossed to the kitchen door, opened it and talked briefly to Pepe. As he returned, Phil appeared at the top of the steps with an enormous man clad in motorcycle gear. Karl went to greet them and everybody at the table rose.

'Maxo, Phyllis, welcome!' said Karl. Phil gave him a dangerous look and kicked his shin lightly – she clearly preferred to be called Phil – but Karl ignored her, saying, 'Phyllis, let me introduce you to one of your *many* uncles. This is your father's half-brother, Angelico. I don't believe you've met.'

21
No Plasters

The rest of the evening passed swiftly and at a high emotional pitch. It appeared that Enrique had kept his and Peggy's involvement with his various offspring fairly compartmentalised, to avoid the wrath of various husbands. Angelico himself didn't know who his real father was until sometime after the death of the man he had thought was his father. By then, Enrique was also dead and so Angelico's mother eventually told him the truth herself. He had chosen to tell no one at all until Karl came to hear that he was back in town and told him about Alex and the house. That's when Karl had cooked up the idea of inviting Angelico to the regular Monday night dinner.

Alex was buzzing around the room at breakneck speed. He spent most of the time hugging people and insisted that Karl took countless photographic permutations of him and his 'cousins', who had become immediately inseparable. There was a Latin intensity to it all that was so unfamiliar to me that I hovered on the margin.

While Alex was telling Maxo and Phil the story of his house and his new-found ancestor, Penny and I drifted out onto the terrace to take the air. The garden lighting had been dimmed so that it mixed with the moonlight to spread a gentle, shadowless glow.

Penny walked down the broad steps to the pool and sat facing me on its raised edge. She inhaled deeply and savoured the air, her eyes shutting until she breathed out again. As I looked towards her I was aware of the whiteness of the marble steps extending to the edge of my vision in each direction, as if I were sitting on the lower skirts of a great pyramid and she was the Sphinx.

'I hope you didn't feel too intruded upon by that little interrogation earlier,' she said. 'It came out of concern rather than any desire to pry.'

I nodded.

'I know something of how you feel, from when Carey died; but they say that losing a child is the worst thing, the hardest thing to bear.'

Her tone was comfortable and intimate, her expression soft.

'It feels like that,' I said.

'Have you allowed yourself to talk it through with anyone? Clearly not with Selina and your father, but what about other people? Your sister?'

'I've talked a little with Lolly. She's the breakaway faction in the family. She thinks the rest of us are emotion-bottlers and in a way she's right; I find it easier to just try and get on with things.'

'That's not working too well for you at the moment, is it?' She said this very carefully so as not to imply that I was at fault.

'Not really, no. Though tonight, in *there*,' I nodded towards the room behind me, 'was the first time I've done anything like that. I mean, I couldn't stop myself. It's very unlike me.'

'Excuse the cliché, but no man is an island. Did it make you feel any better?'

'I think so. I can't really sort everything out in my head yet. What you said about Selina, about her maybe feeling guilty herself... That makes the beginnings of some sense to me.'

She sat forward, her hands clasped together. 'The beginnings of sense can sometimes be the hardest part to grasp. Maybe the rest will come more easily now. Grief can be a very frightening thing at first, Michael, but when it starts to run its course it can also start to work a little magic.'

She produced the word 'magic' with a half-whispered, bedtime story flourish.

'You're reminding me of something Karl said last night,' I replied. 'About how you always apply emotional first aid. It's appreciated, you know.'

Penny laughed and rocked herself forward to her feet. 'I quite like that. So I'm Nurse Penny, am I?'

'With your box of magic plasters.'

'Oh no. No plasters, Michael. A wound heals faster if it's allowed to bleed a little. So let it bleed and then let it breathe; there's plenty of fresh air around here.'

22
Peggy's Palimpsest

A while later, Penny made her excuses and went back to the guesthouse. She was expecting new guests the next morning and wanted an early night. But the rest of us went to Alex's house to see Aunt Peggy's 'surprise'.

It took only a few moments to get the large picture off the wall. It was the same dark abstract I had noticed earlier, painted on canvas and stretched over a borderless wooden frame. As we lifted it I was aware that its centre of gravity was shifting unexpectedly; something heavy was swinging from its rear. We pulled it carefully into the strongest patch of light in the hallway and while Maxo and I held it upright, Angelico went behind it and unhitched the mystery object. He emerged moments later holding an ornate frame, a satisfied smile on his face. He held it with its back to us for a dramatic moment before saying 'Guess who?' as he turned it towards us.

For a painting that was clearly well over a hundred years old, it looked almost as good as new. It was naïvely done and showed two elderly men, one white, one Hispanic, with identical houses behind them. They were holding hands.

'Amos and Juan,' Alex and I said together.

Angelico held up his hands to silence us all. He cleared his throat and said, 'Actually, though this is rather a wonderful piece of family history, it's not the main surprise. You need to know a little background first. Because of the layout of this house, there's a secondary attic reached through the oldest part, above what is now the kitchen. It's extremely cramped, more of a cubbyhole, and its entrance was concealed by asbestos when Peggy bought the place. In the course of having it removed, workmen found a hatch, so naturally she explored. She found this painting wrapped in paper inside an old trunk. It verified what she'd already worked out about Amos's story because of what it shows. Though sweet, it's of no real artistic merit or value, I think; it's probably the work of a reasonably gifted amateur, maybe a friend of the two men. Maxo, would you mind holding it flat for me, please? So that the back of it is facing upwards? Thank you.'

He had us all gripped again as he removed some retaining clips at the back of the picture and took out a thin sheet of wood, which he handed to me. Then, as carefully as a midwife, he reached into the darkened recess at the back of the frame and lifted out a frameless stretched canvas.

It was Amos again, but this time on his own. He sat in a high-backed chair wearing stiffly formal clothes, facing slightly towards the right-hand edge of the frame. This time, Alex was speechless; the painting was clearly of a far superior quality to the one it had been hiding in. It glowed richly in the dim light.

Sue spoke first this time. 'I'm certainly no art historian, but that looks serious. I mean, d'you think it's by someone famous?'

'I don't know,' replied Angelico. 'Peggy was delirious when she found it, she was sure that it must be valuable but felt that Amos would have had a good reason to hide it inside the other painting. Almost as if to say, "If you don't like the picture of me and Juan, then screw you, you'll never find the other one!" It's fantastic, it's the perfect reverse metaphor for the *love that dare not speak its name*, to hide the respectable picture inside the shocking one. And so much better if the hidden work is of value, because the visible picture of the two men as lovers keeps the prudish from discovering the more valuable one. Instead they bundled it into an attic and forgot it!'

'Did she ever have it, like, evaluated?' asked Sue.

'I certainly suggested it when she showed it to me. But she wanted to be in on Amos's joke. Eccentric as ever, she decided to rehide it, then put it inside her own painting. After all, she and Enrique had outraged her family enough for her to feel some sympathy with Amos. She once referred to it as her "palimpsest".'

'Her what?' asked Phil.

Karl replied. 'Palimpsest. It means something that is hidden underneath something else. Artists and scholars used to use the same canvases and parchments again and again to economise on materials, so their work built up in layers. And sometimes the technique was used in order to hide things on purpose.'

'Do you think it's worth anything? I mean, not that I'd want to sell it, but if it's valuable it should be somewhere safe.' This was Alex.

Angelico looked uncertain. 'I'm no art historian either, but it looks pretty good to me. Karl, what do you think?'

Karl took a long, appraising look before answering.

'It appears to be unsigned, which doesn't really help – and it's very much not my period. But it's undeniably fine. With your permission, Alex, I would like to show it to my friend Marty. He's a rather illustrious New York art dealer who has a vacation home down here. He's not in residence at the moment but I'll call and ask when he's next due in town. In the meantime, may I suggest that you allow me to put it in my safe. Of course, we trust everyone *here*, but...'

He looked around him like a detective examining a roomful of suspects.

'As they say in the navy, loose lips sink ships – and this is rather too exciting to expect everyone to retain their discretion. Alex?'

'Sure, please do, I would really appreciate that, Karl. God, I don't know what to say. I don't know if it even belongs to me. Aunt Peggy's will said house and *contents*. I guess this is a "content", isn't it?'

Maxo and I rehung Peggy's large abstract on the wall while Alex started to reassemble the other two pictures, but halfway through he stopped and said, 'Karl, do you think it would be OK to keep Amos and Juan here with me? This is their home, after all, and we can wrap the other painting up for you to take in the car. I want to hang them in my room. I think it's time they saw the light of day again!'

'That's rather a touching thought. I see no reason why not. Angelico, would you care to escort me back safely?'

After a profusion of kisses between Phil and Angelico, he and Karl stepped carefully down the front steps to the car, Angelico holding the freshly wrapped painting like a new-born baby with Karl hovering nearby as if he were the father. Alex offered the rest of us a drink, which I accepted before realising that the others were making their excuses, so within five minutes we were alone together on the back deck with cold beers in our hands.

Alex pulled the two mattresses out from inside the house, placing them close together, and then lit a joint as we sat down. He looked up at the sky, exhausted and content, the thin stream of smoke that curled from his mouth backlit by a shaft of light coming from the kitchen to form a lazily drifting ectoplasm. Slowly he slid himself into his mattress until he was lying down.

We didn't speak for a short while, he staring up at the stars while I looked across at him, deep in thought. Then he said, 'Chill-out time,' and handed me the joint. I took a drag and held it down briefly before exhaling and handing it back to him. I didn't really want it – being mildly suspicious of it after the way I'd felt earlier that day – but neither did I want to make an issue of it; I didn't want to break his spell. We continued like this for a while, with me taking another couple of shallow puffs until a slight buzz set in and I followed his eyes upwards. The moon had gone and the sky had turned to dark, star-dotted crystal. The air was warm, the storm that afternoon having cleared all humidity, and the last thing I remember before drifting off was feeling as if I could see forever.

I woke some time later. There was now a slight chill in the air, the first light of dawn glimmering in the eastern sky. Alex and I had moved closer during our sleep and were lying on our sides facing each other, his hand stretched out and almost touching mine. I lay and watched his peaceful face for a while before getting slowly up, tiptoeing into the house and fetching a rug, which I placed gently over him. Then I let myself quietly out and cycled back to Penny's, where I put myself to bed.

23
Heading Out of Town

I spent the next day on my own, cycling around the town, swimming and thinking. Alex and Sue were working the evening shift at the café, so Penny and Karl invited me to dine out with them that night, but I pleaded tiredness and got an early night.

Something must have clicked into place while I slept because when I woke the next day I found that I knew exactly what to do next. I didn't question it or even think about it; I was simply appreciative of the certainty, after so many days of emptiness and flux. So I forced any doubts to the periphery of my mind in order that I might act before I could reconsider.

I went first to the offices of the Union Bank on Duval and then to a small cybercafé further down the street where I ate brunch and sent an email to my solicitor. Then I went to a jewellery shop and purchased a pretty antique brooch in the shape of a dragon, asking for it to be wrapped. By the time I had done all of this, it was early afternoon and an acceptable hour to call my cleaner in England, which I did using a newly purchased phonecard. She wasn't in so I left her a detailed message, then called my bank and gave them instructions. They needed a fax confirmation so I went back to the cybercafé and paid to use their machine.

Thinking of the extra clothing that I had acquired, I bought a small weekend bag and hurried back, reaching the guesthouse at around 2.45. There were three messages for me in my room: one from Angelico with a number for me to call; one from Alex saying that I should drop by the café whenever I was up; and one from Penny asking me to find her when I got back. I packed quickly and tidied my room, then locked up and crossed the main deck towards the reception area. There was no one there so I rang the bell on the desk and a man I did not recognise appeared.

It was the night-clerk, Sam, who said he was covering for Penny while she was out dealing with a crisis.

'I'm checking out,' I told him. 'Do you know when Penny'll be back?'

'She shouldn't be too long now, she's been out for a couple of hours. Which room number?

'Eight.'

'Ah, OK, that makes sense. You must be Michael. Hi.'

He extended his hand and as I shook it he continued, 'Penny said to tell you that you're welcome to stay. She's had a bit of a problem with some of the other guests and she's had to ask them to leave early, so there's a room available for another five nights if you need it.'

'That's very kind but I'll be checking out anyway. What sort of a problem?'

He leaned forward conspiratorially, as if someone might be trying to eavesdrop on us.

'It was the people in the room next to you, the ones from Wisconsin. She found them doing something unacceptable so she asked them to leave.'

I shuddered, my suspicions confirmed. 'What were they doing?'

He leaned closer, ready to whisper news of some obscenity. 'She caught them this morning, on the corner of Duval and Southard. A full public performance. She was suspicious when they arrived because of all the gear they were carrying. She was on her way to the drug store and there they were.'

'Doing what?'

'Preaching,' he said. I paused for a moment, taking this in before replying.

'That hardly sounds perverse.'

'Are you kidding? They were all like, "Key West Is Sodom and Gomorrah" and "The Lord Will Judge You for Your Sins" and "Satan Dwells Within Your Citadel" and shit like that. The man had a microphone and this, like, battery and amplifier and everything. He was going on and on while the two women tried to collect money. I mean, really. These crank fundamentalists come down here thinking they can save our souls. Assholes, I say. Excuse my language but fuck 'em, I think they're *far* more perverted than anyone here. I'm sure it's like a kinky little holiday for them, like, they're really repressed or something. They come for a cheap thrill to, you know, watch the faggots in the zoo.'

'But what about the chicken?'

He looked at me as if I were a lunatic.

'Chicken? What chicken?'

'I overheard them on their deck yesterday. They were talking about charging their battery and how when the man got "up and at it" he went on for hours and so on. I thought they were swingers. Then he said, "Welcome to Sodom and Gomorrah, now hand me that chicken," or something like that. I couldn't take any more, God knows what I was imagining!'

Sam laughed explosively. 'Michael, we have only just met, but I think you might just be weirder than them. What did you think they were doing with the chicken? No, don't tell. Anyway, Penny is furious. Now, how are your little twin nephews? I took the message the other evening.'

'They're doing very well, thank you. But what's Penny up to at the moment?'

'She's cycling around town like a mad thing, making phone calls, tipping everyone off about the fundamentalists. It is her avowed intent to make sure no one else gives 'em a room on the island – and she has the contacts to do it. Said she was gonna run 'em out of town even if it took her all day. That's my girl! Whip the bastards with a rainbow flag until their asses sting!'

Sam giggled over this image as I paid for the three nights I'd agreed and wrote a note for Penny. Then I handed him the package with the dragon brooch and the key to Carey's bike and asked him to give them to her with the note. I also asked if he could spare me an envelope, which he did.

'Tell Penny I'll be in contact very soon and say thank you to her from me. Nice to meet you!'

'You too. Go carefully!'

I unlocked Alex's spare bike from the railings outside and pedalled until I reached the back gate of the café, where I locked it to the railings and wrote a short note. Placing it in the envelope along with the bicycle key, I addressed it to Alex then slipped around to the front and dropped it through the mailbox. I walked quickly away without looking back.

Within a couple of minutes I was back on Truman, the name for the final stretch of Interstate 1 as it runs southwest through Key West to its conclusion near the ocean. I hoisted my bags onto my shoulder and turned northeast, heading out of town.

24
Just a Salad

Several blocks further on, I came to the first destination on my list, The Key West Cycle Store, where I hired a bike from a grungy young man with scabby knuckles who called me 'Dude'. Then I cycled to Alex's house where I hopped over the gate at the rear with my bags and, finding the back door open as usual, left them in the hallway. After that I cycled around looking for a bookshop until a smiling old lady directed me to Flaming Maggie's where I bought some books on local architecture and plants. Then I went to Fausto's and bought the ingredients for a meal for two and a bottle of cold champagne. Back at Alex's it took a couple of careful trips to get my booty over the fence, after which I emptied the groceries into the fridge and dialled Angelico's number.

It rang for a while and I was about to give up when he answered, breathless.

'Good afternoon, Angelico. It's Michael, Alex's friend from the other evening. I was wondering if I could pop round and take a look at the stuff in your garage with you?'

'Well, hello, Michael, what a timely call. I just finished dragging the whole lot out into the yard. I have a houseboy, strapping Felipe, who kindly offered to help. I also still have the U-Haul that I used to get my possessions down from Rhode Island, so we've loaded most of it up already. I was hoping you'd call so that we could bring it round. You see, Felipe will be returning the truck for me tomorrow morning so I was rather hoping to get this over to you today. Otherwise poor Alex will have to hire a vehicle and he hardly looks as if he can afford to eat, the dear boy!'

Within half an hour Angelico and Felipe had arrived and I was helping them carry the bagged items up the front steps. When we had got them all inside we opened one of the bags to find that each piece was meticulously labelled. Then Angelico produced a large manila envelope containing carefully annotated diagrams that showed how everything should be reassembled.

By this time it was nearly six o'clock and the sun was beginning to dip. We were all sweating readily so I offered the two visitors a cold beer but they declined, Angelico saying, 'I have a hot date this evening and I have to go beautify, but please call me tomorrow. There are some things we should discuss and you'll probably need some help working all this out. I'm quite certain that under all this apparent order' – he pointed at the envelope – 'lies total chaos. Like me, my handwriting is elegant on the surface, but hard to fathom.'

He winked, then raised himself onto his toes to kiss me on both cheeks before rounding up the keys to the truck, various extraneous pieces of paper and the small leather handbag with which he'd arrived. Then, as quickly as they had appeared, he and Felipe were gone.

I was in the kitchen when Alex appeared an hour later. I had prepared a meal and laid the rickety table on the back deck. He came in through the front door and I heard him whistle to himself in surprise as he saw the half-unpacked planking and sections of wall in the front hall. I expected him to call my name but he didn't and the next thing I heard was him running up the stairs.

I heard the shower start then four or five minutes later it stopped and after a brief pause I heard his feet on the stairs again. I was still in the kitchen when he came in, humming something mournful to himself as he rounded the door. He was naked.

'Aargh!'

He screamed and covered his genitals in a reflex action, then started laughing.

'My God, what are you doing here? Penny called and said you'd packed and gone. She said you left her a note saying you'd decided to do some bleeding and breathing, something to do with a conversation you had with her the other night? Then I found the bike. I thought I'd lost you.'

'Didn't you get my note?'

'What note?'

'I put it through the letterbox at the café.'

'No, I mean, I only check that in the morning. It goes into, like, a box inside.'

He moved excitedly across the room and grabbed me, holding me close with his arms reaching up around my shoulders. I returned his embrace briefly then, uncomfortably aware of his nudity, I gently separated from him. Looking a little embarrassed, he sat down on a chair and tucked himself away.

'So what did the note say?' he asked.

It was my turn to be embarrassed. I'd chosen to write the note rather than talking to him because I'd found it easier to express myself that way. Now I was aware that I had little option other than to tell him its contents accurately, since he would certainly read it the next morning. I coughed nervously.

'It said that I've decided to stick around for a while and that I'd like to take up your offer to stay here. It also said that I'd like to work a little with you and Angelico on the house, just to see how things go. And it suggested that if you were free tonight I'd make us dinner here, which I've already done on the off-chance – but please don't worry if you have other plans, it's all cold, just a salad really – and it also said that...'

I coughed again. Damn, why hadn't I realised that he might not have read the note?

'Said that...?' prompted Alex.

'It also said... look, sod the note. Listen, Alex. I overheard you talking to Penny about me on the phone a couple of days ago. While you were upstairs here.'

Alex looked horrified but I continued.

'I'm really sorry. I sort of got trapped in the hall while you were on the balcony upstairs so I heard pretty much everything. I realised then that you had the wrong end of the stick, which is partly why I said all that stuff at Karl's the other night – so you'd know what my situation is. Anyway, what it said in the note was, I'd like to move in for a little while, until I've done some stuff on the house. But to be honest, what I meant, what I should have said, was that I'm only prepared for friendship. Nothing more. Which might not suit your... might not suit you. In which case I'll just leave.'

He stood up and moved slowly over to the door and reached behind it to pull out a large dishcloth, which he wrapped around his waist.

Then he walked over to me and put both his hands on my shoulders, looking into my face and saying, 'It's me that owes you an apology. You turn up here in a terrible state, mourning and depressed, and I let you down by being so pushy. Whatever I thought I was doing, it seems rather immature now. I have a habit of being too spontaneous. You must think I'm a real jerk.'

I started to reply but he hushed me with his finger and continued with a grave look on his face.

'So here's what I suggest. I can't undo our embarrassment at what you overheard and what I misunderstood – and that's really not your fault, by the way. But what I can do is to say, please, please stay here as my friend. I absolutely promise to behave and not to make you feel uncomfortable ever again. Truly, I mean it. And I'd love to have dinner, if the offer still stands.'

25
Alone in My Bed?

I spent the next week or so working on the house, often with Angelico's guidance. We decided to do some pressing external works before tackling the internal reconstruction and with his contacts we managed to get hold of some salvaged Dade County pine to match the original timber. Evenings were spent with various combinations of my new friends and nights were kept in solitude in the room next to Alex's, which he never entered without knocking.

After many hours around a variety of dinner tables, I had discovered more about all of them, as well as about myself. Alex, with his impossibly well-balanced upbringing, his close relationship with his parents and his innate desire to please and to see other people happy. Karl, with his obvious need for a substitute family, determinedly *sui generis* and appearing to have existed in outline only before Carey came along. He described his previous life with broad impressionistic brushstrokes, purposely leaving much to the imagination. He and Penny went to some lengths to bring me out of myself but, while other people chipped in with bits of their own histories and experiences, Karl restricted himself to life with and post-Carey, augmented only by brief references to his previous relationships. He was so adept at shifting the focus of conversation away from himself that it took me a while even to notice that he was doing it.

Penny was a little more forthcoming, telling me about her opera career and her life touring in Europe, though I often sensed that she too was holding something back.

Sue was less intensely Californian in the way she spoke than Penny, more common sense than psychoanalytical, and therefore more like the people I was used to. Her hippy parents had been surprisingly careless with her as they'd travelled around, indulging themselves in a succession of religious and drug-induced experiences. They had even left her with a friend's parents for a few months when she was just two years old so that they could visit an ashram in India. But, when she was older, they had found it hard to accept her lesbianism, her mother thinking that it was an over-reaction to her rape and subsequent abortion and her father simply not understanding how any woman could not want a man. She had a quiet determination when she spoke about them, as if they were naughty children, but I could tell there was plenty of residual resentment in her. And I came to think what a good mother she would make; she'd seen how not to do it, the perils of her unstructured childhood contrasting with my growing perception of my own overly structured experience. I thought that she'd had it rather worse than I had, since she didn't appear to have had anyone sensible around her as she grew up. She seemed to have got most of her craving for order and conventionality from a variety of TV shows, though they were mostly about offbeat families who portrayed conventionality from an angle. *Bewitched* and *The Partridge Family* were her favourites, though when I said of the latter, 'But surely they went around in a bus too,' she looked rather surprised, as if she'd never noticed the connection before.

I also discovered an interesting similarity between Alex and Sue: neither of them had any siblings, their parents having decided for similar ideological reasons that having more than one child was irresponsible. Sue felt that the real truth in her case was that they had found caring for her to be too much of an interference with their freedom. So much for ideology. In any event, it became clear to me that Alex and Sue's relationship, if not a conventional marriage, was rather more than a friendship; they had effectively adopted each other as brother and sister.

*

I spent a lot of time with Angelico and quickly became fond of him. He was an extremely kind and big-hearted man with a wide range of knowledge and an extensive collection of anecdotes that kept me amused while we worked. It also transpired that he had a passion for Noel Coward and we spent many slightly silly hours singing along with him as he oozed out of a portable CD player while we worked.

It turned out that Angelico's 'hot date' wasn't Karl, as I'd assumed, but a forty-something model called Andy who was halfway through a painful slide from glossy magazines to knitwear catalogues. Karl had met him in California the previous year and had been 'keeping him for a rainy day', which had obviously now arrived since he'd invited him to stay for a while.

On Friday night of the following weekend, Angelico invited Alex and me to dinner to meet Andy, who got drunk and spilled his midlife crisis over the table and, as it happened, over me.

His therapist had told him that he could never allow himself to be successful until he managed to free himself from the disapproving internalised voice of his father. Something along those lines. Anyway, it sparked a 'coming out experience' session between the three of them. I sat on the sidelines listening as they swapped stories, apparently unperturbed by my presence, as they discussed the ways in which straight family and friends had reacted to their revelations. As we shared a very mild joint, Andy started talking about his 'clincher'. This turned out to have been, of all things, a Little League baseball game. It was a longish story but the gist of it was that at the age of nine he'd dropped a catch at a critical moment in a critical game and his dad had called him a fairy. That was it. Their relationship was never the same again. And as I listened, I found myself thinking; is that really it? You had one bad moment with your dad and it crippled you for the rest of your life! I had a thousand bad moments with my father and *I'm* still here.

Just as I was thinking this, Andy said, 'Anyway, I'm still here and at least I got honest with myself about it early on. I mean, I know a load of guys who got *married* rather than admit their gayness to their families or themselves. That sets up all sorts of shit. The human mind's capacity to deny the obvious is totally fuckin' infinite.'

He talked on about himself for a while and my attention drifted. Then he took me by surprise.

'So what about you, Mike? Angelico told me you were married, but didn't you ever do it with a guy?'

I saw Alex flinch slightly from across the table before intervening.

'Don't you think that's a little private, Andy?'

'Privacy?' he slurred. 'It's an alien concept to me, I'm an anal disbursive. Besides, we're among friends here, and Mike may have something to add to our shared experience?'

His voice rose to push home the question. Alex sat back, an apologetic expression on his face.

I thought about my reply for a moment, uncomfortably aware that, though Andy was drunk, it was not in fact unreasonable to pull me out of my observer's role. So I went ahead.

'Yes and no. I suppose it depends on what you mean by "doing it".'

The three of them shifted slightly in their seats.

'You've probably heard about how British boarding schools are rampant with homosexuality. Well, I went to one and it wasn't. We had girls in the sixth form and a surprising amount of normal – I mean to say, heterosexual – sex went on. As far as I knew, there was no homosexuality at all. It was all good, bracing, healthy stuff – you know, rugby and cold showers and so on. But there was one chap, he was in a different house to me and I hardly knew him. Anyway. After most of my friends had left school, I stayed on to do Oxbridge. It's a sort of special exam you used to have to do to get into Oxford or Cambridge, so not many people stay on to do it. I was actually going out with a girl called Clare at the time, but she'd left the school and was doing a gap year thing on some Australian sheep farm. So we had these special tutorials in very small groups and we had to do workgroup sessions between tutorials with other people doing the same subject as ourselves. He was the only other person doing my subject.'

I paused to take a drag of the joint, and Andy asked, 'What was his name?'

'Why do you ask?'

'Because people have names.'

'His name was Andrew.'

I was aware of an aggressive edge to my voice and felt sure the others must have noticed it, but Andy appeared unaware, saying, 'That's cool. Could've been me.'

I looked across the table at him and thought, 'Yes, it could have been you but I'm glad it wasn't.'

Then Angelico said, 'Go on.'

So I continued.

'My parents were stationed abroad at the time and Andrew asked me to his home for half-term. We had a project to work on and I was getting to quite like him. He was funny, he had an offbeat, clever sense of humour and appeared very self-assured for his age, much more than I was. It turned out that his parents were away on holiday, so we had the place to ourselves. The second or third night we were there, he raided his brother's room for some porn mags and we had some whisky and got quite drunk. We looked through these magazines and he suggested that we should read some of the stories out loud. After a while he started rubbing himself, eventually he took his thing out and we masturbated together.'

Andy had rolled and lit another joint by then, and was taking a long appreciative drag, nodding his head. He handed it on to Alex and said, 'God, I love that word, it's so *English*.' He experimented with it in a torturously bad attempt at an English accent, distorting his vowels. 'Maasturbate. Maaasturbate. Would you like to *maaasturbate* my *thing*? Excuse me, Dad, I'm sorry, but I like to *masturbate* with other boys.' Then he took me by surprise again. 'Did you kiss him?'

'No, of course not.'

I was aware of the absurdity of my reply even as I said it, but Andy was in his own world by now.

'My therapist says that kissing is much more intimate than genital sex. He says the mouth is our most sensual space or some shit like that. It certainly is with me. Though my ex-boyfriend,' he leered inexplicably at Angelico for a moment, 'says that "therapist" actually means "the rapist", only they fuck with your *head*. Anyway, no kissy stuff with the lovely *Andrew*. So did you blow each other?'

'Andy, I think that's probably enough for now, don't you?' This was Angelico, quietly serious.

But I had always been taught to stick up for myself, so I said, 'It's OK, Angelico, I'm a big boy, I can look after myself.'

'That's the spirit!' said Andy. 'So come on, *big boy*; any *sucky licky fucky*? Did you do any *big boy* stuff?'

I reached for the joint again reflexively, feeling that, despite my claim, I wasn't looking after myself as well as I'd hoped. But the fighting part of me wasn't going to be unnerved by this irritating victim of a man. He made me want to strike back by being more adult and reasonable than him. Though, at the same time as I was trying to look unfazed, I was also frantically trying to calculate what all this might mean to Alex.

'A little sucky on his part and a small amount of licky on my part and none of the other at all, since you ask,' I said.

'And did you like it?'

'Well, I obviously liked it enough to do it, didn't I?' The aggressive tone was back in my voice.

'Chill, man, shit, I'm just asking. So, did you do it again?'

'Once or twice.'

'Any fucky later, then?'

'No.'

'Kissy?'

'No.'

'Sounds pretty tame. But here's a little question, which you can choose not to answer if it's too, you know, in your *face* or something, since you sound a little oversensitive. Didn't you ever think about it before that time at school? Like, didn't you ever whack off while thinking about your classmates or anything like that? Your balls must've been bursting for years. Had you screwed the girlfriend?'

I was still unused to this sort of conversation. After a week or so of Oprah I suddenly found myself on the Springer show. Having no idea of the rules, I had no idea of what might come next, which was very disorientating. The net effect was that I just kept on answering his questions.

'No, I never made love to Clare; in fact, she stayed in Australia with someone she met there.'

'And the classmates?'

'I suppose I had one or two crushes on people. I might have thought about them a little.'

'But did you ever whack off over girls?'

'Sometimes.'

'But other times it was over guys, right?'

'Maybe. Sometimes.'

I was aware that Alex was looking at me fairly hard from across the table and that my face was burning. I looked at my watch, scrabbling to find an excuse about needing to get up early, which would have been ridiculous because it was not yet ten o'clock.

Andy continued. Like a lot of unhappy people, he had a finely tuned nose for trouble.

'So, did you get married to please your family?'

'No. I wanted to have children.'

This was only half-true and Alex and possibly Angelico would know it, but I excused myself the shorthand.

'And did you?'

'Yes. One.'

Alex was preparing to intervene again but Andy wasn't really interested in anything that didn't relate directly to his own situation so he moved straight past the issue.

'Cool. So have you ever done it with other guys since you got married?'

'No, not at all.'

'Do you ever like, fantasise about it? Like, are you bi or something?'

Suddenly a new strategy suggested itself to me, one that I've used many times since. I simply turned the tables. It's the best way to win with people like Andy who in truth mainly want to talk about themselves.

'What about you, Andy? Did you ever make love with a woman?'

'*Fuck*, no. Are you kidding?'

It worked like a dream. Within seconds we were being treated to the full details of how a cheerleader called Shirleen or Shirley-Anne, I couldn't tell from his slurred delivery, had tried to give him a blow job when he was in high school and then told all his friends that he couldn't get an erection, and what a negative long-term impact this had had on his self-image, provoking a defensive narcissism that led him into the wrong career path when really he should have been a lawyer or a big-shot Wall Street financier, and so on and so on.

Listening to him was like wading through discarded chewing gum and I soon gave up trying. His over-familiarity and self-indulgence were simply too much for me to take and I could feel no sympathy for the obvious comfort he found in the role of victim. I felt like telling him to shut up and get on with his life but, not wanting to offend Angelico, I bit my tongue.

As Alex and I cycled home, he drew level with me and said, 'Well, I don't think *that's* going to last. Poor Angelico. He's invited him to stay for three weeks! It's too painful to contemplate. I mean, I feel sorry for him and everything but really...'

I swerved past a fallen palm-frond in the road and rejoined him, saying, 'I can't say I liked him very much. He seemed to be almost entirely self-obsessed. I've never heard so much psychobabble crap. I mean, when you or Penny talk about people's feelings, that's what they sound like. Feelings. But Andy manages to pathologise everything until all his feelings are disordered.'

'He was certainly getting off on your little story, though, Michael. You are a dark horse, aren't you?'

'Not at all, you never asked.'

'We have a deal, right? Just because I'm trying to stick to it by not leaping all over you doesn't mean I'm not interested in that sort of story. Obviously. Whenever you want to tell more, I'm all ears.'

I pondered how I ought to respond to this as we continued to pedal, Alex's rear mudguard filling the quiet street with a rusty squeak on each revolution of his wheels. Should I tell him more? I tried to remember Penny's phrase from the day I'd met her... 'oversharing', that was it. I decided that I'd already shared enough that evening. It could wait.

We reached the house less than a minute later and I pleaded tiredness, going straight to bed – but it was a while before I went to sleep.

I woke early the next morning, showered and went quietly past Alex's shut door. It was Saturday and the streets were quiet outside as I cycled to the Waterfront Market for milk and croissants.

While I pedalled, I thought back to my weekends in England; how Selina and I would go to the supermarket together while Jim slept in, and how I'd take him breakfast in bed when we returned, staying to chat with him while he ate. Simple pleasures, gone but not forgotten.

The sky was a little overcast, beginning to look like rain, and I made a mental list of things that needed doing to the house, things I'd left uncovered that would need making good temporarily if it were to rain heavily. By the time I returned, it was around 8.30 and the postman was just cycling off down the street. I looked in the mailbox to find a mixture of circulars and junk mail. But there was one envelope addressed to Alex with the name of a Miami clinic on it. I made a pot of fresh coffee, put some butter, jam and croissants on a tray, and took it all upstairs to his room.

He was still sleeping so I opened the curtain gently and placed the tray on the dressing table. There was a tissue on the floor, which I kicked aside as I sat on the edge of his bed. By now his eyes were open but he was dozy, so I sat and waited while he came around. It had been a warm night and he was covered only with a sheet, his curving shape clearly visible underneath. As I unconsciously allowed my eyes to roam over him, he smiled lazily, yawning and rolling onto his side to face me.

'Breakfast is served, m'lud,' I said.

'Why, thank you, Jeeves, that is most kind. What time is it?'

'A little before nine.'

'Hmmm. Day off, Pablo's turn to do Saturday at the café. Cool. I can help you with the house.'

'There's a letter for you. From Miami.'

He looked at it in my outstretched hand, as if in preparation for an ordeal, and said, 'I have to pee first. Excuse me.'

He scrabbled out of bed holding the sheet to himself and I suddenly had the most powerful wish that he would drop it. I was so close to reaching for him then, but the moment passed as he went through to the bathroom. I could smell the air in his wake as he went and it was the scent of locker rooms and male sex, mingling tantalisingly.

I waited for him to finish in the bathroom. I heard him pee and then the flush and a running tap and when he returned the smell had gone, replaced with an astringent soapiness.

Just as he was about to get back into bed, the telephone rang and as he reached for the handset by his bed, the sheet slipped from him. Tiny beads of water shone in his pubic hair and his cock, fat and half-tumescent, swayed just below the horizontal. We both froze as he followed my eyes to it, and it twitched and started to rise, its head extending towards me. The phone continued to ring.

Whatever might have happened next was arrested by the sound of the answering machine clicking in from the hallway below and my father's voice booming out through the gloom.

'I'm sorry to disturb you. My name is Douglas Stuart, I am Michael Stuart's father. I got this number from his cleaning lady. I need to speak to him, so if this is the correct number, would you please tell him to telephone me at home. I shall be here all weekend. Thank you.'

I heard the machine click and the tape whirring into rewind.

'Michael, are you OK?' asked Alex. 'You're as white as a *ghost*.'

26
All Donations

'Damn.'

'I thought you told the lady not to give anyone your number.'

'I did. That's just so absolutely typical of my father, pushing people around until he gets what he wants. If the phone rings again I won't answer it and if you pick up on him, please just tell him it was the wrong number or that I've moved on or something. Sorry.'

I looked back at his descending cock and shook my head.

'Look, Alex, get back into bed. Don't you think you ought to read this? I'm sorry that he rang and disturbed you.'

An angry look crossed Alex's face. 'No, Michael. I'm not letting you fool yourself on this one, so don't even try. He did not disturb me, he disturbed us.'

I exhaled in frustration, nodding slowly.

'OK, OK. Us, he disturbed us, you're right. Look, I feel terrible about this but I just... Well, I can't. Not after that. He's taken the wind out of my sails.'

'Well, let me blow some back in.' He sounded almost petulant.

'No. Come on now, read the letter. It's important.'

He climbed back onto the bed, this time not bothering to cover himself with the sheet, and sat half-upright against the wall, facing me. Then he took the letter from my outstretched hand. He turned it around in his hands a few times as if it were a fascinatingly complex piece of origami, before eventually peeling it open. A thin, medicinally blue flash of static flared from the flap of the envelope as the glue was pulled apart.

His face was in neutral as he started to read to himself, then his lips began to move silently and his brow furrowed into a deep frown. When he got to the end his hands dropped briefly to his lap before rising again to return the letter to me.

'You're a doctor. Sounds like I'm fucked to me.'

I scanned it quickly, taking in key words and phrases.

'Sorry to... standard test... extremely low count... unlikely that conventional... possibility... in vitro.... further investigative...'

I shuffled up the bed towards him and took him in my arms. He gave in reluctantly at first but soon collapsed into me and started to sob.

'They'll all be so disappointed. Sue, Penny. Even Karl. I know it's illogical, but I really feel as if I've let them down. They want this so badly, particularly Penny. Fuck, I feel like a seedless grape or something. Half fruit, half fucking *eunuch*. It's so unfair. And it'll end up with me losing the house, which I just can't bear. I can't bear the thought of having to go back to being like a factory-farmed chicken, all cooped up and robbed of any choices, everything planned out for me until the day I die. Grad school, career, pension... I want *this*. I want my freedom.'

I continued to hold him quietly for a while as his chest and shoulders convulsed. Eventually I spoke.

'It's not as bad as all that. The letter says that you and Sue might be able to benefit from IVF. You could have a child that way.'

'Sue won't do that. She has very bad memories of the clinic where she had her termination. Penny practically had to drug her to get her to go for her tests recently, and it set the whole thing off again. So now she's even more insistent about wanting this to happen naturally or not at all. She will not undergo any procedures or artificiality. Fuck. What will we do? Is there anything I can do to raise my sperm count, Michael? Anything at all?'

I tried to switch to bedside manner but it fell away quickly.

'Your count is very low. I know this from when Selina and I tried for a second child. Mine was normal but I know the ranges. IVF is your only chance, and even that wouldn't be certain. But I've just had a thought; there could be another way. What exactly did your aunt's will say about the baby?'

'It said, my wife has to have a baby within three years of our marriage. Which doesn't leave an awful lot of time. Otherwise the house reverts to my third cousin, Elspeth, who is an absolute cow and who really disapproves of me, *and* she knows I'm gay, so she's already, like, totally onto me. She's already spoken to Aunt Peggy's executors about it, washed all my dirty linen in front of them. Shit, I hate this.' He grabbed his cock and tugged it, as if trying to rid himself of it. 'After what Angelico told me, this house means even more to me now. I mean, what with Amos, Juan and everything. And the sick irony is that Elspeth is the sort of person who would've put *them*' – he nodded towards the portrait of the two men on his wall – 'straight back in the loft.'

'Alex, listen to me. This is your Aunt Peggy we're talking about. Eccentric? Yes. Stupid? No!'

'What do you mean?'

'Come on, you worked it out the other night when Angelico made you really *think* about Amos. You heard everything Angelico said. Think. Think how your aunt's mind worked.'

He looked blank and confused, so I continued. 'The will says that your wife has to have a baby. It doesn't say you have to be the father. Think of all Peggy's "children": Phil's dad, Angelico, all the others. They weren't hers at all, not biologically. She knew you were gay, she worded her will like that on purpose. Sure, she wanted the name and the dynasty to continue, but only according to *her* rules! I think Amos would approve!'

I paused while this sank in, then spoke again before I could check myself. It may sound crazy but it made sudden, clear sense to me; after what had just not happened between Alex and me as a result of my father's interruption I felt as if I owed him something. And I provided myself with plenty of let-out clauses, aware that I might be being reckless. I couldn't stand by and see him so desolate; I just couldn't.

'Would you want to have a baby if it weren't for wanting to keep this house?' I asked.

'Definitely. It's what Penny and Sue want. And it's not just them, it's all of us as an extended family. It's all the stuff I said a couple of weeks ago about not wanting to miss out on what straight people take for granted.'

'Good. Now here's a suggestion. I'll need to talk to my lawyer about it, maybe take some legal advice in the US too. And I'll really need to think about it, talk about it with all of you, but *I* could do it.'

'Do what?'

'I could... you know... with Sue. If she'd have me, when we know each other better. I mean, I'm a bit out of practice but I'm sure I could manage.'

Alex looked at me incredulously.

'You mean, you would father my child?'

'Like I said, there'd be a lot of thinking, talking and advice-taking first, but it's a possibility. Why not? It's no stranger than most of the rest of what goes on around here.' I smiled, dizzy at the thought of what I was proposing.

'But you've known us for such a short time. How could you make that commitment?'

I thought for a moment and then answered in what felt like a measured tone.

'I've got several answers. It feels as if I've known you for much longer than I have. I think you'll make a fantastic family. And if the legal situation is OK then it may be that there is no commitment other than the one you were already prepared to take. So the baby could have three uncles instead of two. You, me and Karl.'

Alex's incredulous look was switching slowly to regret. 'Michael, you're sweet and adorable and I love you for thinking of this but it's, it's... it's insane. You can't just go around fathering random babies to make your friends happy.'

'Why not?' I was enjoying myself now. 'Why can't I? I have nothing to lose apart from a paternity suit and, as I said, I can take legal advice. Maybe there's something Sue can sign to indemnify me. Whatever. Alex, I lost my son. Maybe I'd like to have another one.'

'You could get married again.'

'Maybe I don't want to.'

'Don't you think that could be very dangerous emotionally? To give your child up into another family?'

'Possibly, but give me a break! I've only just thought this up and I'm not claiming to have covered all the angles yet. Anyway, maybe I'd want to feel like a part of that family. It's much nicer than the one I grew up in. Listen. Let's think and talk about this while we work on the house today. Then if we feel there's anything worth pursuing, we can share it with Sue and Penny.' I took a little good-humoured dig. 'You know how you all love to share.'

Then I nodded at the letter and said, 'And I'd suggest that you don't tell them about that until you've decided what you want to do.'

27
Knock on Wood

The clouds were thick and swollen when we got outside, so we did some patching and tidying up outside the house and when the rain eventually came, mid-morning, we headed off to swim in the ocean. The air was still pleasantly warm but the downpour had cleared the beach at Fort Zachary Taylor so we had the whole wide sea to ourselves. Apart from the occasional boat on the horizon, we might have been on our own private island.

We swam offshore for a few hundred yards without speaking and then, while we were treading water, Alex paddled round in front of me and kissed me on the mouth for one brief moment before swimming off. I caught up with him and, as I tried to grab his feet, intending to tickle them, he dived underwater and attempted to pull my shorts off. But I resisted and when he surfaced I smacked him playfully but firmly on the head and said, 'Down, boy!'

As we reached the beach again, Alex squawked and pointed at the water in front of him, shouting, 'Portuguese man-of-war!' Looking down I saw, glistening in the shallows, a fat translucent creature like a dim-sum dumpling made of pale purple plastic.

'These things are an absolute nightmare,' he said. 'Time to get out. When there's one around, there are always loads more and they sting like crazy. They say that if you get stung you have to pee on it, or get someone else to. Yuk.'

It had stopped raining while we'd been in the water, and the sun was just starting to reappear, so we sat on the beach for a while. After some time I plucked up my courage and said, 'What happened this morning. Before Dad rang. I don't quite know what came over me...'

He interrupted. 'Nothing, as I remember it.'

I gave him a grown-up look and carried on as if he hadn't spoken: '... but I feel rather bad about it and I feel as if I owe you an explanation.'

'OK. Shoot.'

'Look,' I said, staring down at a stone on the beach in front of me. 'I'm not very good at this sort of thing, but what I want to say is this: I've done *it* before, at school, as you heard last night. But there could have been more. I forced myself to stop wanting more, for Jim and Selina's sake. There was a man...'

'Yes?' Alex said, quietly. 'There was a man?'

I paused, knowing I would never feel ready to say this, so I might as well say it now. 'There was a man. Nearly fifteen years ago. He swam at my local pool and we used to shower together after swimming. And I... well, I wanted to. He wanted to as well. It was clear. But I made a concrete decision then that I would not do it. I was married, with a very sick young son and a very worried wife, and it wouldn't have been fair. It just would not have been fair to any of us. So I did nothing.'

'I can understand that,' Alex said. 'But this whole situation hasn't been fair to you at all. And things have changed now, haven't they? For whatever terrible reasons, you're free to make your own choices now.'

'Alex, I know it looks as if I'm ready to do it again but I'm not, not really. I'm so much happier than I was when I arrived that I have to pinch myself sometimes, and that's all down to you lot. But there's a lot of unexpected stuff going on and I'm naturally cautious. *If*, and I have to emphasise the *if*, anything more is going to develop between... us, then I need much more time. The sex thing is, well, it's obviously there and more strongly than I thought. Maybe clumsy Andy dislodged something last night, I don't know. But I do know that I have some in-built things to deal with before we go any further. I'd hate it if we were to just, you know, spontaneously do it and then I felt bad afterwards and didn't handle it well. Sex is one thing but living with the implications of it is another.'

Alex was silent, looking hard at me as I gazed out to sea. I felt miserable, unable to clarify anything to myself or to him. 'I just don't know how to explain this. I'm sorry.'

'I do,' he said.

'Pardon?'

'I know how to explain it. Or at least I think I do. Should I try?'

I nodded without looking at him, still gazing at the sea as its colour shifted slowly back from grey to blue in the gathering sunlight. He continued.

'Last night at dinner when the three of us were having the usual coming-out confessional, what I was trying to say got lost in Andy's stuff. Poor bastard, can you imagine getting to his age and still being so fucked up?'

'Yes.'

'I didn't mean it like that.'

'Whether you did or not, it's true. I am fucked up and it's hurting your feelings. Go on.'

'What I was trying to say was, well... people always think it was really easy for me because I have such liberal, enlightened parents. But it wasn't like that. I never totally shook off the feeling that their acceptance was maybe a little more political than instinctive. And parents aren't the only people around either, there's all sorts of other people's reactions. So there's fear and guilt for everyone, Michael. Everyone who has to deal with this feels like a freak at some point, and that's how I know what you're trying to say. Because I've felt like a freak too. You don't want to make love with me, because you associate making love to another man with that guilty, freaky feeling. Shit, Michael, it was written all over your face when your dad called. And you don't want to associate that sort of feeling with me. Am I right?'

He seemed to be holding his breath.

'Right. Yes, I think that might be right.'

He breathed out and continued. 'Good. OK, then there's two things that I can say that'd maybe help you. Firstly, *not* feeling guilty and *not* feeling like a freak is *not* something that comes from the outside. Having parents or friends who are cool with it might make it easier but in the end what matters is what you can accept in yourself. Which is not a process that can be hurried or forced, especially in the over-forties!' He laughed. 'Secondly, don't forget that I've only known *you* for a short while, too. I may have developed some feelings for you but that's my privilege, not your responsibility. This whole thing is made more complicated by your having lost Jim, we both know that. So I have a suggestion. Let's revert to Plan A.'

'Plan A?'

'That you continue to live at the house, work on it some, we be friends. I can handle my side, really. It won't be particularly easy but few things worth having ever are.'

He paused.

'I kissed you in the sea a few minutes ago. As far as I understand it, I'm the only man, apart from Jim and your father, that's ever kissed you.'

'Apart from Jim and my grandfather.'

'OK, apart from Jim and your grandfather, I understand. So maybe I'd like to keep it that way? And though I really appreciate the thought – what you suggested this morning about the baby – I think it might be a good idea to put the idea on hold for now.'

'Why's that?'

'Until you've had time to settle. It's not fair on you to do this implicit deal where you won't go to bed with me so you make up for it by helping me out with the baby.'

I was shocked that he'd seen this.

'How do you work *that* out?'

'Come on, Michael. I wasn't born yesterday. And you need more time to work things out before starting up new complications for yourself.'

I lay back until my eyes had switched from the ocean to the sky. A fringe of green leaves from the trees behind us framed the blue.

'Where did you get to be so good at this, Alex? How is it that things I have to unearth like a...' I struggled for the metaphor then spat it out in frustration '... like a blind archaeologist, are so clear to you, at your age?'

He thought, propped up on his elbows in the sand besides me.

'I was going to say from my parents, but that's not strictly true. They gave me the theoretical outline of it, the intellectual infrastructure, and they taught me about having respect for other people, and manners, which I think are very important. But I think it comes from a mixture of places. From books: Edmund White, Michael Cunningham, Armistead Maupin...'

'Didn't he do that TV thing? I never saw it but people talked about it, I think. It rings a bell.'

'*Tales of the City*? Yeah, he wrote the series of books it was based on. I have them all back at the house. You should read them. They're huge fun, of course, but they were a lot more than that to me: they really helped me to turn the freakish feeling into something more positive. I'll lend them to you. But to finish answering your question, the biggest source of any insights I might have, at least into myself, is Penny.'

'Penny?'

'She is one well-thought-out lady. Watch her closely. She shares her own history just in as much as it helps to illustrate some point that she thinks it'd be good for someone else to grasp. She almost never dumps her own stuff just for the sake of it. You know, sometimes it can be breathtaking, it's like watching a great, graceful eagle teaching her chicks how to fly.'

'Eaglets.'

'Teaching her *eaglets* how to fly. My, we are a little controlling today, aren't we, Doctor!'

It was a statement rather than a question so I didn't reply.

'Anyway, Penny is exactly the sort of woman I'd like to have as one of the parents of my baby. She doesn't *need* to be a mother, she already is one, to lots of people.'

'What about Sue?' I asked.

'Oh, Sue would be tremendous too. Talking of control freaks, she can be a little controlling sometimes, but hey, who can't? It's her way of ensuring that her environment remains orderly, which is no bad thing for a child. Look Michael, I don't take this lightly. This isn't a whim or a Save Alex's Real Estate scheme. This will be a big part of all our lives. If it happens. Knock on wood.'

He reached out towards a small, smooth piece of driftwood near his feet and held it to him for a moment, then I reached across and touched it too.

I was amazed, during those last few days of peace, just how easily Alex and I made the readjustment. I had been sitting on my hands for years, but I was surprised and warmed by his patient ability to do the same thing. He was considerate in a host of small ways. He kept a discreet distance between us and even remained more than usually clothed – which was beginning to have an effect opposite to what I think he intended.

It was a busy time in all sorts of ways. Alex had told the others about the result of his sperm test and had also raised my interpretation of Peggy's will, which created some relief. We kept silent, however, on the issue of my potential involvement with the paternity so as not to raise people's hopes and expectations. Alex told me that he did have a quiet discussion about it with Penny, who agreed firmly with his own approach. She never raised the issue with me and I don't think Sue knew anything about it. And so I came to see that the order around Sue's life, though ostensibly created by Sue herself, was often Penny's quiet work.

Pretty much the last thing that happened during this happy period was a carefully orchestrated dinner one Monday night at Karl's. Mondays were his favoured choice because that was the only day off that Sue and Alex reliably shared, so it was the only evening he could guarantee getting his little family together.

Andy was no longer on the scene and Karl and Angelico had been working in tandem. Angelico had devoted some of his time to discovering who owned the twin house, while Karl had managed to track down Marty during one of his short visits. Marty's provisional opinion was that the painting of Amos might be by a woman called Jane Maria Potter. She was one of the most successful of a family of nineteenth-century American painters, specialising in portraits of wealthy patrons. The excitement was that she often did *pairs* of paintings – both halves of a married couple – and Marty thought that the way in which Amos was looking out of the frame suggested there might be another painting somewhere. We debated whether it would be of Amos's wife Jessica or possibly of Juan, and Angelico pointed out that, since Potter had never married, we might be lucky.

Privately this reinforced the impression I was developing that gay people like to think that most apparently straight people are really gay after all, just hiding something. It was as if, having discovered something as exciting as homosexuality themselves, they wanted everyone to have some.

In any event, Marty had disappeared back off to New York with the painting; he wanted to show it to an expert friend who was travelling in Asia and wouldn't be returning for a few weeks. But he did say that according to his memory, few works by Potter had come on the market since the early 1990s, at which point they'd fetched significant prices.

Angelico had become more and more convinced that the key to the other painting might lie in the twin house, so he'd redoubled his efforts and eventually turned up some information. Juan had left the house to a Cuban cigar workers' charity, which was registered in Havana. After the US and Cuba severed relations, the house got caught up in a long-running but now dormant legal battle as to who owned it. Juan had also left a sum of money for its upkeep, which was now in the hands of a local law firm whose trust department was unwilling to allow anyone to visit the house but did confirm that the house had been regularly maintained, its contents in storage following an earlier burglary. No inventory was available despite a call from a friend of Angelico's posing as a venerable art historian trying to track down a 'rare piece of America's cultural heritage'.

The evening on which they told us all this was fantastic, a typical example of Karl and Angelico's natural showmanship. If I had known what the next day's mail was going to bring, I would have lingered over it even longer than I did. But somewhere out of sight, wheels were turning; the letter was in the post.

Book II
Falling

28
Bad News

I got up early as usual and cycled out for breakfast things, checking the post when I returned. There was only one item, a padded bag addressed to me, with a Toronto postmark. I opened it to find two envelopes, one fat, with 'Good News' written on it and another thin and clearly from England. Selina's sharp handwriting had been scrawled over by Lolly with the words 'Bad News?' in black felt pen.

I opened the good news first: photographs of the twins, pink, wrinkled and smiling. I laid them out on the table in front of me, wishing that Alex was not at work so that I could show them to him.

Then I opened the bad news. It went like this:

Dear Michael,

I hope you are all right, wherever you are. Aside from all the legal stuff, which as far as I know is going ahead as planned, there are some things I have to tell you. None of them are comfortable and they don't show your father or me in a good light either. You often marvelled at how completely confident I am. Well, it was the only way I could carry all this off. Before I go any further, I also need to apologise for the way I behaved at the hospital the night James died. I was crazed and I didn't know what I was saying, so whatever it sounded like at the time, please don't think that I was blaming you in any way for not being able to do anything. We've both known the risks for years, it quite clearly wasn't your fault.

Firstly, I have moved in with Douglas. I'm sure there's some biblical penalty in store for women who lie with their husbands' fathers but, with James gone, I want to have another child and at my age I need to hurry. That's a detail really, or at least it is for now and it's not the main reason I'm writing. There's no easy way to do this, so here goes.

When I was working for your father, before you and I met, we had an affair. I was fascinated by him, always have been, despite his not being an easy man, but you know about that. Out of respect for your mother, he knocked the affair on the head almost immediately, and then he introduced me to you. Also, he was terrified that you might be homosexual, wanted to make sure you didn't go that way. Don't ask me why, he was never clear about it, it was 'just a feeling' he had. He hasn't spoken about it for years now. It would be ironic, wouldn't it? With Douglas being such a man's man? Anyway, he practically begged me to seduce you, kept asking if you'd 'made a move' yet.

Michael, in all the years that you and I were married, I never slept with him again, I promise you. But I – he and I – did do something much worse, so unfair to you that I've really only begun to fathom it since James died. We didn't plan it as such, it just unfolded. I'm not asking for your forgiveness, I'm not asking to be understood, I just think that finally I have to tell the truth and that you have always had a right to know it, and your father thinks you should know too.

At that big party at the base, the night that you and I first had sex, I was desperate and that's why I was so pushy with you. A couple of weeks before, Douglas and I had had a relapse at work, unexpectedly and without taking precautions. It was a bad time of the month to make that mistake and I was terrified that I might be pregnant. I know it sounds mad now but I was only nineteen and I was scared and not thinking very clearly. I was pretty keen on you, as you know, but you seemed to need an extra push and I've always been good at getting what I want, or what I thought I wanted. I thought I could somehow just fudge the issue of who the father might be in my own head. (Not that I think that's an acceptable excuse now.) When it turned out that

I actually was pregnant, Douglas saw the logic of the arrangement – that's why he bullied you so much about marrying me.

This is getting messy and I didn't intend to write to justify my part in the unjustifiable, so I'll cut to the quick. What I'm trying to say is that I had tests done fairly early, so I've known for nearly twenty years, and so has Douglas. Jim wasn't your son, Michael, he was your brother.

You won't want to read any more, I am sure. And what else could I ever say? So, goodbye, Michael. You're a very sweet, very kind man, far better than I deserved really, and I am very, very, sorry.

Selina

P.S. I have dropped all claims under the settlement, it seems the least I could do.

29
A Time of Loathing

Alex returned much later to find me lying drunk on my bed, the letter by my side. I handed it to him and he read it through a couple of times. Then he lay down beside me and held me for a while until I fell asleep. I woke in the middle of the night fully clothed and alone with a sheet pulled over me. The next morning in the kitchen, he tried to hug me again and I shrugged him gently away.

Over the next few days Jim came more sharply into focus as I thought of him in a new and even more painful light. In a strange and inexplicable way it felt as if he had deserted me for my father, and so I came to think of how like my father he had been. So physically confident, so brave, so present. And though in truth he had had none of my father's arrogance or scorn, I somehow lost the sense of his ever having been truly mine and of his ever having loved me, which was more than I could bear.

I felt brutally betrayed. As a result I became unable to trust anyone at all. I was unkind to the people around me, often puzzled and even irritated by their forbearance, but they were mostly waiting for me to come through in my own time.

Penny, Alex and Sue were all agreed that, whatever Selina said, whatever the mere biological facts, Jim had been my son in every meaningful sense. In acting as his father for all those years, I had become, with enormous love, what the role required and that was that. But to me at that time these were nothing but bromides; the fact was that I had lost my son for a second time. Penny said my father had stolen the first twenty years of my life and Selina the next twenty and that now I needed to reclaim it for myself, but this sounded like therapy-speak to me. A thick set of shutters had gone down.

Once, I tried to write to Dad and Selina, but the ink dried on my pen as I attempted to imagine what I might say. I even made a comment to Alex and Penny one evening about feeling resentment at the way my father and Selina had used me as part of their breeding programme, not realising until after I'd said it what this might mean to Alex and Penny themselves, in terms of my possible involvement in their plans for a child. However carefully my friends tried, I was not ready to accept their clear understanding of my situation and I could not accept their help, so full of loathing had I become.

30
Horny at Atlantic Shores

My belated adolescence started one early evening, soon after the letter arrived. I'd quickly developed the habit of starting to drink at lunchtime, everyone else being at work and there being nothing else to do to keep me from thinking in too much detail.

As I walked half-drunkenly down Duval, I passed the Bull and saw a sign for the Garden of Eden, a clothing-optional rooftop garden. I went up and wallflowered for half an hour, lurking next to an obscene hibiscus plant with open trumpets and jutting stamens, until two pretty girls in their early thirties came up and chatted to me. They were fully dressed, unlike many women there, who were topless. They were friendly, not too pushy, and they didn't try to get into my head. So when they asked me to join them at Atlantic Shores the next day I said, 'Sure, why not?'

I left the Garden soon afterwards and noon the next day found me parking my bicycle in the car park at the Shores and walking up the steps to find the girls already sitting at the bar. We started drinking margaritas, switching to Killer Koolaids after a while, because one of the girls thought it was an amusing name for a cocktail. By two o'clock the place was buzzing with mainly naked people, music pumping out to sea. After a while we got three sun chairs and lay around talking and drinking in the glaring sun, observing and discussing the pierced and painted bodies around us. I kept on glancing over at the pool meaning to swim but carried on drinking instead. Everything got funnier and funnier, a peculiar mix of very adult and very childish humour. The man running the kitchen announced that people's orders were ready with lines like 'Dave, your cheesy wiener's up,' which seemed funny at the time.

At one point the woman who ran the bar grabbed the microphone and announced in a deadpan voice: 'Jeff, who has parked his pickup truck in the middle of the lot, please move it. Jeff, whose pickup is selfishly blocking everybody else by parking right in the middle of the lot, please move your pickup so that these poor people can get their cars out so that they can get home so that they can feed their kids. Otherwise their kids will go hungry and be forced to rob your mansion, selling your antiques and stereo equipment to buy crack cocaine which they will then sell to your bottle-blonde new boyfriend, who will pay for it with money that he has stolen from your wallet, thereby punishing you eventually if indirectly for your crime... So, Jeff? Please move your pickup. Right now.'

An embarrassed-looking man with extensive metalwork joining his nipples stood up and took a bow as he pulled on his shorts, the whole crowd cheering and clapping as he headed off towards the car park. Then a male voice came over the tannoy.

'Thanks to Judy for her eloquent announcement. And aren't we pleased to see that Judy has no control issues, ladies and gentlemen?'

It was one huge, sexy, sleazy daytime party. The flags on the pier were stiff in the breeze, the ocean was slopping lazily around the legs of the deck, the sun was blazing and the drink kept flowing. One of the girls had a tattoo of devil's horns poking out over the top of her bikini bottoms. After a while she slipped them off to reveal the rest of the picture, clearly visible around her shaven mound. I refused to remove my swim-shorts and even had to fight the girls off as they tried drunkenly to get them from me.

A while later the one with the horns stopped talking and laughing and lay back on her sun bed, completely naked. She unscrewed the cap of a bottle of sun cream, then put her thumb over the nozzle and shook the bottle, squeezing it sharply so that a thick rush of cream shot out over her belly and breasts. She rubbed it in slowly, looking me in the eye as she did so, then she shook the bottle again and out shot another stream, up her inner thigh and onto the devil's forehead, lips and chin. I was starting to tent in my shorts and she noticed me adjust myself.

She leaned across and said, 'We're staying nearby. You wanna come party with us?'

I nodded.

The car park was incredibly hot as we crossed it, lying below the level of the breeze and coated with macadam. By the time we reached their hotel room I was sweating. It was dark inside and so it took me a while to realise that, though the king-sized double bed was empty, another figure lay in a single bed off to one side. It didn't move so I ignored it, and anyway the two girls were working on me already, slipping my shorts down, rubbing the mix of sun cream and sweat between us into a slithering, lubricating film. The girls took it in turns to suck me for a few minutes while I used my tongue and fingers on them, then one of them slipped a condom on to me and soon I was inside her.

Moments later, while I was moving in and out, I felt a hand creeping in between my legs from behind. I half turned to see a man on all fours behind me, his arm extended.

'Who's he, what's he doing here?' I asked, aware of the slurring sound of my voice.

'That's my boyfriend,' one of the girls replied. 'Relax, it's what he likes to do. Be nice to him and he might blow you. I'm told he's really good at it. Says it's a guy thing.'

31
Out Late

The sexual geography of Duval quickly becomes clear to most visitors who stay in Key West for more than a day or two. At the northwest end, the point at which the cruise ships decant their passengers and where people gather to watch the spectacular sunsets, is the sexless zone. This is where tours on the Conch Trains start and, after an hour and a half of snaking through the streets, their passengers are taken back to where they started, to the heart of a family-orientated complex of restaurants, gift shops and museums.

A few blocks further up Duval, things start to warm up a little at the clothing-optional rooftop Garden of Eden, full of straight tourists and visiting naval personnel looking to experience a little Key West spice without getting too close to their boundaries. Which I suppose is why I started there. Another few blocks and the more curious explorer will discover Wax, off in a side street. Fashionable and European in flavour, fashionably ambiguous in terms of clientele, it has something of a reputation as the place where people who are basically straight might go to experiment, just a little, with something else. Three more blocks again and the drag-and-gay zone starts, moving from the mainstream tourist-friendly Divas nightclub and drag show past a variety of increasingly strongly flavoured and increasingly gay bars. Continue for another quarter mile, past the Scrub Club, and you reach Atlantic Shores at the southeastern end, where groups of all configurations are as likely to witness the dawn together as the sunset. My jump from the Garden to the Shores had kick-started me, and now I proceeded to fill in the strip between them.

*

My progress down the street began a few nights later when I walked into Bandidos, a bar whose interior was shielded by a partition near the entrance, and which charged a two-dollar cover. Outside were xeroxed pictures of lap-dancing boys, steroided into prize beef. I went inside and drank bourbons for a while, watching two young men gyrating on a small podium at the end of the room, grinding and hypnotising their way into me. One of them was a big Latino with a handsome, straight man's smile. From time to time other men would approach him and rub under his towel before placing their dollars in his sock and retreating, flushed. Sometimes he would reach down to fondle a customer's groin, whispering something in their ear.

I'm sure it was some sort of professional trick he had and that every man in the place felt the same way but it seemed that he was particularly focussed on me. I sat a few yards away looking mostly at him, and he appeared to hold my gaze for most of the time. Twice he smiled at me and indicated with his head that I should come over, but I just smiled drunkenly back and stayed where I was. After half an hour or so I left.

I returned the following evening but he was not there, so I went home and imagined him instead. But I was back the next night and so was he and soon I was approaching the podium. I stood smiling dumbly in front of him while he moved his hips close to my face, rubbing his hands up and down his thighs and squeezing his nipples.

Then he lowered his head towards me and said in a thick Latin American accent, 'You a little shy, aren't you?'

I nodded. He leaned forward and took my right hand, placing it on his inner thigh as he ground his hips further towards me until I made contact. I was hard in my own underwear now, and he reached forward and rubbed me. It was only for a few moments, but it was enough to send a stain spreading across the front of my trousers.

He realised what had happened and said, 'Boy, you *real* excitable. That normally a private extra, understand?'

I nodded again.

'I can do a *really* private dance for you, your place or mine, normally two hundred dollars but for you one-fifty. I like you, and you really quick as well.'

He winked, then fondled my ear before standing up again. I took a twenty-dollar bill from my back pocket and slipped it into his sock and he smiled and winked, raising his eyes to the next man.

I didn't return but later that week I slid further southeast into another bar called the Zone and sat drinking beer out of the bottle while the other men cruised around. Occasionally someone would approach me and try to start a conversation but I'd just smile and ignore them. I'd already learned that the briefest hint of an English accent could be used as a crack for aggressive would-be conversationalists to widen into a whole stream of questions, so it was better to stay quiet and act surly.

One man in particular kept hovering close. He was around my age and had a well-muscled chest and arms, every detail showing through a very tight white T-shirt, including his aggressively obvious nipples.

He was playing the same ignoring game as me so eventually I said, 'Hi. Where are you from?'

'Boston.'

'You been here long?'

'Got here last night. Man, this place is dead. It's normally much better'n this.'

'You've been here before?

'Yeah, I come this same week most years. I always book the same room at the same guesthouse. Where're you from?'

'England.'

'Uh-huh.'

I was glad that he showed no interest in talking, though it was clear he was interested in other ways, so when he said, 'I'm gonna check out the back bar. You wanna come?' I said 'OK' and followed him through into another, much darker room.

It was full of men standing silently watching pornography in the gloom. Three or four monitors were positioned at head height around the room and all heads were turned towards them as a silent video fantasy played itself towards a conclusion. The soundtrack was turned down, replaced by Madonna pumping from hidden speakers, 'Tell me love isn't true, It's just something that we doo-o-oo.'

On the screens a group of young, all-American jocks had silent conversations in a locker room. Soon they were rubbing themselves and opening their flies to reveal their semi-distended penises. They progressed briefly through oral sex to full-blown buggery, one particularly well-endowed man screwing each of them in turn, smacking their backsides silently as he did so until finally, silently, faces contorting into ersatz ecstasy, they all came.

Throughout this, two separate things were going on. Firstly, I was on some level repulsed by the banal and sexless sex. Secondly, the man was standing close behind me and I could feel his breath hot in my ear. He started by moving his hand around under my arm until his palm lay flat on my chest. Then he explored a little, cupping and stroking, briefly locating and squeezing my nipple. I had a sense that he was trying to work out whether what lay under my baggy shirt was sufficiently well toned to be worth his while, but I was already half-gone on bourbon and didn't try to stop him. He seemed satisfied with his discovery process so now, under protection of the darkness, he lowered his hand to my trousers and started to explore. At the same time he pressed his groin into my backside from behind, and started to pump his hard-on back and forth in time with the action on the screen.

From time to time he whispered wetly in my ear, 'Yeah, feel that, you know that's what you want! ... Yeah, you like that fat cock! ... You know you want to suck that fat cock!'

The permutations of this small set of words went endlessly round, like the experimental vocabulary of a child.

When the locker room scene was finished, he went to the bar and came back with two beers, resuming his position behind me. I could feel that he was still hard but, as the next movie began, he became more insistent. The opening scene showed a big, hairy man chained by his wrists to an anchor point somewhere above him so that he was raised on tiptoes. A similar man in leather trousers and a leather waistcoat and cap smacked him gently all over at first then started a strange, pummelling motion. The first man spun and writhed, but did not become erect. From time to time the two men would kiss aggressively, the captive having his head pulled back by the nape of his neck, his hair too short to grab hold of.

My new companion was rubbing his hands all over me now in a shimmying motion, pushing his hardness at me through the fabric of his jeans and my chinos. Sometimes he put his hands in my pocket and felt me there. The man on the screen started to whip his victim's buttocks and back with a leather flail and I heard a hot, wet whisper in my ear, 'Let's hit the backroom, bud.'

I followed him the length of the bar, not knowing for certain what he was talking about but perfectly able to guess. A red light shone in a small passageway at the end. Off to one side, through a thickly hanging set of plastic curtains that made me think of the wholesale meat units at Smithfield Market in London, lay a darkened void.

He pushed me through into a space the size of a large cupboard and I heard a slobbering, grunting noise all around me. As my eyes adjusted to the darkness, I could dimly make out a padded bench around three sides of the room. Propped in the corner, a man dressed like the aggressor in the video was being attended to by three other men. They were sucking and kissing and licking, one was kissing his boots.

Before I had time to notice anything else, I had been pushed to my knees and my companion was unbuckling in front of me. I couldn't see his cock, but when he forced it into my mouth it was as cold and hard as marble. It was perfectly comfortable, being quite small, and soon I was moving my head to his rhythm. He held me by the hair, once briefly even by the ears, as he pushed himself into my mouth again and again. As he did so he repeated his mantra, entirely to himself, 'Yeah, suck that cock, you like that cock, you like that fat cock, don't you...'

After a while my attention strayed. I could see another man, silhouetted against the red light from beyond the curtain, standing on his own facing in our direction and masturbating mechanically with exaggerated strokes, like a toy soldier beating a drum. Without removing my mouth from its duty I unbuttoned my own fly and started to masturbate too. Soon the other man was lying on the floor between my legs, his neck arched and straining up as he sucked me. And soon after that we all came. It seemed like everybody in the room came at once, like in the first video, and after a few moments of wiping and buttoning, we filed out to make room for the next shift.

Out in the street again, me unchaining my bike from a railing, he turned to me and said, 'Well, you sure got what you wanted tonight, didn't you.'

It was meant as a statement rather than a question, but I replied anyway as he walked away.

'Yes, I suppose I did.'

When I got home a few minutes later, the light was on in Alex's room, music creeping out from under the door. But I crept past to my own room and closed the door quietly behind me.

For a few weeks after that, the pattern developed. I quickly stopped having sex with women, focussing on the gay bars instead, where I learned a host of tricks and techniques. For example, I quickly learned to avoid local men. They all knew each other, the same old faces; an encounter with one of them would inevitably lead to the discomfort of seeing them around afterwards. Besides, I didn't want to get to know my sexual partners at all; the opposite was true. So I specialised in spotting who was new in town. I'd cruise them for a few evenings, eyeing them across the bar but not talking to them until I had counted five or six nights, which meant that they were probably about to leave town. Then I'd approach and see where it went. And I never used my real name.

I also learned to perfect 'the flick' fairly quickly, having experienced it myself. 'Flicking' is what men do in bars when they are trying to decide whether to have sex with someone but they can't tell what extent of musculature lies under a baggy shirt. So they find out by 'accidentally' brushing their hands very quickly across certain key areas. Reach across for cigarettes, glancing the hand off the chest and see if those big pecs are really just flabby tit. Allow your elbow to rub the side of the torso to identify any possible problem with love handles. Wait until they're seated and find a way to separate the six-packs from the barrel-bellies. Some guys then graduate to squeezing the front of their would-be partner's trousers, like Mediterranean women at the fruit market. All this saves disappointment later, when at two in the morning you find yourself in bed with a blob, thinking about that other guy in the bar earlier to whom you should have devoted more attention. It's a harsh world, and it suited my mood.

I went along like this for a while, doing little in the daytime other than swimming and tanning, a little work on the house but not much. I'd put Angelico off by now, saying I could work without him. After a few weeks, I was staying out late every single night. I knew most of the hot tubs at most of the guesthouses on the island. But I never stayed the night, I never kissed anyone and I never took anyone back to Alex's. And, though he clearly had a good idea of what was going on, we never discussed it.

Book III
A Shot at Redemption

32
The Prince of Pride Street

It was Pride Street Mardi Gras, a week of festivities organised by a group of bars and involving drag queen beauty parades and a variety of other contests and entertainments.

I noticed on the first night that every time anyone bought a drink in any of the bars, they got given a string of beads. Fairly soon it became clear that some guys had more beads than they could have drunk their way into and inquiry revealed that there was a barter system in operation. If you were reasonably good looking, particularly if you were in good shape, you could win beads by showing people any part of your body they wanted to see. The drag queens had huge swathes of beads to give away and were liberal with me to the point that I soon had enough of the smaller strands to trade them for the huge fake pearls that represented the next-level denominator. At one in the morning on Saturday, the Prince of Pride Street was due to be crowned, being the person with the highest bead-count.

I got a little high at home before going out on Friday night, smoking in the early evening twilight. By the time I hit the bars at eleven I was well primed and after a few beers I was flying. I'd worn my beads from the two previous nights, a heavy garland of white pearl necklaces, and more and more people were steered my way, wanting to trade beads. Soon I had shown myself to pretty much everyone in the place and then, as people paid for more rounds of drinks, they'd come back for more. By 12.30, when it was becoming clear that I might win, I had switched to bourbon and was wildly drunk, dancing and showing my stuff. I went out back with one of my opponents and he traded me his collection of beads, two-thirds the quantity of mine, for a favour. This sealed my lead and at one o'clock I was crowned Prince of Pride Street.

I stripped to my recently acquired boots and underwear for the ceremony, which took place on a dais at the back of the bar. After it was done, I shed my beads and climbed up onto the counter. Soon my Calvin Klein undershorts were stuffed with five-dollar and ten-dollar bills and I'd had a lot of hands on me. I bent down to talk to one man, who offered me a hundred dollars to go back to his hotel with him, and as I stood up again and resumed my hip-writhing dance, I looked out across the bar and saw a familiar face near the door. It was Alex. He waved at me, an odd expression on his face, then turned and left.

33
I Want to Get Inside Your Head

A few days after that, I woke late to find a note in the mailbox from Penny. Alex had gone to work so I was alone in the house. I'd planned to spend the afternoon at the beach, then hit Duval in the evening, but Penny had other plans.

The note said: *'Please join me for an unusual view of sunset from the east of the island. Meet at 6.30 at White Street Pier. Call if you can't make it, otherwise I'll see you there. Love, Penny.'*

I toyed with the idea of claiming another engagement but in the end I decided to go along. I wasn't feeling sociable but the wording on the note intrigued me. So at six o'clock, after a very long swim, I put on some chinos and a clean shirt and pedalled off down White Street. I'd never been to the pier before, my preferred beaches being elsewhere, so I was surprised when I arrived to find a large sign at its foot saying 'Key West AIDS Memorial'. I had arrived before Penny, so I started to look around.

The pier is formed of a string of interconnecting concrete rectangles leading far out over the ocean. I skirted the memorial and headed out to the last of these, a huge square the size of a parking lot. Kids on blades and boards circled lazily around while seagulls echoed their movement overhead and the sun sank in a reddening sky over the island. There was a warm, salty breeze, as warm and salty as blood. I looked briefly out to sea, eastwards towards the Old World, before turning back to face the New.

Seeing Penny arrive in the distance, I strolled back towards the mouth of the pier. She wore a flowing white dress with a plunging *décolletage* and a floppy hat, like an English lady might wear in a garden. She spotted me and waved, then turned to lock her bicycle. By the time I reached her she was sitting down on a bench looking at the ground in front of her. I sat down beside her and kissed her on the cheek. She was wearing the dragon brooch I'd bought her some weeks before, which I thought was a cheap trick.

'Long time no see,' she said.

'It's only been a week or so.'

'Make that two.'

'Sorry.'

She kissed my cheek and said, *'De nada,'* then took my hand in hers.

'Michael, while we watch the sunset, I want to tell you a little more about myself. I'd like you to know me better and I think it may be of some use to you to hear it. The schedule is: here' – she gestured around her – 'for a while, and then we'll maybe go and have a drink at the Casa Marina.'

'Sounds good to me.'

'Good. Now, about me. Straight to the point. You've probably noticed that I have a strange accent.'

'Not strange,' I replied, 'just variable. It changes from Southern Belle to Brooklyn Broad and back depending on what you're saying. I'd put it down to your stage training.'

'Well, in a way that's right. But there's more. Come.'

She stood up and took my hand, leading me a few paces into the open space in front of us, towards the sea of black marble from which I had averted my eyes when I arrived.

Spread out before us on the ground for several yards in each direction were hundreds of polished slabs, set in the ground. Many of them had names engraved on them, around twenty per square, and some were still blank.

'I come here once a month or so, to see Carey.'

She pointed towards one of the stones.

'There, right-hand side, fifth name down.'

I read across and down until I found it. It said 'Carey Herrnstein.'

'But your surname's Heron. Oh. I see. Heron, Herrnstein.'

'That's right. Heron is my stage name, Penny Herrnstein was already taken on the register when I first started performing.'

'So you're actually Jewish then, like Karl? Or German?'

'Jewish. Born in England a few years after the war had ended. My parents had escaped from Germany a few years earlier, but their parents didn't make it. They're still there on another memorial, not unlike this one.'

'I'm sorry.'

'There's nothing to be sorry for, Michael, because you and I, you and Carey, have all suffered the same thing in some ways.'

'By which you mean?'

She paused for a moment.

'A few weeks ago, just after you arrived, you said at Karl's one night that your father's father was killed in service during the war while your father was a child.'

'Yes, that's right.'

'And don't you think that affected him? Made him, you know, made him like he is? Like he's behaved towards you, your sister, your mother? Have you ever wondered about that?'

'I suppose it must have had some impact. Lolly always thought so. He never spoke about it. He just hates the Germans.'

'Ahh, hate. Well I suppose that's what so much of this comes down to.' She looked up for a moment, towards the darkening eastern horizon. 'Here's a very potted version of my history, which I think is relevant to your own. Both my parents lost both their parents to the death camps. It's a long story but my parents were childhood sweethearts, from the same town near the Dutch border, and a local German businessman smuggled them out and away into the refugee network just before things got too bad. Soon they were in England. That was in 1938. In 1945 after the end of the war, they married. In 1946 they finally found out what had happened to their parents in the camps. As you might expect, the confirmation of what they had feared for so long had a devastating impact. It's not an unfamiliar story. Anyway, they worked hard, had me and moved to America in 1954. A little later they had Carey. On reflection they should have stopped after the first child, because they found it so very hard to function as parents. Simply put, they'd had too much loss.'

'I suppose that's understandable,' I said, aware of a growing need to escape.

'Yes, I think it is. And over the years I've done my own work, worked through it, which was hard. Mother is still alive, living in California. Dad died soon after Carey.'

'That must have been terrible, I'm very sorry.'

'You have no idea. You see, Dad killed Carey.'

'But I thought you said Carey died of AIDS?'

I pointed down towards the inscription. Penny's eyes followed my finger and she said, 'Well, that's why we're here.'

'I don't understand.'

'I hope you soon will. You see, my parents were damaged, so badly damaged by what they'd lost and how they'd lost it. Mother has made some progress over the years and in fact she's been better since Dad died. But what happened to them was an open wound that, for Dad at least, never healed, never even really became a scar. Like a lot of Jews of their generation, all he could do was focus on survival. And he could never *quite* love. That would have been too painful, too much of a risk. He couldn't risk another loss, you see. So he was unbearable with us. He drove and drove. Our schooling, our friends – in so far as we were allowed any – everything. I think he was trying to make us perfect, hard, inviolable.'

I was switching off, blocking her out, so my reply was automatic.

'I think I see.'

She turned towards me.

'Do you really? Do you see it yet, Michael?'

'What do you mean?'

'Do you see what this means for you?'

I just stared at her.

'I don't think I do.'

She took both of my hands in hers and led me back to the bench.

'Michael, like I said, Dad killed Carey. He provided him with almost nothing as a kid, other than material support. He pushed and pushed until Carey broke. He ran away from home at the age of seventeen and went wild. He lived in New York and did everything that was going. This was the mid-70s and, as it turned out, that was a very dangerous time to be a promiscuously gay young man. But he was lucky for a while. He was negative when they first started testing for HIV in the 80s. And that's the point. *He would not stop until he caught it.*'

She stopped for a moment to let this sink in.

'The way I look at it is, he was doing three things. Firstly, he was desperately searching for a man to love him, to give him what his father never could, though Carey could never admit that to himself. Secondly, he was doing everything he could to shock and offend my parents, who made it very clear that they did not approve of his lifestyle. They utterly refused to see him at all once they knew what he was up to, even up until he died. He was supposed to reproduce, to renew the bloodline that the Nazis had tried to extinguish. So by being gay he was committing the gravest sin, colluding with the enemy to stamp us out. Thank God Dad never knew about me!' She laughed, hoarsely.

'Then thirdly, on some level he loathed himself. Total lack of any sense of self-worth, brought on by our parents' frozen emotional rage, their siege mentality, compounded by his having internalised such strong disapproval of what he was doing. So actually, when I say that Dad killed him, what I really mean is that Dad showed him how to do it and handed him the gun.'

I knew where Penny was going now, and I didn't want to join her. I had to fight a strong urge to leave. But there was absolutely no escaping what came next. She stood again, took my hand as if I were a reluctant child and led me back to Carey's inscription.

'Michael, I don't know all the circumstances, only what you've told me. But I do know what you've been up to lately. It's a small town. I also know you're a doctor, and I know you're probably well informed about safe sex. But so was Carey.' She stopped and looked around her again, as if she were about to sing something big and sad.

'I was here the night this memorial was dedicated. It was a beautiful evening in early December, a few years ago. There were hundreds of candles, hundreds of people. And all around here' – she gestured, a huge sweeping motion, gathering in the world – 'were brothers, sisters, friends, lovers, mothers and fathers. And how many of those parents had created that nightmare for themselves? How many had pushed their own children into the excess that killed them?

'You know, that night, the night of the dedication, people were discreetly craning their necks to read all these names, like people at a party trying to see if there was anyone here they knew. And I overheard one woman saying, "Why are some of them blank?" and her friend replied, "Those are for the next ones." So what I am asking you is, think about this. I know you'll resent hearing it, and you can see it's not easy for me to say it, but if Carey's death can mean one thing, if I have one way of turning it into a gift, then I give it to you now. Don't be one of the "next ones", Michael. Don't let your father drive you that far. I've seen it before and I'm sorry if I appear to be interfering but I cannot bear to stand by and watch it happen again.'

I wanted to argue, or to run, or simply to rewind back to that morning when I'd received the note, then call and say I'd be busy. But I was cornered between Penny and Carey.

Finally and mechanically, I replied, 'I know the risks. HIV these days isn't the death sentence it was. With the correct cocktail of drugs it's more of a chronic disease, controllable. Besides, I have fairly safe sex. Much safer than most people.'

Penny stared me down for a few moments, a dangerous look in her eye. She was angry now.

'Don't be cute with me, Michael. You know *exactly* how stupid that is and you know *exactly* what I mean. The highest rate of contraction of HIV at the moment is in the younger age group, kids who think it's an old man's disease, and you're currently behaving like an angry nineteen-year-old. You have the same look in your eye as Carey did and it scares me. I know about this, I'm involved with AIDS work; there are a lot more people still to die. You might be able to fool yourself but you cannot fool me.'

'But...'

She spat her next words. 'There *are* no buts, and I *am* going to finish. Even if you were right, this is not just about AIDS; it's about you and what you're doing to yourself and the people who love you. Alex, for example. If you can't get your father to love you, love yourself. You don't have to exorcise something to lay it to rest.'

I tried again. 'But it's the sheer availability of sex in this town, it's unavoidable, it's corrupting.'

She rounded without pause. 'It's not the availability of sex that's corrupting; it's what drives you so blindly to take it, THAT is what corrupts you. You are brutalising your own sexuality to protect yourself from emotion.'

'Penny, I can't do this. I appreciate what you're trying to say, and I really am sorry for you, for what you, your parents, your brother have been through, but I just can't do this. I don't look at things like you do; I don't have the vocabulary. This stuff about loving myself and so on. It's just not me. It's... it's too Californian. It's psychobabble. It's just not how I see things.'

Her anger rose a dangerous notch.

'Is that it, Michael? Is that your daddy's voice speaking? Would it be too weak, too homosexual, to give yourself a little understanding. Would Daddy think you were a pansy? My God, you're as bad as your father. Well, I'll *give* you a new vocabulary. Love. Loss. Denial. Love. Betrayal. Pain. Love. Do you want more? Do you want me to rub this in, to rub your father's voice out until you can hear your own? Take some responsibility for yourself now! Don't let him have it his own way, always, ever. No one with your educational advantages is as emotionally illiterate as you make yourself out to be, unless they make a choice to be so, as an avoidance strategy.'

I tried to speak, but Penny raised her hand to silence me before continuing.

'And are you really telling me that in all your professional life, you've never learned any psychology? Is a heart really no more than a lump of muscle to you? Maybe you're just hiding behind professional arrogance. Whatever, you cannot run away from this forever and the longer you avoid it, the worse it will get. You're forty-three years old and it's time you grew up.'

She paused for a moment, breathing into the coda, breathing more easily, calming us both.

'My final point. I think you have fallen for Alex as much as he's fallen for you, but you're scared to admit it to anyone, not least to yourself. I think you're partly scared of opening yourself up to getting hurt again, to which I'd reply "No pain no gain". And I also think that the similarity in age between Alex and Jim spooks you. To which I'd say, "Look who's been the father here!" Alex has looked after you with more love and with more care in the past three months than your father managed in over forty years. Think about it!

'Now, come on. End of subject. Neither of us can take any more of this right now, so let's go. You need time to think about all this alone, if you want to. If you can.'

It was nearly dark. I don't know why I followed her, I just did, as bruised and silent as the violet sky. And as we unlocked our bicycles and pedalled off past the Casa Marina, all thought of having a convivial drink together forgotten, I looked up and saw a thin sliver of moon. It hung in the sky like a sabre.

34
A Letter and a Lesson

I got back to the house to find a bright green envelope lying on the floor, right in front of the door where I couldn't miss it, with my name on the front in Alex's handwriting. I expected him to be back by now, but the house was silent and dark.

Dear Michael,

This is tough, so take a deep breath alongside me. Penny told me she'd be speaking to you this evening (I didn't put her up to it, honest!) and I know from experience that she can give quite a going-over. So I'm giving both of us some much needed space by going home to my parents for a long weekend – I haven't seen them since Thanksgiving. I'll be back on Tuesday afternoon but I'm going straight to work so I won't be home from the café 'til quite late.

Anyway, to the point. As you found out when you overheard me talking with Penny on the phone months ago, I fell for you pretty much at first sight. And I would like to apologise if I came on too flirtily (is that a word?) too soon. I tried to be sensitive to your situation because I care about you and for a while I think you started to reciprocate the way I feel. I talked to Penny a lot more about it at the time, after that day at the beach, and she agreed that I should put my own stuff on the back seat until you'd dealt with your feelings about Jim to a better degree. I tried to do that, and I really hoped that persuading you to stay on here might give you something constructive to do, what with the house and whatever, and give you some core of a family feeling with all of us. Somehow that has not worked out as I hoped, and I feel as if I failed you somewhere. I just can't see the place where that happened, though that letter from Selina looks like it was the starting point.

So, what I am saying is that I love you, Michael. I've never said it out loud to you, and it's probably time I did. I love you, I love you, and I love you. There, that's it. But (and this is quite a big 'but') I cannot stand to carry on with things like they have been recently. I appreciate that you don't bring it home, but seeing you on the bar the other night was too much for me and of course I know some of the other stuff that goes on. God, I sound like a spy or voyeur here and I'm really not, it just filters back to me through people.

So here's the deal. I need for you to show me some kind of respect and affection. If you can't love me as a lover – and let's face it, there's no reason why you should – then at least please try to be a friend. Just don't cut me out like you're doing at the moment and please don't carry on being so self-destructive, it pains me to see it. There are no conditions attached, it's not like I'm saying 'be my boyfriend or leave', I'm just saying, 'talk to me a little' and let's sometimes do stuff together. Dinner, out or at home like we used to, Thursday night movies outdoors at the Shores, maybe even a ride on the Conch Train. You can have your boyfriends and I'll no doubt some day move along and have mine, but we have to at least be friends if we're to carry on living in this house together. If you can do this, you are always welcome here, but I am accustomed to living in a home, not a house.

I love you very much in several different ways, enough to adapt if I have to. OK?

Alex

A numb feeling settled on top of the anger and resentment I felt at Penny. I pulled a cold beer from the fridge and went out onto the front porch. The sliver of moon had moved higher in the sky and gave just enough light to boost the streetlamps around the graveyard. Such a strange light, half warm orange and half cold blue.

Feeling as if Penny and Alex had lured me into a trap, I sought release by lighting a joint. But, even as the first wave of relaxation hit me, I couldn't help but think back over all the things she'd said at the pier, formulating a half-theory that the whole performance was a set-up, related to the baby, and was somehow wrapped up with Alex, Sue and Penny's plans. Then her voice came into my head – as if she'd heard what I was thinking and was giving her reply.

'Is that Daddy's voice, Michael? Saying that no one ever does anything out of love or affection, only because they want something?'

So I thought about love and affection, and I thought about Alex. I certainly had affection for him. How could anyone not feel that for him? But love? Could I allow that?

My head was confusingly full of voices. My father's, Penny's; I found it hard to accurately identify my own. So, before I became too stoned to lose the moment, I did something clinical and diagnostic. I thought back along a line of facts. And the facts were that the first time I'd thought Alex was touching me intimately, I'd had an erection. It wasn't Alex, it was Lunch, though I hadn't known that at the key moment. Nonetheless, it had taken one joint and one hangover to open up a possibility that I had suppressed for years. Penny replied again: 'Which you allowed your *father's* voice to suppress.'

And Alex had offered me far more than sex, a far more forbidden fruit than mere sexual release. Now I was fucking with different men every night, provided they didn't know my real name and provided we didn't go any further than sex. But between Karl's party and Selina's letter, there had been a period when things had felt different, when I had half-acknowledged the possibility of something more with Alex.

So Selina's letter had been the turning point. And what impact had it had? At the exact point where I had been getting more comfortable with certain possibilities, I'd been hit with betrayal and renewed loss.

These had been some of Penny's words from earlier that evening. Loss, betrayal. What had the others been? Pain? Denial? Love?

Such frustrating words, such an abstract vocabulary. They were as hard to grasp as my father's: duty, honour, service, respect, obedience. I preferred the concrete certainties of cock, fat, suck, ass, fuck, and that was what I needed now. I extinguished the joint, downed the rest of the beer, and headed off into the night, leaving the empty house behind me.

Later that night I ended up in bed at some guesthouse with a slightly overweight, nondescript man of around my age. I'd been desperate for a conquest but the dope and drink had made me play my hand badly. The cute guys had already paired off and left together and I had a slight feeling that I was doing this man a favour, so I was less than fully enthusiastic, though he seemed nice enough. Except he kept trying to talk, asking questions about me, which was not what I wanted at all.

After a little heavy petting, he said, 'I want you to stay the night, not just an hour or so. I don't like to do, you know, to do just a quick impersonal sex session.'

'I can't.'

'Why not?'

'I have a roommate.'

A vision of the empty house crowded in on me and for a moment I was tempted to agree to stay with him. But he pushed too hard.

'Roommate or boyfriend?'

'Just a roommate. What's it to you?'

'Well, no one worries about getting home for "just a roommate". And it's pretty clear that your thoughts aren't here with me. I don't know where they are, or who they're with. Maybe with your "roommate"?'

'Can we just forget this stuff about my roommate? Please? It's irrelevant.'

'OK, I think you should go then.'

He spoke quietly but firmly.

'What?'

I couldn't believe he was throwing me out; I was doing him a favour by being there. But he continued, 'To be honest, I don't often do this. And when I do, it's never with guys as hot as you. But I want to be with a person rather than just a nameless body, however great that body is. And not only won't you stay the night, you're not really even here right now. Whoever you're thinking about, you should be with him. Whatever, I'd like you to leave, please.'

35
Night of the Iguana

I had a pretty bad weekend, cranking up my consumption of booze and dope until I found myself spending more time in backrooms than in bedrooms. Not only did I not want to know their names any more, I didn't even want to see their faces. But I couldn't blot out Penny's voice. So on Tuesday when the phone went at lunchtime as I groped my way downstairs for the first time that day, I suspected that it would be her even before I answered. The sound of her voice crystallised a growing feeling I'd had that she wasn't done with me yet, and I was preparing to resist. But she was, as usual, far too smart to be outwitted. She had a hook.

'Hi, Michael, how are you?'

She didn't give me a chance to reply.

'I'm calling to ask if you're free this evening. No more lecturing, and I think when you hear about the schedule you'll want to come.'

'Try me.'

'First, I want to take you somewhere where you'll find out something you've always wanted to know. It's time you came to terms with Alex's secret second job, and if I'm not wrong we'll be able to see him in action late this afternoon. Then I want to take you to the theatre. You'll be safe there; I never make a sound during a performance unless I'm on stage. And afterwards comes the best bit, I promise.'

'What are we going to see at the theatre?'

'*Night of the Iguana*, by Tennessee Williams, one of Key West's adopted sons. Have you seen it before?'

'I don't think so.'

'Good. I think you'll like it. Afterwards we'll have dinner at the

Rooftop. Something extra-special is happening there, and I want it to be a surprise. OK if I pick you up at around 6.30?'

By now I was resigned to whatever she had in store.

'OK, 6.30. But why do you need to pick me up?'

'You'll see.'

She arrived punctually. I'd spent the afternoon swimming and tanning at the beach and was feeling healthier than I had done of late. I had a slight sense that I'd need to be in training to deal with her.

We kissed as usual and she said, 'Oh Michael, don't look so terrified. This evening's going to be exciting and fun, quite unlike last week, I promise.'

We set off, and after a few blocks, on the corner of Simonton and Eaton, Penny stopped.

'I told a small white lie. Before we get to Alex, there's one other thing I would like to show you.' She gestured towards the huge concrete building in front of us.

'This is the Old Stone Methodist Church. It was rebuilt in 1877, in a very unusual way. The previous church was made of wood, but the minister didn't want to miss a service while the new one was being built, so they constructed the new stone church around the old wooden one. And when they'd finished, they dismantled the wooden one and carried it out the front door.'

'What do you want me to make of that?' I asked, surly at the renewed lecturing.

'Oh, nothing in particular,' she said, fake innocence sitting serenely on her face. 'I think it makes a nice metaphor for all sorts of things. And now it's three blocks to our next brief stop, then on to the theatre. I'm rather pleased with myself, I think I have the timing perfectly.'

We set off again and Penny continued. 'Michael, one night at Angelico's you took me aside to ask what Alex's other job is. You didn't say what your concern was, but you hinted. You were worried that he was working as a stripper, a private dancer maybe? Am I right?'

I nodded, saying, 'I suppose so. I mean, he's so secretive about it, embarrassed, and whenever he leaves for work he carries a tiny bag with something in it that he never lets me see. I suppose it must be what he wears. But it's none of my business what he does to make ends meet.'

Penny looked at me quizzically before speaking, as if to say, *'Don't kid yourself, of course you give a shit what he does.'* But she decided to play it gently, saying, 'Well, Sue and I had the same thought until one day I saw exactly what it is he does. He doesn't know that we know, so don't ever tell him that I showed you. I don't know why he hides it so – and in a town this size, he can't think we won't find out one day. Maybe he's worried that one of his friends will turn up and he'll suffer some kind of performance anxiety. Maybe he thinks the costume is too embarrassing. Whatever. Anyway, we're here and we're just about on time.'

We'd reached the junction of Duval and Front Street, the sexless zone. Penny tucked us into a small lane on one side so that we could watch unobserved. We were quiet for a while, then a Conch Train trundled down the street and into the depot opposite. The driver's voice issued from the string of loudspeakers down its length.

'Here we are, back where we started, ladies and gentlemen. Thanks for taking the tour and I hope you enjoyed it. Sally will have your photographs ready in the booth to the side after we've stopped. I've enjoyed showing you Key West, this is Andy your driver and guide, signing off for the evening, which I hope is a very pleasant one for all of you.'

But it wasn't Andy, despite the slightly disguised voice. It was Alex. And, as he stepped from the driver's cab in his short-sleeved Conch Train driver's shirt with embroidered badges on its shoulders, I had a sudden urge to sweep him up.

Penny held me by the arm, one finger to her lips and said, 'Remember, Secret Squirrel.'

'Secret Squirrel,' I replied.

*

Soon we were being shown to our seats near the front of the theatre. I'd seen some of Williams's plays before but *Night of the Iguana* was new to me. Two lonely people, a man and a woman, shackled by their pasts and their failures, live through a few hours of tropical storm in a run-down hotel in Mexico. While the locals capture an iguana, chaining it up under the porch until they are ready to slay and eat it, these two characters work through their demons. There is some focus on sexuality, unfulfilled on her part, compulsive on his. And in the end they reach a form of resolution, a way forward, which is symbolised by cutting the iguana loose from its chains. This was Penny's point, I assumed.

As we left, she turned to me and said, 'So, what did you think?'

'I thought the performances were very good indeed, far better than you'd expect somewhere...'

'... as provincial as this?'

'Somewhere that isn't a major city. Look, you know, I did all sciences at school from the age of sixteen onwards but I do vaguely remember doing *Streetcar* for O-level, and I had the same feeling this evening. Everything a little overblown, the symbolism a little obvious. Do you know what I mean? And I also think the last scene is hard to believe.'

'Why's that?' she asked.

'Because these are two extremely unhappy people, with years of doubt and missed opportunity and confusion behind them, behaving in an extremely dysfunctional way – and suddenly everything changes: they share a few home truths, do a bit of *Sturm und Drang*, agree to commit one symbolic act of liberation and suddenly, bingo! Everything falls into place and their inner conflicts are resolved. I just don't think it happens like that in real life, do you?'

Even as I asked the question I realised I'd been set up.

'Ooh Michael, this is so exciting! "Dysfunctional", "Inner Conflicts Resolved". What a fancy psychobabble vocabulary you have when it suits you! Either that or you learn fast!'

'Be gentle with me, Penny, or I may not make it to dinner,' I said, trying to sound half-joking and half-serious but probably just sounding churlish.

'OK, I'll be gentle. But you asked me a question. Do I think it happens like that in real life? Well, the answer is, not often, but sometimes. I think Williams aimed to concentrate a longer process into a play-length piece. I also think that he uses strong symbols to try to illustrate, from the visible tips of icebergs, what the underwater portion might look like.

'But I do think it's sometimes possible to experience change, quickly and dramatically, as a result of one pivotal moment that sparks a response to a long-term build-up of factors. In other words, redemption or damnation can come equally quickly if the circumstances are right. Look at you, for example.'

'Why did I think it would come back to that?'

'Cut the crap, Michael. You asked the question. You want to do this or you don't? We'll be at dinner in a hundred yards, so you choose. We can talk about the weather for two minutes or you can give me a shot at wrapping up my attempt at being helpful. Well?'

'All right, Doctor Herrnstein, I'm fascinated. So go ahead: look at me, for example.'

She continued, ignoring the resentment in my voice, though I heard it clearly myself and it made me feel like a schoolboy trying to disguise some dishonest act.

'You've been behaving totally differently since that letter from Selina. It's a good example of what I just described as a pivotal moment; it catalysed a reaction to a long-term build-up of factors. And since then you've been behaving as if all your long-term factors are bad ones. Your father, Selina, all the circumstances surrounding Jim and his death; your feelings of inadequacy. So, in my final minute, I'm going to tell you how the rest of us see you, and I'm sure that this includes Jim, your mother, sister, grandfather, as well as all of us.'

She gestured around her as if everyone in town was with her on this, then said, 'Look at me.'

I did as ordered. She was magnificent, glowing with energy and certainty.

'We see a handsome, clever, funny, kind, competent, charming, lovable man, a good father, who has been treated like shit by people who should have known better. In other words, we see plenty enough good long-term factors to make a happy man, not a miserable one. Which takes me back to your question. Do I think things happen in real life like they did in the play? Well, I answered, "not often but sometimes", when people are smart and motivated. All that appears to be missing in your case is the motivation. I don't want to sound like a cosmetics advertisement, but you have to believe that you're worth it. So look at what the good guys think of you. They're much better guides than people like your father. Even Selina, Princess of Darkness, said you were better than she deserved!'

We had reached the foot of a wooden staircase that led upwards from the street to the restaurant. But before we went up, I had a question to ask, the same question I had asked Alex some weeks before.

'How do you know all of this, Penny? Where do you get your certainties from? Not about me in particular, but this whole psychology stuff in general.'

'*Dummkopf*!' she replied in an unadulterated Yiddish accent. 'How else? I've been there myself, of course! Only it took me years, so luckily for you I've applied for a shortcut on your behalf. Now take me to dinner.'

'You planned this whole follow-up session like a military operation, didn't you?' I said. 'Talk about belt and braces.'

'You betcha! Belt, braces, whatever. Anything to help you keep your trousers on.'

'Very funny. And you lied to me – you promised no more lecturing.'

'You're worth it,' she replied, tossing her hair in imitation of a cover girl and grabbing my hand to lead me up the stairs.

This section of the evening was clearly at a close.

36
Cutting Loose

After we had climbed the two flights of stairs to the main restaurant area, Penny steered me to a table near the piano.

'Shouldn't we sit outside?' I asked. 'It's such a beautiful evening. And why are there six places? Who's joining us?'

'Trust me. We'll sit here. Now, here's the nice part.' She gestured to the piano and the waiting microphone. 'Phil sings here from time to time but tonight something rather special is going to happen. The other seats are for Maxo, for Phil's mother and for...'

'But I thought her mother never left the house.'

'She's making an exception this evening. She wouldn't miss this for the world. You see, two days ago, a lady checked in at the guesthouse and I got chatting to her. She's in A&R for one of the big New York record labels.'

'A&R?'

'Artists and repertoire. They find new talent and sign it up. She's here on vacation. Anyway, I told her about Phil. She was a little, you know, "Get out of my face, I'm on vacation", but I dragged her along to a show Phil was doing at Blue Heaven and she was amazed. So, get this: she's got her boss to fly down from New York to watch Phil tonight. They're dining with us. Says she can't believe that no one's signed Phil yet. This could be major.'

'You are quite the fairy godmother, aren't you?'

'Interfering old sow, more like it. Don't tell me you don't agree.'

At that moment Phil arrived, too breathless to kiss either of us. She was weaving around more agitatedly than usual.

'Michael, hey, could you give me a little help here? Mom's like, *wedged*. You know, we got her into the cab but we can't get her out. It's *tragic*. I mean, I'm on in like ten minutes or something. And the driver, he's like really *pissed* at me. Are they here yet?'

She looked around her like a frightened rabbit.

'It's OK, dear,' said Penny, 'they didn't arrive yet. Michael, go see if you can help. I'll stay here to meet and greet.'

We trotted down the steps to the street where the cab ticked away. Phil's mother sat, sweating and heaving, on the back seat. She had a high colour, emphasised by heavy rouge, and she was wearing an evening gown that was far too small for her. With the way she was sitting, it looked as if it was restricting her breathing. Maxo stood beside me on the pavement, also sweating. He was wearing a T-shirt with a logo on the back that said, 'If You Can Read This, The Bitch Fell Off.'

Phil went around to the opposite side of the cab and climbed in, then took her shoes off and raised her feet to the small of her mother's back.

'OK, you guys, I'm gonna push, you're gonna pull, and Mom, make like you're thin for a moment.'

Her mother swivelled towards us so we could take one hand each. We started to pull, and with Phil grunting and shoving from behind, we eased her from the cab. She stood uncertainly and then dropped an inch into a tiny curtsy while passers-by applauded. Another cab had pulled up behind us and two women had emerged, as stick-thin as Phil's mother was fat. Phil bobbed over to them.

'Hi, Janice, thanks for coming, it's like, so cool of you to do this. Hey, you must be Sandrine. Thank you, thanks for coming all this way.'

Before either of them could reply, Phil had taken them by their hands and led them over to us. 'I want you to meet my friend Michael, my boyfriend Maxo and my mom, Cynthia. Friends call her Skinny.'

The women shook hands with each of us in turn, repeating our names and theirs. Cynthia said to Janice, 'I'm so sorry about that little performance you just witnessed, looks like it was me that turned into the pumpkin, rather than the carriage.'

It was the first time she had spoken and I think we all did double-takes. She had the sexiest, huskiest voice I've ever heard, the voice of a screen goddess.

'Well, girl,' said Sandrine, 'looks like we came to hear the wrong lady!'

'Well, thank *you*. I weren't too bad in my time, ain't got the breath for it no more. Now, you girls go on up while these gentlemen help this old lady with them stairs.'

Phil showed the two visitors up while Maxo and I did as directed, which took a good five minutes. Cynthia had to pause at almost every step. Her breathing was stertorous and despite her good humour she was clearly in some physical distress. However, after a few minutes at the table, where she sat between Penny and Janice, she appeared to recover. Phil waited with us until we'd ordered.

The Rooftop is famous for its crab-cake appetisers, made with fresh crab, lobster and shrimp, so everyone at the table ordered that. Only Maxo and I ordered main courses and I chose wine for all of us, starting with champagne. There was a party spirit at the table, Cynthia entertaining the two visitors with stories of the bars in which she had sung in the Key West of the 60s and 70s. She was a typical local product: lush, exotic, colourful, entirely uncontrolled. She had the two wafer-thin executives in stitches.

There was quite a buzz in the restaurant that night. It was very full both inside and on the moonlit banks of terraces beyond. But, as Phil's first notes hit, the noise level dropped considerably. She started with her usual warm-up, the wordless vocal wail from *Dark Side of the Moon*, 'The Great Gig in the Sky'. But tonight she pulled off a very particular trick, which you'd have to listen to the original to understand. On the album, the track starts with a wide soundstage as if the singer is at the other end of an arena, with thousands of other people there. Then throughout the piece she appears to draw closer until it's just you and her alone, with her crooning almost in your ear. I'm sure this is achieved with some combination of echo and reverb in the recording studio, but Phil did it with just her voice and a microphone and it was spine-tingling; you only had to see the looks on the faces of the New Yorkers to see that they were caught from the first minute. Next came 'Mack the Knife', sung as a slow, dream-like ballad. Then a trio of Diana Ross songs, starting with 'Touch Me in the Morning', then 'Ain't No Mountain', and winding up with the theme from *Mahogany*. By this time we were well into the first course and Sandrine had discreetly slipped half her enormous crab cake onto Cynthia's plate, though I noticed she was less shy with the wine. New York, rather than LA, I thought to myself.

She beckoned Phil over while the audience was applauding the last of the Diana Ross songs, and said, 'Phil, now you've shown Ms Ross where to get off, I'd like to hear some of your own stuff. Janice tells me it's real good.'

To my surprise and with no hint of her earlier nervousness, Phil replied, 'I really appreciate your asking, but I can't do that in here.' She flicked her hand quickly round the room, like the wing of a small but determined bird. 'The ambience is a little more formal than where Janice heard me the other night. The set I'm doing is aimed square at this type of customer and it's what the management wants. I have to respect that. But, if they ask for an encore, I'll do one song. The rest I can send you on tape, though the recording's not great quality.'

I only heard this because I was sitting right next to Janice. It was not just the fact that Phil had the courage to say it that surprised me. It was her tone of voice. The valley-girl speak and vocal italicisation were gone, as were the nerves from earlier on. This was a quick exchange between two professionals, and they both knew it.

Sandrine nodded. 'Sure.'

The rest of the set was electric. Phil picked favourites from Ella Fitzgerald, Aretha Franklin and Tina Turner, before ending with 'Somewhere Over the Rainbow', which, as usual, she milked mercilessly for tears. As she took her bow, people stood at their tables, cheering and whistling for more. Sandrine had dialled a number on her mobile phone three songs earlier and then left it discreetly on the table, still connected to someone. Now she picked it up again and spoke for a few seconds.

Phil took a few bows and a sip of water, then darted over to peck her mother on the cheek before whispering something in her ear. Cynthia nodded and reached for her napkin to wipe her glistening face.

Phil returned to the microphone and said, 'Thank you, thank you. Now with your permission I'd like to fulfil a request by singing one of my own songs as an encore...'

The audience interrupted her with further cheers and wolf-whistles, the fine-dining ambience of earlier having disappeared entirely.

'This is a song for two female voices, written by me to be sung by me and my mom Cynthia, who was performing in bars around this town over twenty-five years ago. It's dedicated to the unreliable men of Key West... including my boyfriend Maxo.' Phil gestured to him to rise, which he did, bowing to raucous laughter and whistling.

'Mom, do you want to do this standing up or sitting down?' she asked, holding the microphone to her mother's mouth.

'I usually prefer it lying down, honey.' This was met by joyful whooping. 'But since there's an audience, I'll stand. Do we have to share that teensy li'l thing?' She pointed at the microphone, a cartoon look on her face.

'Ladies and gentlemen, we'd like to sing for you tonight, "Two Can Play at That Game". Thank you!'

It was an upbeat romp of a song in which a mother and daughter compared notes on their feckless lovers. Its tune was immediately catchy and memorable and Phil and Cynthia performed it with abandon, dancing side by side, bumping hips together and camping it up for the audience. Having recovered from the stair climb earlier, Cynthia appeared to be in good working order and was surprisingly mobile for a woman of around five-five and close on twenty stone. She also had a fabulous voice, like Phil's but with more honey, less raw. By the end of the song she was sweating profusely and I thought I saw some discomfort behind her smiles and little curtsies.

She stood centre stage and said, 'Thank you all so much, you're very kind. Now me an' my little girl's gonna take a rest. Thank you, good folks. Goodnight!'

They bowed offstage, having thanked the pianist, and returned to the table. I noticed Sandrine say something briefly into the phone before punching a button on it and putting it in her handbag. Everyone but me was focussed on Phil as Sandrine and Janice congratulated her. I was watching Cynthia heave herself back into her seat. She appeared breathless, was breathing shallowly but rapidly. She had a very high colour, which suddenly drained away.

I knew at that moment, the same moment as her right hand moved to her chest, then to her left arm, that she was in serious trouble.

Everything went into overdrive. I grabbed Phil and said, 'I think your mother's having a problem with her heart. Does she have heart problems?'

'Yes. Angina. She's been warned...'

Then I said loudly and clearly to everyone at the table, suddenly aware that I was using a tone of voice they'd never heard before, 'Cynthia may be having a heart attack. Penny, ambulance, now. Write this down...'

She grabbed a pen from the table.

'Tell them: fifty-year-old woman, severely overweight, suspected myocardial infarction, we're upstairs and they'll need to bring the defibrillator up with them. Speed will make a big difference. Now, you three' – I pointed to Maxo and the New Yorkers – 'pull this table out of the way, chair cushions on the floor. Then clear everyone else away and make sure the path to the stairs is clear.' They looked frozen. 'Now, please.'

Cynthia was writhing and within seconds Maxo and I had her lowered to the cushions on the floor and I was loosening her tight dress, keeping her propped semi-upright.

'Cynthia, can you hear me?'

She nodded, glazed terror in her eye.

'You're having a heart attack but I'm a heart specialist and I can help you. Stay as still as you can, try to breathe and stay as calm as you can – it will be better if you can do that. I'm keeping your pulse monitored and an ambulance is on the way.'

I addressed Phil. 'Does she have any tablets or spray for the angina?'

'She had a spray, but she ran out a coupla days ago. She takes aspirin every single day. My God, please, Michael!'

'Phil, someone in this restaurant may have some spray. Grab the microphone and ask, immediately, tell them to bring it to me. And find aspirin too.'

I returned my attention to Cynthia. Her wrist was very fat and her watchstrap too tight, like her clothes, so I took it off, then felt the pulse at her throat. It was jumping wildly. Then suddenly her face contorted and I felt the pulse race, then stop. Her eyes started to roll and she bucked briefly, foam at her mouth. She was going blue.

'Everybody clear, NOW!' I shouted.

I ripped her dress open and alternated cardio-pulmonary resuscitation with pulse taking. There was no sign of a pulse.

I did some quick calculations. The time that had elapsed between the ambulance being called and Cynthia's entry into total cardiac arrest had probably been less than two minutes. I'd expect a response time, given my knowledge of the island, in the region of six to ten minutes. That meant we could now expect help in between four and eight minutes.

Out-of-hospital cardiac arrest victims who receive CPR followed by defibrillation have around a ten per cent chance of survival. Of these ten per cent, between one and two per cent would tick away with every minute's delay in administering defibrillation. And I could hear no sirens. I also knew that tonight was the last night of Mardi Gras on Duval, and that the traffic all around might be more than usually backed up. So she had a six per cent chance at best, which I could almost double if I had a defibrillator to hand. I stood up and shouted to the whole restaurant, 'I need a defibrillator right now. I want you all to run to the nearest restaurants and bars and ask if they have one – some places keep them on hand. NOW! And you.' I pointed to a waitress who stood open-mouthed nearby. 'I need thick rubber gloves, from the kitchen, immediately. Maxo. Unplug that floor lamp from the wall and rip the wires out of it. I want bare wires, separated by at least a foot at the live end, then stand by to plug the flex back in.'

I was back down on the floor, where Phil was holding her mother, keening. I moved her to the side and while people scattered to do what I had asked I resumed my cardio-pulmonary effort. I alternated big pushes, most of my weight now pushing into her sternum, with trying to inflate her lungs. She was quite blue, unmoving, cold and clammy. I slapped her face hard and shouted her name and I kept on going. Another minute must have passed before I heard the first wail of sirens in the distance. Soon after that, I finally got a weak pulse back.

Then a man rushed out from the crowd with a spray, shouting, 'I found it; it was in my wife's handbag, here.'

He thrust it at me and, checking the label quickly, I released my mouth from Cynthia's. Lifting her tongue, I squirted the spray underneath and whispered into her ear, 'Come on, Cynthia, you can do it. You have to stay with us, Phil's going to get her recording contract this evening, you have to be here for her.'

The pulse was weak and irregular, but it was there and it strengthened a little as I spoke.

Within moments the paramedics were running up the stairs and I briefed them as they set about stabilising her. The head of the crew, seeing Maxo standing by with the two bare wires in his hand and the waitress beside me with the rubber gloves, said, 'Yeah, home-made defibrillator! I saw that movie too. Always wanted to try it. Man, would you be in trouble if you did! That is so not legal!'

As they were loading her onto a stretcher a few minutes later, Phil rushing around like a terrier, hugging and kissing me and crying, I heard the muffled ring of a mobile phone. Sandrine retrieved it from her bag and answered it and, after a few moments of conversation, she turned to Phil and said, 'This is not a great time, I appreciate that, but we want to sign you, immediately. We almost never do that, we option people. This is big, girl. Call me at Penny's place when you get back from the hospital if everything's OK. Now, go!'

She shooed her off in the direction of the stairs, where the paramedics were just starting a teetering descent. As they disappeared, the room burst into applause and it took me a few moments to realise that they were cheering and clapping me. Many of them, including Penny, were in tears and many of them came up and held me briefly, saying 'Amazing!', 'You saved her life!', 'My God, I've never seen anything like it!', 'You're should be on ER!'

'Who's the fairy godmother now?' asked Penny, as she gave me a long, long hug.

'All I'm saying, Penny, is that I hope you didn't plan that last bit. That really would have been going too far.'

'Even I wouldn't plan anything as dramatically dangerous as that.' Then she smiled slyly. 'Correct me if I'm wrong, Michael, but isn't that the scuttling sound of a freed iguana I hear?'

37
At Home

I was on a high and I wanted some time to come back to earth on my own. Somewhere out of sight another set of cogs had turned, ratcheting into a new position, and I knew they would not be turning back. But I didn't want to do what I was planning next either lightly or immediately. So I went for a long, long cycle ride.

I pedalled up Duval, past the Garden of Eden and Wax, Bandidos and Divas, past all of the bars of my most recent history. The lights at the junction with Truman were red but I went straight through them and on to Atlantic Shores where I turned left towards the AIDS memorial at White Street Pier. I stopped there for a while to look for Carey's name before cycling on past the airport until I came to the end of the island, where I stopped once more and stared at the strip of water between where I was standing and the rest of the Florida Keys. A stiff breeze was whipping up a little froth, blowing water through the narrow channel. My final glance was eastwards, over the dark seas that separated me from Europe. Then I turned back towards America, that enormous land of defeated frontiers, of conquered deserts and mountains. And after a few moments I set off, pedalling powerfully, towards the heart of my new home.

Alex was asleep by the time I got there. I tiptoed into his room and slipped quietly out of my clothes before climbing in beside him, forming a spoon around his back until he began to stir.

The next morning, as we ate breakfast together on the front porch and as I was about to tell Alex about the events of the previous evening, the telephone rang. Neither of us got up and it soon clicked into answer mode.

'Hi guys, it's Phil. I've been at the hospital all night with Mom. She's really stable now. They say she'll be OK but she has to stay in for observation and she has to lose some weight and stuff. Anyway, that's for later. For now, she's doing fine. Shit, I'm exhausted! Anyway, Michael, you know why I'm calling. Will a simple "thank you" ever be enough? How 'bout a billion times over? I owe you. I have to go now. Sandrine and Janice are coming by. Can you believe all this? They have some sort of contract for me to look at but I'm so tired I can hardly even read. It's the last thing on my mind.'

She laughed suddenly.

'Maxo called the restaurant manager from last night, he was really cool about it all. Says, can he fix the lamp now? Boy, are you one crazy dude! Anyway, gotta gotta go. Love love love, thank you thank you thank you.'

Alex had to leave for work but before he went he insisted that I explain what he'd just heard. He was mostly quiet while I recounted what had happened, interrupting with little 'wows' and 'amazings' while I told the story, and when I'd finished he took a few steps back, looked me up and down and said, 'A lamp, Michael? You were going to plug her into the *grid*?'

'I saw it done in a film once. It was a contingency plan. I've never actually seen it done in real life and I was trying to work out how many joules I'd get from your electrical system but I wasn't getting far; there was too much else going on.'

I could hear how ridiculous it sounded as I said it.

'Oh, I'm sorry to hear they don't teach that at med school in the UK any more. I did it in pre-med. Shit, with Phil's mom you could've fused the Keys from here to Miami.' He sat down and regarded me appraisingly. 'You Englishmen. So conservative on the outside, so wild underneath. I can see I'm going to have to keep a close eye on you from now on, lover boy. A very close eye indeed.'

'You American boys,' I replied. 'So apparently wild on the outside, so conservative underneath. I know more about you than you think.'

'And what do you mean by that?'

It was mean and it was breaking a promise to Penny, but I was sure I could pretend to have found out on my own. Besides, it was irresistible. I tried to imitate Alex's own roughly disguised voice.

'And on our left we see the home of Alex Crawford and Michael Stuart. This is one of a pair of so-called "twin" houses, built in the mid-1800s.'

Alex looked confused.

'Looking over to the left of the *train*, we see the graveyard...'

An expression of horror was chased across his face by mock revenge as he took over from me. 'Up ahead is Duval's most popular male *bar-dancing* venue. And now, give it up for Doctor Michael Stuart, the one with all the beads, Prince of Pride Street!'

'Actually I'm not a Doctor at all, I'm a Mister.'

'What? What the hell were you playing at with Phil's mom then? I thought you said you were qualified?'

'Poor Alex. It's all a bit confusing for you, isn't it? In England, if you've qualified as a doctor and you go on to be a specialist, you become plain old "Mister" again, like me. Now go to work while I wash your *uniform* for you.'

'How did you know that's what I do? Who told you?'

'My secret. I have my methods. Is there anything else you want to tell me?'

'No,' he said, sulkily. 'Nothing.'

'Nothing at all?'

'Yes. I don't love you after all. It was all a terrible mistake. I'm going to work now and you may not see me again. Not until this evening.'

I spent the morning pedalling backwards and forwards between Ace Hardware, the lumberyard and home, getting things I needed to resume work. From time to time the phone would ring but I was perfectly happy to carry on with what I was doing out in the sunshine, not even listening to the messages. It was the first day for a while that I hadn't had a hangover and at lunchtime, though I had a sandwich and a cold beer, I decided against a joint and carried on working. I wanted to have the back deck finished by the time Alex got home.

Around three o'clock, Angelico dropped by. He'd come to congratulate me, having heard about Cynthia from Penny. But when he saw that I was itching to resume work, he offered to stay and help and I accepted.

By six o'clock we'd completed a task I'd more or less abandoned some weeks before. Two rotten supporting posts under the deck had been replaced, Angelico explaining that the deck was probably a more recent addition and made of inferior wood, which is why it had rotted in the stream of water from the leaking gutter above. We'd also stripped away the weakened parts of the decking itself, replaced some battens and a few cross-members and laid new timber on top. It wasn't pretty and would need sanding evenly and treating, but it was done.

We still had an hour or so to go before I expected Alex, so Angelico held a ladder while I ascended, bits of zinc in my spare hand, and re-attached the guttering. Then Angelico left, pleading a previous engagement.

I showered quickly and changed before pedalling off to the Waterfront Market for food and wine. While I was there I saw a bag of barbecue charcoal and had an idea – so I bought some glistening, freshly caught Mahi Mahi.

Back home, I grabbed a bucket of water and a scouring pad from the kitchen and went back into the yard to clean the barbecue. It took longer than I expected and by the time I'd finished it was around 7.30 and totally dark. Alex wasn't home yet so I went up to the top porch at the front of the house and detached the rusting bicycle, unthreaded the fairy lights and took them out to the yard. I was just passing them through the kitchen window so I could plug them in when I heard a voice from behind me.

'GET BACK, he's holding a domestic lighting appliance and it may be live!'

I turned around to see Penny, Alex, Sue, Karl and Angelico beaming at me from the deck. They were all holding items of food. Cold meats, bread, cheese, a salad.

'Surprise!' they shouted as one.

Later that evening when we had eaten everything including the Mahi Mahi – which, as Karl cynically pointed out, is always the catch of the day in Key West – Angelico announced that he had something to show us. He delved into his leather handbag and produced a bunch of keys and a torch with a flourish and said, 'Follow me.'

We filed through the house and into the street where we turned right, right and right again until we were approaching a point directly behind where we had started, by which time we had all guessed our destination: the twin house.

Alex was fizzing with excitement but there was another look on his face too, a look that I couldn't interpret. Something a little guilty, perhaps?

'How did you manage to get the keys?' he asked Angelico.

'One of the guys in the trust department was... well, let's just say he was friendly.'

Angelico reached for the gate and it opened, silently.

'I had the briefest look earlier this evening, just inside the front door. I've been cultivating my friend with the keys for a while but I had to step up the offensive after Karl called me this morning. It seemed as if the moment was right. Please be careful, believe it or not there's no electric light, it was never even installed.'

The streetlight cast an orange glow over what was just recognisable as a replica of the back of Alex's house but without the cottage-like rear portion. Its lines were much finer in this form, cleaner and with greater integrity.

Angelico flicked the torch into life and led us up the steps, saying, 'Let's do the time warp.'

*

The door gave directly onto a passageway with rooms off to either side. I stood back so the others could go first, led by Angelico.

After a few yards the passage opened out into a hall, much narrower than that of Alex's house because the original walls were still in place. But as Angelico flashed the beam of the torch around, it became clear that everything was otherwise the same: the same doors and windows, the same carving on the newel post and banisters, the same fanlight above the front door. If we hadn't all been in such uplifted spirits, it would have been positively spooky.

'We can't go into any of the rooms or upstairs, I promised my friend. But he said we should visit the garden, if I could just find the right key. Hey Karl, hold this for me.'

He handed the torch to Karl who shone it downwards as Angelico fumbled with the bunch, trying key after key in the lock until he found the right one.

The door swung open as soundlessly as the gate had. Somebody was obviously taking the maintenance work seriously.

We stepped out onto the porch and were met by a familiar squawk. It was the same noise I had heard countless times before from Alex's yard but much closer now.

'What the...?' said Sue.

'Parrots,' Angelico replied.

'What? *Parrots*, did you say?'

'I did indeed.'

'What are they doing here?'

'The trustees are apparently very diligent in carrying out Juan's wishes. I was told we should pay them a visit but I didn't have time earlier.'

We took the steps down to garden level carefully, Karl lighting them with the torch. Then we followed its beam as he passed it around in front of us. The central part of the garden was carefully tended but after a few yards it merged into a thick tangle of shrubs and palms. Standing at the margins, in a place that I guessed would remain shaded during the daytime, were two large cages, each containing a parrot.

Angelico reclaimed the torch and showed us the way towards them. Their colours resolved into vivid flashes as the torchlight played over them. In the left-hand cage was a huge scarlet bird, nearly four feet long from the top of its head to the tip of its tail feathers. On the right was a fantastical creature, harlequined in rainbow shades of orange, yellow, green and *eau de nil*. Both birds were staring unblinkingly at us.

Penny leaned forward and tapped the cage on the left.

'Hello, what's your name?'

The bird puffed its chest and ruffled its feathers before settling back on its perch.

She tried again. 'Hi, tweetie pie, what's your name?'

The bird blinked once and looked away.

I tried to help, adding, 'Who's a pretty Polly? Who's a pretty Polly?'

Neither bird seemed interested in talking so we gave up and turned away. As we did so, the inhabitant of the left-hand cage squawked as if to gain our attention and when we had all turned to face it again the bird said, '*Buenos días, Amos. Buenos días, buenos días.*'

The harlequin creature in the next cage drew itself up to its full height and cried, 'Juan, Juan, Juan.'

'Fuck!' shouted Karl, stumbling backwards. It was the first time I'd ever heard him swear. Simultaneously, I realised that Alex was doubled up with laughter, holding on to Penny's arm as if he might collapse.

'Surely they don't live that long, do they?' asked Sue in wonder as the torchlight panned waveringly over the cages.

The birds spoke again.

'Alex. Alex. Alex.'

'Michael.'

Angelico shouted first this time. 'SHIT! Let's go. This is bad *lacumi*. Weird voodoo graveyard shit.'

Alex was rolling on the ground now, wailing with uncontrollable laughter and gasping for breath.

'Alex! What have you been up to?' barked Penny before dissolving into laughter herself.

He lay on his back with his knees raised while Angelico shone a shaking torch on his face.

'That was the best. The BEST! You guys...'

He paused, trying to catch his breath.

'I've been over that wall for weeks now. *Weeks*! I've been teaching them to talk. Shit, I never thought I'd get you all in here at once. Oooh, I'm gonna remember this for *ever*.'

Angelico feigned a kick between Alex's legs then dropped down beside him and started to pummel him.

'You bet you're gonna remember this forever, you little shit, bastard shitty little bastard. I nearly fucking wet myself. Jeeeez!'

Alex rolled away and leapt to his feet saying, 'Ladies and gentlemen, my unwitting accomplice, Angelico. A round of applause, please, for his misguided efforts at making well-connected friends when all he needed was a ladder. And a little *voodoo magic*.'

I noticed out of the corner of my eye that Karl had produced a huge white handkerchief and was mopping his brow quietly in the shadows, but he too was smiling.

After Angelico had recovered we poked around for a while as he explained that Juan's original birds, the predecessors of the two we'd just met, had lasted until sometime in the 1930s or 40s. Juan had made provision for their care and eventual replacement, in perpetuity. The trust people had emptied the house of its contents years before, but Juan's instructions specifically stated that the parrots had to stay in the garden. Their cages were therefore securely chained and they were checked and fed several times a week.

After we'd run out of things to look at and Angelico had restrained Alex from grabbing the keys to go snooping, we locked up and left.

We were halfway home when Angelico dropped back to where I was walking and gestured that we should slow down. As the others drew a little way ahead he said, 'I have some further interesting information. I've been doing some investigating and there might just be a way around the legal issues. So, maybe, just possibly, Juan's house could be for sale!'

38
Turning the Handle

The simple fact is this: sometimes, when something moves within us, we can no longer stop ourselves from being happy. I'd been stumbling from one thing to another, making decisions I hadn't even thought about and avoiding others that I *should* have thought about, but now I found that I wanted to do things differently. So, though I had the outline of a clear plan in my head, I realised it wasn't having the idea or the desire that counted; it was matching the plan to reality – mine and other people's – which would distinguish between success and failure.

The plan required big commitments both emotionally and in terms of time and money, from me and from others. Because of this I spent a lot of time researching its separate elements with a variety of professional advisers. I also bounced it off Lolly and, as it developed, she grew increasingly enthusiastic.

It was hard telling Lolly about Alex and me. I did it on a trip to Toronto to meet my nephews and it was an emotional time in general, meeting James and holding him for the first time.

Unlike Dad, Lolly had never guessed, never had the slightest clue about what I had to tell her, so it came as a real surprise, but she took it in her stride and that helped move things along. I think she was especially keen to encourage me in finding a new life now that she knew about Dad and Selina. She certainly didn't delete any expletives when it came to discussing their behaviour, which was a refreshing change from the attitude of my Key West friends, whose tendency to look for the upside in everybody sometimes got in the way of a good old-fashioned rant. So we talked a lot about 'the bastard and the bitch', getting it off our chests and saying that we never wanted to see either of them again, whatever happened.

My plan developed as Lolly repeatedly inquired how my relationship with Alex was progressing. She was concerned that I shouldn't dig myself into another unhappy situation and repeatedly said that the measure of how sensible it was to go ahead with my scheme would depend on how certain I felt about my future with Alex. I took her advice and bided my time.

I didn't discuss the plan with anyone in the circle of people it concerned, apart from Angelico, whose help I needed.

The hardest part was keeping it from Alex. I bought a laptop, ostensibly for internet access but actually to help me marshal the increasingly complex information and analysis involved. Sometimes I needed to work with printouts and this meant remembering to hide them afterwards. The most difficult thing was countering his questions about the way I was tackling the renovations to his house and my continual delay in replacing Angelico's salvaged partitions. Angelico helped me with this, blinding Alex with the terminology of preservation and assuring him that everything would happen in due course. It was also remarkably hard to keep Alex off the scent when it came to the particular way in which I was clearing and replanting the garden. He couldn't see the point of the empty patches I left, nor the underplanting scheme, which looked strange without the Chinese Fans and Bismarck Palms which Angelico planned to bring in full-grown at a later date.

The closest I got to having to share my plans came when Karl announced over dinner that Marty's friend had returned from his travels and verified the painting of Amos as being a Jane Maria Potter original. It would be worth quite a lot of money at auction, but considerably more if reunited with the second piece, which the expert thought might well exist. Disappointingly, Angelico had got hold of the inventory of Juan's house and there was no record of any painting that matched what we were looking for.

Alex was reluctant to allow the painting to be sold but he thought he'd need the money for the house. Clearly, I needed to stall him. I was about to take Karl aside and ask him to try to delay the auction process, when I had an idea. I suggested that I lend Alex ten thousand dollars with the painting as collateral, on the basis that the second picture might turn up later on, thereby increasing the value of the first. Alex wouldn't agree at first and later that night when we got home we had what amounted to a row.

'I know you made the offer out of the right motive,' he said, 'but I won't allow you to play Sugar Daddy. You know perfectly well that the chances of finding the other painting, if it exists, are pretty small. If I can't afford to carry on with the work on the house, we'll have to stop until I can.'

'Why are you so defensive about this? What's wrong with my making a contribution even if it's only in the form of a loan? I live here too, don't I?'

'That's not the point,' Alex said.

'So what is?'

He looked proud and sure of himself as he replied. 'The point is that you already pay for most of the groceries, you share the utilities and you've paid for almost all the building materials and plants you've used. So don't try to tell me that you want to pay some form of rent in addition to all that. This is a relationship of equals and that's the way I want it to stay. I don't ever want you to have a reason to doubt why I'm with you. Not ever.'

I had to think quickly.

'Do you still want to go back to school, Alex? Do you want to train? To qualify? To practise?'

He nodded as I continued.

'Then you have to take your head out of the sand. You can't afford to keep this place up on your own as things stand, let alone go back to college. Let me help. Please? It's only a loan.'

'You don't mean it as a loan and I know it. When am I ever going to pay it back? I'd rather...' He looked around himself defiantly. 'I'd rather sell this place if I have to.'

'You said you'd never do that.'

'Things have changed. I love this house, Michael, but I love you more and I'm not going to risk having money get in the way of our relationship.'

'And I love you and I'm telling you that money is already in the way. I have it and you don't and that's a fact so let's try to be grown up about this.'

I instantly regretted saying this.

'Grown up? Grown up! Please don't patronise me. I may be eighteen years younger than you but I am plenty grown up enough to be at least a match for you.'

I was starting to panic a little and wanted to de-escalate things. And he was right. So I told him a half-truth.

'I've sold my house in England.' In fact, it was under offer.

'You never told me about that!'

'It was going to be a surprise. I don't ever want to go back there, especially not to that house. So I've sold it and I want to make a contribution here. Anyway, you can't sell this house. It's not yours to sell unless Sue has a baby and I'm quite sure you won't want to give in to Wicked Cousin Elspeth so easily.

'This isn't just a house, it's our home and I want to get old here, with you. Really. Talking of which, I'm going to get old before you, so your turn will soon come to look after me.

'Come on, Alex. Look, forget the second painting. You're right, it's hardly likely to suddenly appear. I have a better idea which should keep both of us happy.'

'Which is?'

'I lend you money against the painting of Amos. You don't sell it until something changes. We'll accrue interest and then, if and when you do get to own the house fully, we convert my loan into a share in the house. If not, we'll sell the painting and you can pay me back.'

He looked vaguely interested for a few moments as he thought it through. Then he blew it out of the water.

'It's no good. I hadn't thought about it clearly before but you've revealed the flaw in the whole plan. I can't sell the painting anyway; it doesn't belong to me yet. Which means I can't offer it up as collateral for a loan either.'

'But Elspeth doesn't even know about it.'

It didn't matter any more; the painting was safe for the meantime and that was all I needed. But I was surprised by Alex's bloody-minded honesty in refusing to accept these plans, and his underlying desire to protect me. It was such a stark contrast to the way that Selina had behaved.

A few days later, while I was completing some work on a spreadsheet, I heard the postman whistling outside and when I went down there was a letter from my solicitor in the UK confirming that the contracts on my house had been exchanged. As I read it I recalled something Karl had once said. It was now time to stop reading the fine print, so I made a few phone calls and the cogs moved on once more.

But this time, I was turning the handle.

39
Showtime

I'd learned quite a bit from Angelico about how to give a performance such as the one I was planning, so I followed his lead and concentrated on getting the narrative in the right order. I spent many hours with my various professional advisers until every part of the jigsaw was in place, bar one. That was out of my control and would have to wait.

I decided that Karl's house would be the ideal place to stage the occasion since that's where so much of the preamble had been revealed in the first place. So I used the excuse of Penny's fiftieth birthday to suggest that we give a little dinner for her, asking whether Sue might like to cook. Luckily, it was a night when I knew Phil would be performing in a local club so she wouldn't be able to join us until later. I didn't want her and Maxo there for the first part; they had families of their own.

A few days before the event, I went back to the jewellery store in which I had bought the dragon brooch, and chose another piece. Then I took Angelico for lunch at Caladesi Catch on Simonton. I needed an ally for the forthcoming evening and I had to brief him, but I still managed to keep one or two surprises up my sleeve.

I spent the afternoon of the day itself checking over the final details and having one last meeting in the offices of a law firm just south of Duval, then I went home and showered, putting on the shot-silk shirt that Phil had chosen for me nearly six months earlier. It was mid-July and the nights were getting to be hot rather than warm, so I didn't take a jacket.

Alex would be meeting me at Karl's when he was through with his Conch Train tour so I cycled across town without needing to hide the four brown envelopes I'd prepared earlier. When I got to the house I slipped them behind the statue of Carey near the entrance and went in.

I was the first to arrive apart from Sue. It was a Monday, the café's day off, so she'd been there for a while preparing the menu we'd planned together. Everything had to be ready in advance so that Pepe could simply finish off and serve. I didn't want Sue out of the room but I needed the meal to be her creation.

I went straight into the kitchen and put my hands around her waist, kissing her neck.

'Well, hey, lover boy! You came just in time, I'm nearly done.'

She was taking some twice-baked lemon soufflés out of the oven, the ramekins steaming and sweet-smelling.

'Can you look after these for me while I go shower? Karl's given me one of the cabanas to use, I think he's nervous at having a woman in his sacred temple of a bathroom.' She laughed. 'Wait for fifteen minutes until they're cool, then put them in the fridge. Apart from that everything's ready, provided Pepe can do the new potatoes.'

'Where's Karl?' I asked.

'He went out for more champagne. He'll be back in a few minutes.'

She slipped out of the kitchen onto the terrace and I watched her descend the steps and circumnavigate the pool. When she'd shut the door of the cabana behind her I went quickly back to the entrance and retrieved the envelopes from Carey's temporary safekeeping. Then I went inside and hid them in a drawer in the petticoat sideboard so that they would be closer to hand when I needed them.

Patting my pocket to make sure that I still had the piece of jewellery, I went over to the wall and opened the concealed bar, helping myself to a gin and tonic. I'd hardly been drinking at all over the past few weeks but tonight I needed Dutch courage.

Angelico arrived a few minutes later carrying a large portfolio case, which he stashed out of sight around the corner of the terrace. He was followed in quick succession by Alex and then Karl and soon we were all on the terrace with glasses of champagne, chatting as we waited for Penny to arrive. Sue joined us a while later; it was the first time I'd seen her wearing a dress. She always looked good, whatever she was wearing, but tonight, in loose-fitting green silk almost the same colour as my shirt, she looked lovely.

We were just about to call Penny when she arrived, nearly half an hour late. She swept in through the entrance and past the pool in a sleek black glove of a dress that clung to her curves as it plunged almost to the ground. Unusually, she was wearing her hair down and I thought I detected that it was a shade darker than usual. She was wearing the dragon brooch.

'My darlings, I am so very sorry to be so late. I couldn't cycle in this get-up and I couldn't find a cab. I've walked the whole way.'

'Did you get any interesting propositions?' asked Alex.

She ignored him.

'Be a love and fetch this old lady a drink. My fifty-first year has already begun and I need assistance with the concept.'

Alex did as requested and, as people resumed their conversations, I decided to do a little groundwork.

'Any interesting new arrivals in Paradise today, Penny?'

'More like hell than paradise, I'm afraid. A couple of dismal dykes from God-knows-where turned up, saw two men kissing in the pool and left immediately. Sometimes I despair of people, I really do. It's no problem, business in general is really quite good, it's just the attitude of some people that disappoints me.'

This was perfect, as if I'd written her script for once.

'Karl was talking about this exact same thing the first night we met,' I replied. 'The whole thing of gay and lesbian separatism. You know, some wanting to do a "united we stand" and others wanting to be utterly divided. It must be hard to cater to all the varieties and permutations without sending out a questionnaire whenever someone tries to book a room.'

Karl joined the conversation. 'A policy of "separate but equal" is hardly in fashion these days but I do think it's wrong to confuse political correctness with what people actually *want*. If I were a lesbian, particularly a lesbian of *my* age, I certainly wouldn't want to remove my bikini top in front of a group of men, not even gay men. Of course, in a totally mixed environment like Penny's, there's the added complication of straight men leering over their wives' shoulders. You know what straight men are like with lesbians and I doubt that most dykes want to fuel those particular fantasies.'

I didn't want to push my luck so I let the subject move on. So far so good.

A few minutes later Karl tried to give Penny a birthday present but I suggested that we wait until coffee and Penny, embarrassed at being so late and fearing that people might be hungry, readily agreed. Soon we were seated around the table.

The first course was an expertly executed French onion soup; salty and caramelised with garlicky, cheese-topped croutons. There were several appreciative comments so it was easy for me to slip in another bit of preparation.

'This is fabulous, Sue. You know, the food in Key West tends to be very good as long as it sticks to seafood and so on, but a diet of fish palls after a while. I've been to a number of the places that have pretensions towards something a little more adventurous but somehow few of them seem to quite pull it off.'

Typically, she looked embarrassed at being complimented.

'Thank you,' she replied. 'You know how much I like to experiment, but the customers at the café are generally pretty conservative.'

Penny nodded her head in agreement, saying, 'If we had the space, we'd have a little restaurant at the guesthouse. Blue Heaven's only a block away and it's always absolutely bursting, so there's clearly a good trade to be had. But Karl needs Sue for the café and we just don't have anywhere to put a decent-sized kitchen. You're right though, Michael. With respect to Karl, Sue's talents are a little wasted at the café. It's the wrong franchise for her skills.'

'I agree totally,' said Karl. 'Of course the café needs a cook, but not necessarily someone of Sue's calibre. Penny's right; her talents are rather wasted; she's basically little more than a glorified short-order chef at the moment. Maybe you should think about it, Sue.'

'But I'm happy there. I like my colleagues, even if one of them *is* my husband. And this may surprise you, Karl, but I'm also quite fond of my big bad boss. Anyway, I don't like to move around too much, you know, like some chefs have a new job every six months. I wouldn't like that.'

I didn't dare catch Angelico's eye as he chimed in, saying, 'Alex took me to this great new place, Caladesi Catch, the other day for lunch. It's a beautiful conversion job from an old synagogue. Big tall space, airy, light. It had me thinking how much I'd like to design a restaurant here in Key West. I did one in Provincetown a few years back, before I became an academic; really chic, lots of bleached wood and a huge open kitchen. I won a prize for it. There's nothing quite like it here.'

Things were going too well too soon so I changed the subject. And though Angelico helped in keeping the direction of conversation safe, from time to time we'd have to look away from each other as he buried a little joke in an apparently innocent comment.

I had to speed things up when I realised it was getting somewhere near the time when Maxo and Phil might arrive. I guessed I had no more than an hour left so I suggested that we might give Penny her presents over dessert. She looked a little confused after my having already insisted that we should wait until coffee but Angelico jumped up before anyone could disagree and rummaged in his bag. Actually, he had no idea what I was about to do; he was just misreading a cue for what he thought was coming.

'Here, Penny. Happy birthday.'

He kissed her and handed her a powder-blue Tiffany box which she opened to reveal a small black velvet bag containing a crescent of silver, a key holder, with a small silver heart attached. While she was thanking Angelico, Karl produced his gift: a string of fresh-water pearls the colour of moonlight, strung on a fine silver chain.

Sue's gift had been agreed and arranged in advance but was yet to be delivered. It was a fifty-year-old parrot, the same age as Penny herself. Sue had a photograph of it and it was magnificent – startling hues of green, yellow and pink.

'I'm buying him from a family in Key Largo. He's called Billy and he used to belong to the grandmother but when she died, he stopped talking. They have an African Grey now, it whistles "Ave Maria". So Billy's sort of, surplus to requirements, which is sad.'

Penny jumped in. 'That night at Juan's house, I fell in love with those parrots, and I've been hanging around the ones in Nancy Forrester's Secret Garden ever since. Have you ever been there, Michael?'

I shook my head and she continued, 'I'll take you, it's the most incredible place, a tropical forest right in the middle of town and it has parrots, lots of them. I've been practising on them and I'm sure I can make Billy talk again. He just needs a little TLC.'

Alex was next and was a little embarrassed to be so short of money that he'd had to buy a second-hand gift. He'd been colluding with Sue and had found a beautiful glossy book about parrots, with everything you might need to know about how to identify and care for various different breeds. We all crowded around for a while and looked at the photographs. Then it was my turn to offer a gift.

So now it was showtime.

I reached into my pocket and pulled out the package from the jeweller's. Alex looked puzzled; I'd said I was going to buy her a silk shawl that he'd picked out in a shop earlier that week.

Karl and Penny were still poring over the parrot book so I tapped my glass to gain their attention.

'Ladies and gentlemen.'

They turned their faces towards me.

'By the end of the next five minutes you're either going to think that I'm certifiably deranged or that I'm rather a clever chap. Please don't judge until you've heard me through.'

I went over to where Penny was sitting and knelt down in front of her, suddenly aware of my heart racing. It was only the second time I'd ever done this, but this time it was my own choice. I opened the velvet-covered box to reveal a diamond ring.

'Happy birthday, Penny. Will you marry me?'

There was total silence around the table for a few seconds until Angelico whistled quietly and said almost under his breath, 'Mad dogs and Englishmen.'

Penny retained her composure as she said, 'I hope that doesn't make me the mad dog, Angelico.'

Then she turned to me. 'Have you lost your *mind*?'

'Don't make up yours yet; wait until you've seen this.'

I went over to the petticoat sideboard and took out the envelopes, then handed one to each of them.

'Take a look inside. I hope this is a present for everyone, including me.'

None of them took their eyes off me as they opened their packages. Angelico was smiling now, starting to realise what I was up to.

'The first sheet is Exhibit A. Go on, take a look!'

It was a photocopy of the deed of sale of Juan's house, with me as the new owner. I gave them a few seconds to take it in and, as Alex was about to speak, I stopped him and said, 'Don't say anything yet. Look at page two, let's call it Exhibit B.'

This was a copy of a letter from an immigration lawyer I'd been working with, summarising the relevant factors involved in marriage and residency. This time, Sue tried to say something but I hushed her and moved them on to Exhibit C, another legal summary but this time covering the relevant parts of paternity law.

Dawn was beginning to break across Penny and Alex's faces but Karl and Sue still looked confused so I went round to where Sue was sitting and put my hand on her shoulder, saying, 'I know it's Penny I'm proposing marriage to, but it's you I thought of as the mother. That's if you want to, of course. I promise I'll wear a bag over my head. Remember Peggy's will? Alex doesn't have to be the father.'

Sue was speechless, understandably, I suppose, so I encouraged them all to take out the final item. This was a thickly stapled bunch of papers, constituting a detailed business plan, equitable to all and already fully funded in outline, for the venture I was suggesting.

'Don't try to read it all now,' I said. 'It took me forever to put it together, though that was nothing compared to how complicated buying Juan's house was. Anyway, I hope it'll make sense to you after you've seen what Angelico has to show you.'

On cue, Angelico darted out onto the terrace and around the corner, reappearing seconds later with his portfolio. He opened it quickly, not wanting to lose the momentum of surprise I had created. I made space in the middle of the table so that he could spread out the large blueprint he had spent so much time preparing.

It showed Amos and Juan's houses, now Alex's and mine, as part of a compound. Angelico had labelled the street side of Juan's house with the words 'Boys' House' and the street side of Amos's with 'Girls' House'. The whole plan was titled 'Penny's Paradise Found: A Guesthouse Compound for Gay Men and Lesbians' and on a strip down one side was a single word printed inside a long rectangle: 'Restaurant.' It would be built on the lane – which was privately owned by the two properties – and would have access from both the street and the compound.

The twin houses were to be converted into one guesthouse with two separate parts, two pools and two hot tubs. Separate but equal.

Intricate arrangements of decking on multiple levels would separate and define the elements, providing space for an additional run of rooms on two levels to be constructed symmetrically and in sympathy with the twin houses. Amos and Juan's houses were going to live again, with the painting of the two men holding hands hanging in the entrance of Juan's house, out and proud at last. The only incomplete part of the plan was the missing painting by Potter, but I was already working on that.

Angelico explained the plans for the compound in detail and I ran over the business plan briefly. The details could wait until their shock had faded. But for now I was anxious to know what their reactions were.

The first question was from Sue. 'If both houses are for guests, where would you and Alex live?'

Angelico replied for me. He knew this part.

'This is just a series of suggestions. We don't have any right to run your lives, obviously, but we thought you might consider turning it into a home for the four of you? Who knows, you might eventually want a larger family, and then Michael and Alex would be on hand to help with the childcare – if that's what you wanted. And you could use the poolside rooms for the guesthouse staff; it's much easier to keep good ones if you can offer accommodation, even better if it's off-site.'

Their responses were slow to come at first, as the complexity of what I was proposing sank in. But I could soon tell from the pace of questions and the rising level of noise and good humour that the jury was at least actively considering my case. I knew I had Sue interested because her face had lit up and stayed alight almost from the moment I'd explained the third page. At one point she even said, 'But how am I going to run a restaurant and have a baby at the same time?' which was a question I hadn't thought of. But Penny replied quietly, 'We'd find a way.'

Alex's face was like changeable weather. He was darting between Karl, who was examining the business plan in some depth, and Angelico, at whom he fired a rapid succession of questions about the houses and the new additions. Sweetly, he kept shooting little glances at Penny as if to gauge her reaction. It also seemed that the questions he asked her carried an undertow; he was looking for signs of her approval.

The table was still buzzing when Phil and Maxo appeared. Phil saw the blueprint first and said, 'Wow, what's that, Karl? You planning to build an addition here?'

And Karl answered, 'No, Phyllis. The plan is Michael's. He wants to throw Alex out of his home and fill it with lesbians, sleep with his wife, marry her girlfriend and build a restaurant in the middle of the road next door. But it's not as mad as it sounds. Not quite.'

40
The Final Piece

I didn't dare to dream for the next week as they all reached their decisions. It was a long, clear sunrise as facts, numbers and feelings were checked, analysed and felt, but if there was no immediate 'yes' then at least the possibility of it was there from that night on.

To distract myself from the anxiety of waiting, I threw myself into working with Marty's friend on tracking down the final piece, the missing portrait. While he put discreet feelers out in the trade, I spent hours online, numbing my brain with Boolean search-strings and achieving nothing other than an encyclopaedic knowledge of the life and works of Jane Maria Potter. Well, not quite encyclopaedic – the missing portrait remained hidden.

Karl took me aside a few days after Penny's birthday and said he'd had an idea and wouldn't take no for an answer. If Penny, Sue and Alex agreed to my plan, he wanted to play his part. Firstly, he wanted to give Penny and me the portrait of Juan or Jessica, whichever it should turn out to be, as a wedding present. So I had to find it. The second part came out of his observation that Alex's financial position was the weakest of all those involved. Even if he kept the house and raised money against it, he would be burdened with debt and unable to go back to college.

Karl's plan was simple. He would wait until Alex's trustees handed the house over to him fully, thereby releasing the painting of Amos for sale. Then he, Karl, would anonymously bid at the auction. Unless the bidding got out of hand he would buy the painting as a christening present for the baby and reunite it with its partner – if we had managed to find it by then.

I had been hoping to purchase both paintings myself but I could see what Karl wanted; there was a sense in which he might feel left out of what was going on and this would be the perfect way for him to cement his inclusion in the family as an uncle. So I encouraged him. After all, his claim on them predated mine.

Marty's friend trawled through any number of catalogues from museums, shows, university collections and auctions, but had no luck. Then one day at a trade fair he chanced upon another dealer of his acquaintance who, years before, had been asked to value a painting for insurance purposes. Though unsigned, he'd identified it as a Potter and said that it was a portrait of a Hispanic male, probably from the 1870s. It was in a private collection in Texas and the dealer was able to dig up a name and address from his records.

Karl insisted on making the call himself. It was to be his wedding present and he didn't want me knowing how much he'd paid for it. But he couldn't get a phone number: it was unlisted. So he called Angelico, told him to pack an overnight bag, and the two of them drove off together to the airport.

I heard nothing from them until they returned two days later, when Karl called me and said, 'Would you like to come and see what might one day prove to be your wedding present?'

I didn't leave a note for Alex telling him where I'd gone in case he followed and saw the painting. Karl wanted to keep it as a surprise. So I pedalled furiously across town but, when I let myself into Karl's house, I found nobody there.

I walked around a little and could find no signs of life so I decided to have a swim. I stripped off and threw myself into the water but after a few lengths I became aware of a commotion at the edge of the pool. Treading water and brushing the hair from my eyes, I looked over towards the cabanas where Angelico, Karl, Peggy, Sue and Alex stood, holding two paintings between them.

I forgot that I was naked as I leapt streaming from the water, shouting to Karl, 'But I thought you wanted to keep this as a surprise!'

Penny replied for him. 'This silly old man called me from his hotel in Texas last night. He wouldn't part with his money until he knew whether I was going to marry you or not. I don't know if it's strictly legal for us to get engaged until your divorce comes through, but Karl has decided to turn Juan here into an unofficial engagement present.'

She reached into her pocket and produced the ring I'd given her.

'Now cover yourself up. Then come over here, kneel down, and ask me again.'

41
What Goes Around

Key West sweltered in the August heat and many of the hotels and restaurants were shuttered for their low-season break. Penny and Karl decreed that the guesthouse and café should shut up shop too, while we all decanted to Provincetown with Angelico for a week.

We spent hours walking in alternating sunshine, rain and fog on the National Seashore, picnicking amongst the dunes. And we took the boat to Martha's Vineyard where we cycled around for a day, feeling quite at home.

Provincetown itself was remarkably similar to Key West, but with coral reef dives replaced by whale watching, and palm trees and tropical birds swapped for marram grass and skylarks. We even saw some familiar faces from Duval working their low season out in the short northern summer, keeping their rainbow flags flying at the other end of the continent.

We visited the restaurant that Angelico had designed and, though the food was not a patch on what Sue could produce, the building itself was just as he had described – award-winningly beautiful. It was filled with a comfortable crowd of wealthy WASPs and intensely political-looking New England lesbians, doors open on all sides to allow the breeze to tickle hanging bunches of wind-chimes into life.

Cape Cod had more of the sea about it than Key West – more beach, sand and salt, more bleached wood and gull-cry – and after the heat from which we had escaped it seemed deliciously refreshing. It reminded me of the north Norfolk coast where I'd spent such happy summers as a child.

In the early evenings Alex and I wandered hand in hand through clapboard shops where floating skeins of new-age music filled the air and incense and crystals packed the shelves. And whilst he and I were falling further into each other, I sometimes spent a little time alone with Sue.

When the others returned to Key West, Alex and I headed further north, to Toronto. It seemed a natural time to introduce the central part of my new family to the only living part of my old one that I still cared for.

I'd expected a warm welcome, a friendly, possibly slightly awkward 'getting to know you' period. Things started well when my brother-in-law Pete put on a star performance at the airport, kissing us both on the cheek and hugging Alex as if he were his own long-lost brother. Lolly had stayed at home with the twins, both of whom had summer colds. It was less than an hour's drive and we were soon pulling into their driveway.

But Lolly didn't come to the door because she was sitting in the hall by the telephone, staring silently, the twins asleep in a buggy beside her. As we walked in, she stood up slowly and hugged me before saying, 'I didn't want to answer it at first. I was in the kitchen and I didn't want to speak to her when I heard who it was. Then I... just couldn't.'

She reached towards the answering machine and pressed 'Play'.

'Hello, Lolitia. Are you there? Peter? It's Selina. Listen, please can you call me at home? It's your father, Lolitia. He's been feeling unwell on and off for a while and it was getting worse...'

A crack appeared in her voice but she paused and regained control.

'He wouldn't have anyone make a fuss. I finally got him to the doctor last week. He had a scan on Friday and they operated today. It's no good, when they opened him up it was in his left lung, bloody cigarettes. It's spread. Everywhere. Please call me. Please?'

42
Decision Time

Lolly never did return the call and for a while I thought I wouldn't either. But on the connecting flight from Fort Lauderdale to Key West a week later, Alex made a noise something like a sigh and turned towards me.

'You know, Michael, all the stuff you said to Lolly this past week, you'd never have talked like that six months ago. But doesn't it make you think?'

'Think what?'

'That you should take your own advice? I don't want to raise a raw subject but... the fact that Lolly has to block this out, for whatever reasons – and frankly they don't sound like bad ones – you don't think it's good for *her* to block it out, so what does that mean for you?'

I didn't even want to think about my reply. 'Lolly and I both had a miserable time with him, but it's over. God knows he was dreadful enough to her. She didn't tell you this but when she was sixteen she had a boyfriend who died in a light aircraft accident and Dad wouldn't even let her go to his funeral because he didn't approve of her having boyfriends at that age. Can you believe it? But even Lol didn't have to deal with... you know, with Jim, Selina, the whole thing. Not directly, anyway. So maybe she is blocking it out, but I don't think I am. I think I've dealt with it as much as I ever will. I've done my thinking, and I don't want to know. So, like I say, as far as I'm concerned it's already over.'

Alex remained silent for a few minutes and I stared out of the window, trying to keep my mind as blank as I could and hoping he would let the subject drop. But of course, he didn't.

'But it isn't over, is it? You haven't made your peace with him, and it's very hard to do that when somebody's gone; it'll make it harder for you in the long run. Think about it. You could call when we get home. Even just a phone call might help, there's nothing to lose.'

I sat in angry silence for the rest of the journey. Make my peace? Kiss him on the forehead so he could drift away feeling absolved? Make my peace with *him*? *Just a phone call*?

While we were unpacking later that evening I exploded with pent-up resentment and repeated what had been boiling over in my head. And Alex said, 'From what you've said, it sounds unlikely, but would you call him if you thought there was even a one per cent chance of him showing any remorse? Apologising? Maybe even telling you that he loves you?'

'I don't want his fucking love,' I said. 'He can keep what little he has for himself.'

I slept on my own that night, bruised and resentful, arguing away the night in fitful spurts of sleep and wakefulness. And in the morning I called Selina.

We were both businesslike, me cold and her trying to hide the fact that she was bleeding down the telephone. He was getting worse. They said he possibly had less than two months. He'd been asking for me. Would I speak to him?

'No. Tell him I've moved on and that you couldn't get hold of me. But you've got my number. If anything changes, call me.'

Three weeks later, she did.

And so it was that, just over seven months after I had originally arrived at Miami International Airport, I found myself back again, with Alex at my side. It was his first trip to England.

I slept only for a short while on the flight, sitting with my thoughts in the half-light of the dimmed cabin and glancing from time to time at the animated map on the LCD panel in front of me. A miniature aeroplane, its wings occasionally changing their angle in little spasms, arcing us across the Atlantic towards the fresh, clear dawn of an English day in early October.

We landed at Heathrow just after 6 am and, with no luggage other than what we were carrying, had cleared immigration and customs within half an hour. By seven o'clock we were in a black cab heading around the M25, my eyes flicking backwards and forwards at the passing trees and bridges, taking nothing in. From time to time Alex reached across and squeezed my hand.

Reaching the Royal Marsden at around a quarter to eight, we drew up under the concrete porte-cochere behind an ambulance. It was cool as we stepped out, and I breathed great gasps, lungfuls of courage. A woman with no hair sat in a wheelchair in the shadows to the side of the door, a middle-aged man standing close beside her. They were both smoking.

Alex handled the navigation. Lifts, antiseptic staircases, crowded noticeboards, and long, long corridors. I tried somehow to shift my focal length shorter, tried to make the inevitable door, room, bed, recede into the distance. But here it finally was.

The first thing I saw when I walked in was Selina standing at the window, her back to the door. She turned to face us, haggard and free of makeup.

'Hello, Michael. Thank you for coming. He's been waiting for you. I'll leave you with him.'

She crossed the room towards the door and, as she reached me, she suddenly stood on tiptoes towards my ear and murmured with an unfamiliar intimacy, 'I think he's been holding on for you through the night. He doesn't have long now. He's been refusing morphine today. He wants to be clear in his head.'

She left the room and I shifted my focus over to the bed. My father lay on his back, stuck all over with tubing and surrounded by hardware. His head was turned towards me, eyes open and clear. He had aged beyond belief since I'd last seen him, at Jim's funeral. His skin was an unnatural grey colour with a blueish tinge, purple bruising around the needles. His hair, usually thick and white, was patchy though evidently freshly brushed.

'Hello, Dad. How are you feeling?' My tone was guarded. I knew him too well to believe that he would ever be weak enough to be entirely safe.

He beckoned me over with the slightest wave of his hand, indicating the chair by the bed. I obeyed, sitting slowly, not taking my eyes off his. I placed my arm tentatively onto the bedclothes, and to my surprise he slowly moved until he was able to grip my hand with his own.

'Welcome back, Michael. Thank you for coming all this way. I appreciate it. It's important.'

He coughed gently and I heard a soft rattle in his throat as he tried to breathe. Then he looked over my shoulder towards Alex.

'And who is this?'

I steeled myself for an attack.

'This is Alex, he's a friend of mine from America, he offered to travel with me.'

'A friend, eh? Alex... Was it your voice on the answering machine when I telephoned?'

Alex nodded, without speaking.

Here it comes, I thought. But he remained quiet for a moment, then looked up towards Alex and gestured him over with his head. Alex approached the bed and stood beside me. He placed his hand firmly on my shoulder.

My father looked him up and down for a few moments before saying, with a very faint cough of a laugh, 'Jesus, Michael, he's practically young enough to be your son. Still, I suppose it's no worse than Selina and me.'

At first I felt as furious as all hell at this. His apparent attitude towards Alex, the casual mention of his relationship with Selina, as if it were a joke. If he had not been so ill, I think might finally have hit him.

But instead I sat perfectly still while he continued to look Alex up and down, an intense scrutiny, years of thought to squeeze into a few moments. Then he closed his eyes and concentrated on his breathing. Eventually, he opened them again and stared once more at Alex.

'I'm glad I met you, Alex. Look after each other. Michael could do with a little love.'

He switched his gaze slowly between us for a while, then said, 'I wish I had done that myself.'

'What, Dad? Done what?'

But his eyes had closed again.

I thought he was resting, but gradually the grip of his hand faded.

A few seconds passed as I took this in, as I took in the alarm that had started to buzz, as I made my diagnosis. I carried on staring at his closed lids until hot tears forced their way through my own eyes in angry jets.

'Not now, Dad, not *now*. Not now! I want to know what you *mean*!'

I was almost choking on phlegm and tears, Alex's hand on my shoulder. 'Come on, you old bastard. You owe it to me. You fucking owe it to me. You can't *do* this.'

Alex moved around in front of me and, half standing, half crouching, drew me close and rocked me from side to side as I cried into his collar, mumbling all the while, 'What did he say? What did he mean?'

I continued like this until Alex spoke. 'Hush, now. It's over now, Michael. It's over and, for whatever you can make of it, he's finally given you the best he could.'

43
Dad's Swansong

We stayed for a few more days, waiting for Dad's funeral, which was very different from what I had anticipated. He had left one last surprise. I had to call Lolly in Toronto and read it to her – which was hard but, I think, good for both of us.

My Dearest Daughter,

Selina has been hoping that you would call her, having told you the nature of my condition, but you have chosen not to and I can understand why. As you know, I have never been a man for regrets, preferring to believe that it is better to live with the consequences of actions than to cry over spilt milk. But I find myself lying here with so many things unfinished.

You certainly know by now about the situation with Selina, Jim, Michael and myself and I am sure that this cannot have endeared me to you further. On reflection I haven't been very fair to you, or Michael, at all. In fact it is Selina who has forced me to see this. She's a tough woman but this year has been something of an epiphany for her and so she has taken to regret in a relatively comprehensive manner herself and I can no longer avoid sharing some of it myself. I want to be very clear about what I have done.

I don't think any of us is surprised that I have not made a very good father; it's not in my nature. I like to run a tight ship and children are hard to fit into that sort of a scheme. But the fact that I have always found their unpredictability hard to deal with doesn't mean that I don't have feelings. So I don't regret what I did over the years; that's how I am. But I don't have much time left, and I finally have to face my regret over the things I didn't do. Primarily this concerns the fact that I never told you, or Michael, that I love you or that I am proud of you.

I am proud of Michael for having been such a good father himself, and such a good man. And I am proud of you for having had the guts to stand up to me so robustly over the years. You're tough as hell, and isn't it ironic that this should be the final tie between us? You're my daughter through and through; you've never done a single thing you didn't believe in.

From what Selina says today, I may get to see Michael one last time but barring a miracle this letter is the last contact I will have with you, and I have something to ask of you. Selina is pregnant. At some point in the next few months you and Michael should have a new brother or sister and I would like it if you could try to know the child. It will need a family, and you and Michael are the best I could wish for, whatever you might think of me.

Goodbye Lolly. I love you.

Dad

He had dictated it to Selina, and it was odd reading his words in her hand. But when I'd finished reading it to Lolly down the phone, she and Pete booked a flight and headed off to the airport the next day with the twins. So Lolly came home at last, arriving the day before her father's funeral.

Epilogue

A year later to the day, we held a service at the Episcopal Church of Saint Paul on Duval.

A lot had happened during those twelve months. I had become a carpenter, spending my days renovating our beautiful old houses in the tropical sunlight and breezes, ending up where I should always have started. I had learned about the climate, materials, pests, construction techniques, architecture and history – everything that I would need to know in order to do what my grandfather had taught me, which was to take something broken and make it whole again.

Plenty had happened to the others too – to Angelico, Karl, Penny and Sue. But that's another set of stories. What I would say is that Phil was still appearing all over town, though mostly on video screens these days, and known only as Phyllis.

We were putting the finishing touches to the new guesthouse and restaurant, and were to hold a grand opening reception there after the service. The natural profusion of its decks and gardens was already hung with candles and garlands, champagne was chilling and food had been prepared to welcome our guests.

Selina had arrived with Lolitia Anne the night before. The baby was four months old – barely three months older than my infant son, Carey Stuart Crawford. Lolly and Pete were there too, with the twins. So it was quite a family affair.

St Paul's has been around in one form or another for over a hundred and seventy years. It has been destroyed by hurricane and fire time and again but Key West's tenacious islanders have always rebuilt it. So it was a fitting place to hold this most particular of ceremonies.

The first part was a service of remembrance and celebration for my father – and for Jim, my son and brother. It was as Jim's original funeral should have been, a thing of light. At my request, Phil sang her version of 'Somewhere Over the Rainbow', which had Selina, finally, in tears.

The second part was a double christening. As the cool water trickled over the foreheads of my new sister and my new son, I stood at the font beside my ex-wife, my wife, my lover and, of course, the proud new mother of my child. And, while the priest said the words to guide our cycle of death and renewal forward, my mind's eye drifted up the aisle and out of the door. It moved slowly up into the sky, a balloon rising gently against the blue, looking down in ever-increasing circles at this rainbow toy-town, this amazing place, this island of mending hearts.

Also available

Bend Sinister:
The Gay Times Book of Disturbing Stories

Edited by Peter Burton

A deeply disturbing collection

This collection, nominated for a Lambda literary award, is packed with chills and thrills from thirty gay writers. It ventures into the world of the sinister and the disturbing, with flashes of sheer horror.

Authors include: Sebastian Beaumont, David Patrick Beavers, Perry Brass, Christopher Brown, Richard Cawley, Jack Dickson, Neal Drinnan, Francis King, Simon Lovat, Stuart Thorogood, Michael Wilcox and Richard Zimler.

Across a range of nationalities and approaches, one thing is guaranteed: something out of kilter, something dangerously askew.

"A collection of startling originality... a welcome addition to the canon of gay literature" City Life

"[An] excellent anthology of horror, fantasy and crime... a chillingly good read" ★★★ Big Issue

"A lively, eclectic collection... Highly recommended" The List

"Breathtakingly different... incredible 'tales of the unexpected'" Our World

"A superb collection of disturbing tales" ★★★★ OUT in Greater Manchester